Prais

Treasure among the ....

"Jemimah Hodge has guts, heart and a brilliant sense of direction when she's on the trail of something buried. Cash delivers a thrilling ride from start to finish. Riveting."
— Chris Rogers, author, the Dixie Flannigan series

"The essence of northern New Mexico—Santa Fe, Taos, the Enchanted Circle, Chimayo, Espanola, Ojo Caliente, Georgia O'Keefe's beloved Abiquiu—permeates the pages of this nonstop murder mystery starring Forensic Psychologist Jemimah Hodge and her sidekick lawman lover. The trail of death leads from a corpse at a casino to a second corpse loaded with clues that pull us into the back story revelation— when she died, Victim Number Two was in the midst of a sexual rebirth. Congratulations to Marie Romero Cash, for painting new shades into the rich New Mexico canvas."
—Robert J. Ray, author of the Matt Murdock Mystery series

Deadly Deception
"A superb investigative thriller .... Readers will appreciate this entertaining whodunit"
—Harriet Klausner

Shadows among the Ruins
"Shadows among the Ruins is a fast-paced and old-school fun mystery read, highly recommended."
—Midwest Book Review

"This 'who-done-it' has cops, a surprise ending, great dialog, and stunning vistas. This is the kind of book to dive into in front of a fire or to take on a plane and tune everything out."
—*Tradición Revista Magazine*

"Cash is an author who knows Santa Fe inside and out, from its Canyon Road art dealers selling million-dollar paintings to its drug-dealing bar scene and hard-working cops. She's not afraid to pile up the dead bodies and sling the slang around."
—Wolf Schneider, Reviewer for *New Mexico Magazine* and former Editor-in-Chief of the *Santa Fean*

"Marie Romero Cash writes about Santa Fe with a local's razor-sharp insights, and peoples her exciting mystery with a gallery of colorful, authentic New Mexico characters. The plot moves with the speed and force of a Southwestern thunderstorm."
—Kirk Ellis, Co-Executive Producer/Screenwriter, HBO's *John Adams*

"A gifted writer has entered the ranks of the best of Southwest Mystery Writers. From the first chapters I found myself caught up in the action, stifling a catch in my throat, actually hyperventilating. This book has the kick of a high-powered rifle."
—Tal Streeter, sculptor and author of many books, including A Kite Journey through India, Art of the Japanese Kite, and Paper Wings Over Japan

"*Shadows among the Ruins* is a great read whose real characters and honest dialog capture the intrigue of New Mexico. Throw in a great plot with a surprise ending, and mystery lovers will be clamoring for the sequel. Marie Romero Cash has taken the gift for prose she demonstrated in Lowrider Blues and applied it to the mystery genre with spectacular results."
—J. Michael Orenduff, Author, The Pot Thief Murder Mystery Series

Treasure among the Shadows

Treasure among the Shadows

A JEMIMAH HODGE MYSTERY

MARIE ROMERO CASH

Seattle, WA

Camel Press
PO Box 70515
Seattle, WA 98127

For more information go to: www.camelpress.com
marieromerocash.camelpress.com

Cover design by Sabrina Sun

ISBN: 978-1-60381-907-7 (Trade Paper)
ISBN: 978-1-60381-908-4 (eBook)

Library of Congress Control Number: 2013936708

Printed in the United States of America

**Other Books by Marie Romero Cash
in the Jemimah Hodge Mystery Series:**

Shadows among the Ruins

Deadly Deception

To all the treasure hunters out there who still believe in the Tooth Fairy

To Forrest Fenn, who did what no other person has done in this century by giving everyone a real treasure to search for as well as providing me with the idea for this book

To my children, Gregory, Anthony and Audrey, who continue to cheer me on

PREFACE

Several months ago, searching for a good book to settle down with after publication of my first mystery, *Shadows among the Ruins*, I cracked open a memoir written by an esteemed colleague, Forrest Fenn. It was titled *The Thrill of the Chase*. One of the fascinating things about it was that in between the lines were clues to a million dollar treasure Fenn planned on hiding.

I first met Forrest in the 1980s when my then husband owned the Cash Ranch outside of Cerrillos, New Mexico. My stories are based in that area, which lies near the Ortiz Mountains and has an historical Indian ruin on the property. It wasn't too long after the Cash Ranch was sold that the acreage containing the San Lazaro Pueblo Indian ruin was broken off from the main ranch and offered for sale. I called Forrest to tell him, and the rest is history. Browsing through the pages of his magical memoir, I wondered, where does the line between fact and fantasy begin to blur? I couldn't wait to read this book and map out a story about a misguided treasure hunt based on Forrest's very real one.

There is a wonderfully mysterious element associated with something buried. History books are filled with stories of hidden treasure, real and imagined. The treasure in Forrest Fenn's memoir, *The Thrill of the Chase, is* a real treasure, and at the time of publication of this work of fiction, it has not been discovered. Treasure seekers were standing in line to try their luck at unearthing this incredible pot of gold at the end of the proverbial rainbow. Major news media were featuring his story on air, in print and on the Internet.

Bear in mind that the places I mention where a treasure might be buried have little to do with the *real* treasure in Fenn's book. My poem containing hints to the treasure is my own invention. The magnificent bronze chest he describes could be found in an unlikely and isolated spot or right there under your nose. One of the clues indicates the treasure is hidden "in the mountains north of Santa Fe." Well, as Forrest said to me, "*Alaska* is north of Santa Fe."

The hunt for Fenn's treasure has already become an urban legend.

BOOK ONE –
THE HOUSE OF CARDS

CHAPTER ONE

It was a typical February Day. Locals referred to the month as *Febrero Loco*, crazy February, because the daily weather was as unpredictable as a roulette wheel. It was unseasonably warm and just to be on the safe side, the air conditioning at Buffalo Thunder Casino, north of Santa Fe, was cranked up.

The casino was gearing up for the upcoming Valentine's Day, pulling out all the stops with promotions geared toward attracting patrons with the cherry red Toyota Camry give-away. Blackjack modules formed a large circle around the Craps and Texas Hold'em tables. The electromagnetic field and the thousand flashing lights could easily illuminate an entire city. Waitresses attired in short frilly skirts and low cut tank-tops stopped at each console to offer cold sodas, water and coffee, and friendly smiles to encourage tips.

She walked through the automatic doors, the strong odor of cigarette smoke assaulting her senses. Vanity precluded her from wearing sorely needed eyeglasses and she squinted her eyes in hopes of seeing a familiar face, preferably male and old enough to buy her a drink. She navigated her world in a blur, peering out of heavily made-up brown eyes and beneath thin, perfectly arched eyebrows. Dark red lipstick and a heart-shaped face framed by recently touched-up auburn hair completed the picture. She was dressed in black pants, a sparkly jacket and stiletto heels. The first was to hide the extra ten pounds she carried and the second was to give her four-eleven height a boost.

She found her favorite slot machine in a corner next to the lounge, where she could sometimes score a few drinks and maybe a place to stay for the night. Of late, she frequented the casinos on Highway 85, staying until closing and hitching a ride back to Santa Fe, where she hung out in the laundry rooms of motels on Cerrillos Road. She was not a hooker. She was a forty-year-old woman down on her luck, having burned all the bridges behind her. She was desperate to win a jackpot to get her back on her feet.

She glanced out of the corner of her eye at the man playing next to her. He was exactly her type—brown-skinned, tall, sleeveless t-shirt to show off bulging biceps, tattooed arms, long hair and a neatly trimmed goatee. Before the night was over, they were snuggled in a corner of the lounge, sipping rum and Cokes. If she played her cards right, she had a good idea where the evening was going to end up.

CHAPTER TWO

Santa Fe County Sheriff's Deputy Rick Romero could see the crest of Sun Mountain from the living room of his adobe house in the South Capitol area of Santa Fe. More a big hill than a mountain, it was one of Romero's favorite places. He had spent his childhood years scaling its piñon covered trails up to the top, where he could view the entire city. Not so these days. The mountainside was peppered with massive houses built by recent transplants to the City Different. Santa Fe wasn't different any more. Romero thought it had begun to mimic every other tourist destination in the Southwest. Trendy galleries and gift shops surrounded by more trendy galleries and gift shops.

Romero was in his early forties and had been a Santa Fe County sheriff's deputy for more than fifteen years, starting at the bottom rung of the ladder and working his way up to Lieutenant Detective. For the past three years he had been in charge of the substation in Cerrillos, a small burg south of Santa Fe. His almost six-foot frame was muscular but trim. His dark curly hair had a tendency to grow out of control, and deep hazel green eyes competed for attention with a heavy row of lashes. Even as an adult, he hadn't forgotten how his classmates in elementary school had teased him. They were relentless. *Little Orphan Annie, curly locks awhirl. Does your mommy dress you like a girly girl?*

His parents were of Spanish descent, and that was his first language. Being bilingual caused a number of problems.

3

Between his looks and fractured English, *hey stupido* was another moniker he was branded with, and the words, *"Who taught you to talk mocho like that?"* followed him through junior high. The constant teasing served to propel him forward at a pace that all but completely eliminated any hint of an accent by the time he graduated from high school. He rarely spoke *Spanglish*, except in the company of family and friends. On the other hand, his light complexion bore little resemblance to the stereotypical Hispano, and it didn't bother him a bit when people wondered if he was *raza* or *Gringo.*

Dressed in blue warm-ups, Romero was about to take off for a jog when the house phone rang. He hesitated before answering, knowing that early-morning calls were either from local fundraisers or one of his deputies, and he was not in the mood to hear from either. He succumbed when his cellphone started to ring. It was Detective Artie Chacon.

"This better be important, Artie. You know it's my day off and I was about to head out."

"Tough break, Boss, but you'd better head back in."

"Can't Sheriff Medrano handle this? I haven't had a day off in weeks."

"Already called him. He said to call you."

"All right. What is it?" Romero plopped himself on the couch in the living room.

"Dispatch got a call a few minutes ago about a body being discovered out past Cerrillos near the Ortiz Mine. I'm on my way there."

"I'll meet you out there."

Romero hung up, reached for his keys, and then dialed the number of Jemimah Hodge, the forensic psychologist for the county.

"Is this a social call, Detective?" she said. "I was about to head out for a meeting." Jemimah occupied office space at the County Detention Center where the Sheriff's Office was housed.

"'Fraid not, Jemimah. Just got a call about a body found out near your ranch. Looks like we're going to be working together on another case. I thought you might want to get in on the start of the investigation."

"I sure would. Let me make a few calls to clear my calendar. Can you pick me up or should I meet you there?"

"I'm about fifteen minutes out. I'll honk when I arrive." He grabbed a banana from the kitchen counter. It might turn out to be a long morning.

The crime scene was already taped off as Romero and Jemimah drove up. Artie Chacon was standing by his squad car.

"Bring us up to date, Artie."

"Not much to tell. That fellow over there was gathering rocks in his truck, saw what appeared to be an arm sticking out from under a pile and contacted police. We're waiting for the coroner to arrive so we can see if there's anything else under those rocks."

Romero lifted the yellow tape so Jemimah could scoot under and followed her to a rocky ledge where the witness indicated he found the body. The County Coroner's van drove up before they reached the spot.

"Hold it right there, Romero. You know better than to disturb a crime scene," said Harry Donlan, Santa Fe County's Chief Medical Examiner.

"Not disturbing, Donlan. Preliminary investigation."

"My ass. You people gotta learn to be more careful. Follow the rules."

Donlan was a hulk of a man with unruly gray hair, rosacea reddened cheeks and an intimidating manner. Romero had become accustomed to the coroner's rants. He winked at Jemimah.

"Yes, sir. I understand."

Donlan directed the techs to remove the rocks covering the body, careful to preserve any blood evidence that might still be present. After about an hour, he knelt next to the partially nude body.

"Homicide, for sure. Female, somewhere in her thirties, maybe older. Bullet hole right through the head. I'm not seeing any brain matter or any indication that she bled out here. Looks like she might have been strangled first. Whoever did this was in a hurry to cover the body with rocks. Lots of postmortem bruising. Hard to say whether this is the scene of the crime or if she was dumped here. She's still wearing jewelry, so we can probably rule out robbery." He motioned for the techs. "Check this area for personal effects belonging to the victim and get those bagged."

The coroner shifted the body, feeling her clothes for pockets. "Nothing here but a player's card from one of the casinos." He handed it to the tech, who secured it in a plastic envelope and handed it to Romero.

"Amy Griego," he said. "Not much to go on. Artie, see what info you can obtain from the casino. I understand they need some sort of identification when they give these cards out to their patrons."

"I'm pretty sure they keep a record of driver's licenses in that regard," Jemimah said. "You can play without one, but if you want to gather up points, you need a card. They also photo the ID if you win a jackpot."

"Why, Dr. Hodge. I didn't know you frequented such establishments," Romero said.

"Hey, don't knock it. They're great places to take guests for a good meal and some quick entertainment," she smiled.

"We're done here, people. It's all yours, Romero," Donlan said, directing the techs to bag the body. "Nothing else we can do." He left the area without another word.

Romero and Jemimah walked around the scene. Romero gestured at some tracks. "The ground here is covered with fine gravel. I can see there was a vehicle here, but I doubt if it's possible to make an impression." He glanced at Jemimah, who had her hand over her mouth. "You all right, Jem?"

"Sorry. I never seem to get used to being around dead bodies. You can still make out her outline on the rocks. There's no telling what this poor woman went through before she died."

CHAPTER THREE

Romero was window shopping in downtown Santa Fe, where most every shop window was decorated with red hearts and cupids. It had been a while since he'd been on San Francisco Street, just a few blocks down from St. Francis Cathedral where he had been married so many years before. Looking back, he knew the marriage had been doomed from the beginning. His wife was a popular girl, always ready to party, but he was just getting established in law enforcement. At every turn she complained that he was never home and that his job was more important than she was. After the divorce it took a month-long drinking binge and a series of AA meetings before he could once again begin to face each day sober.

It was Valentine's Day and he was trying to understand just what it was women want men to do. No easy task for this handsome native of Santa Fe, because despite his looks, he was shy and reserved where women were concerned. It had taken him a long time to loosen up sufficiently to consider dating again. Then a year ago he found himself drawn to Jemimah Hodge, a Utah transplant by way of Texas who dropped into his life when they worked a case together. She was also the County's highly skilled forensic psychologist, and now that they were in a relationship, he wanted to get her something nice.

Coming out of his reverie, Romero caught a glimpse of his high school friend David Garcia, who stood under the portal of his upper-end jewelry store in the middle of the plaza.

"I hope you're not here on official business, Officer." Garcia smiled, holding his hands up in mock surrender. With boyish good looks, Garcia appeared younger than his years. Dressed in a tailored dark suit, he leaned forward to embrace Romero.

"Hey, David. Long time no see, *compadre.* Actually I'm just here to finger the merchandise."

"Looking for something special? Don't tell me you're getting ready to make the leap? 'Bout time." Garcia directed him through the doors of the shop.

"Sorry to disappoint you, Davey."

"Well, are you thinking about it and just need that extra push?"

"Just need something for Valentine's Day. That's all."

"Something sparkly ought to do the trick."

"Maybe, maybe not," Romero laughed. "I'm not sure if she's into bling. Let's see what you've got."

"For you, *amigo*, pretty much anything." They walked together toward the glass cases.

Early that evening on his way to meet Jemimah, Romero checked his jacket to make sure he'd remembered to slip the black velvet pouch into his pocket. Nothing like showing up empty-handed on this lover's day celebration. He felt like a teenager, hoping the diamond heart he chose would be well received. His jeweler friend kept nudging him toward the engagement rings, but he wasn't ready. Not yet. It had taken long enough to corral this filly, and he didn't want to spook her. He chuckled as he recalled a conversation he'd had with Tim McCabe some months previous as they discussed women in general, and Jemimah in particular. Tim McCabe was a transplanted retired lawman from Idaho who assisted the sheriff's department with cold cases. He and his wife owned a high-end gallery in Santa Fe. Romero and Jemimah had both developed a strong relationship with him over the past two years.

"Here's the advice I promised," McCabe had said when the two of them met for coffee. "I think you should approach Jemimah a little at a time. Kind of like breaking in a wild horse. Let her come to you. Keep your reactions to a minimum. Don't spook her. Just give her a lot of room, and reel her in a little if she goes too far afield."

Romero smiled. "That's quite an analogy there, Tim."

"Listen, I'm just an old cowboy with a limited knowledge of women other than my wife, and I'm not even sure I'm an expert on her any more. But I do know horses, and I know Jemimah knows horses."

"You saying women are a lot like horses?" Romero motioned to the waitress.

"I'm saying Jemimah is intelligent, strong-willed and stubborn. The last filly I broke had those same characteristics. Get the connection?"

"Yes, sir. I think I do."

"Well then, once you learn to stop letting her irritate you about every little thing, you might get something going."

He had followed Tim's sage advice to the letter. So far, it had been right on point.

CR

Jemimah was already in the parking lot of La Choza, a small Mexican restaurant at the edge of the rail yard park where they had their first date. She greeted him with unbridled enthusiasm.

"You're in a cheerful mood," he said. "Good day at work?"

"More like long day." She smiled. "Just happy to be off work for the weekend".

As they walked to the patio entrance, she shifted her

sunglasses to the top of her head. She was wearing skinny black jeans and a plum-colored tank top, her hair pulled back into a stylish ponytail. As they waited to be seated, she leaned forward to kiss him.

It was going to be a very special night, he hoped.

CHAPTER FOUR

Jemimah Hodge was smiling as she arrived at her office late Saturday morning. She was wearing the diamond heart Detective Romero gave her during dinner. She fingered it gently, thinking how happy she finally was. They had spent a romantic night together.

It had taken a long time to get to this point in her life, and she couldn't ask for a more fulfilling relationship. No thanks to her childhood. Her parents were dyed-in-the-wool fourth generation members of the LDS Mormon church, leading a normal life until her father decided to relocate the family to a small community in Utah and join a fundamentalist cult that embraced polygamy. Within a few years, he added two additional wives and several children to the flock. By the time Jemimah was sixteen, she lived in fear that she, like many of her friends, would be married off to someone three times her age. Her one saving grace was a mottled skin condition that made her appear less attractive to potential suitors.

Months before her eighteenth birthday, her mother and one of the wives drove her to Las Vegas, Nevada, for a consultation with a dermatologist. Her father encouraged the appointment—Jemimah would be more marriageable without the skin problem. While one of the wives was at the fabric store purchasing bolts of cloth, Jemimah's birth mother sat with her through the appointment. The physician assured them the samples of the new drug he prescribed would clear her complexion of the red blotches covering most of her skin. He could almost guarantee it. Jemimah thanked him and placed the sample packs in her backpack. The nurse directed them to the front desk, where the young trainee asked them to wait while she retrieved the file.

Feigning nausea, Jemimah told her mother she was going upstairs to use the bathroom. Her mother stood up to accompany her. In a life-changing moment, the receptionist motioned the mother to come forward to arrange for payment and complete the insurance forms. Jemimah assured her she would be all right; after all, she was just going to the bathroom.

Jemimah had raided the family savings jar in anticipation of this opportunity. She found an exit on the second floor at the end of the hallway, bolted down the stairs and into the street. She sprinted down the main drag, terrified that the women would find her and take her back home to face severe punishment. Out of breath, she jumped onto a tourist bus, which slowly edged its way down the Las Vegas strip. The bus driver directed her to the Greyhound station, where she dashed to the ticket counter seconds before boarding a bus to Los Angeles.

Jemimah never looked back. She arrived at the Los Angeles bus terminal and found her way to the public bathrooms. She sat in a stall and cut off her waist length hair, disposing of it in the trash. By the end of the week, she had rented a small apartment and found a job waiting tables at a nearby diner. She had no desire to return to her former life. *I'd rather starve than ever go back to Utah.*

She was fully aware that by now she would not only have been ostracized by the sect, but excommunicated as well. She looked in the mirror one morning and found that her complexion had begun to clear. She was no longer the unattractive wallflower she had been for so many years.

Life moved forward for Jemimah. She stopped worrying

that her parents would continue to look for her. She was of age and they could all go to hell for all she cared. She would never forgive her father for entertaining thoughts of marrying her off to an older man. She had no respect for someone who would sacrifice his first born in the name of his ill-conceived religious beliefs. In her first year at UCLA, a brief marriage to a man she soon realized was a control freak much like her father made her more determined to focus on working toward a degree. The doctorate in psychology would serve her for a lifetime.

Twenty years later, Jemimah was enjoying a successful career as a forensic psychologist, initially in Dallas, and now in Santa Fe. She had honed her skills, working on high-profile cases with the Sheriff's office and the State Police. Although her job description indicated her task was to assist police by profiling criminal suspects, she found herself spending additional hours investigating on her own, and it wasn't unusual for her to be thigh deep in a high-profile homicide case.

And, what more could a woman ask for? She was healthy, happy, had a great job, and was falling in love.

CHAPTER FIVE

That Monday, SFCSO detectives met with Sheriff Medrano to discuss the recent murder.

"All right, people. Put the donuts and coffee aside and let's get started. Apart from the logical conclusion that we're dealing with a psycho here, what have you people dug up regarding the victim?" said Sheriff Medrano. "The morning headlines managed to freak out half the county. 'Killer still at large. No leads or suspects.' Damned phone lines have been lit up like a freakin' Christmas tree."

Detective Romero stood up and cleared his throat. "The victim had a casino player card in her pocket. We had to check it out before identifying the body and notifying any next of kin, just to make sure it belonged to her."

"What did you find out, Romero? Speed it up here." Sheriff Medrano had known Romero since he first entered law enforcement and took delight in lighting a fire under him.

"The card had the name Amy Griego. When we ran it through Motor Vehicle, a number of women with the same name came up, none with physical similarities to our victim. We then contacted the Pojoaque Pueblo Police in the hope that they could run the card through the casino's system to determine if they had a record of the woman's driver's license."

"Any luck?" said Medrano.

"They provided us with a copy of her driver's license identifying her as Meribel A. Griego. The address listed was that of her ex-husband, who said everyone knew her as Amy. He hadn't seen her since their divorce almost a year ago. He gave us the name of next of kin, her mother, who it turns out also hadn't seen her for some time." Romero distributed photocopies of the driver's license.

"All right, now did anything show up at the crime scene? I assume your guys have run a comb through it?" said the sheriff.

"Nothing. We're pretty sure the body was dumped there a few days before. Coroner said the victim had been dead for less than a week before the body was discovered," Romero said.

"You people know what to do. I don't have to lead you by the hand. This case has attracted statewide media, and they're not going to give us any breaks. We've got someone floating around out there who is probably looking for his next victim and everyone in Santa Fe is locking their doors and peeking through drawn curtains."

❧

Romero assigned a three-person team to the case, Detectives Martinez and Chacon, and asked Jemimah Hodge to join them at his office, where his secretary, Clarissa, had set out coffee in the conference room.

"What did you dig up on the victim, Artie?" Romero said.

"Divorced mother of two, currently unemployed. She's got a short rap sheet, mostly petty theft from previous employers, jewelry and such," said Chacon. "She was involved in an altercation with another woman a few months ago at Buffalo Thunder Casino. Spent a few nights in County for that and then bailed out. Case was dismissed after she promised the judge she would attend anger management classes."

"Same casino she had the player card from?"

"Yeah, they probably just kept her out of there for a month. Casinos like their regulars to come back no matter what the circumstances, and they usually do. She'd been a customer for a couple of years, and according to the manager, she was really into slots."

Romero shifted to Detective Martinez. "Any luck in obtaining surveillance tapes from the casino for the days leading up to the murder, Clyde?"

"Working on it, Boss. Right off we were made aware we're dealing with the Pueblo police first and then the casino."

"Why?"

"Each individual Pueblo owns their casino and has jurisdiction over any investigations that directly affect them," said Detective Martinez. "So we have to go through their police department, such as it is, in order to obtain any information from the casino."

"Well, keep at it. Go see the Governor of the Pueblo if you have to. Every day that goes by gives our killer another opportunity," Romero said. "Dr. Hodge, set up interviews with as many of the family members of the victim as you can. See if you can get a cellphone number from them. Woman with two kids is bound to have some contact with them."

"You would think so. I'll see what I can do."

As the detectives were kibitzing with Clarissa at the front desk, Romero pulled Jemimah into the kitchen. "I've been waiting to kiss you all morning."

She smiled. "Now, now, Detective. No hanky-panky on county time. Wouldn't want to be the subject of Sheriff Medrano's next rant." She gave him a quick peck on the cheek and left.

CHAPTER SIX

The Historic Preservation Department for the State of New Mexico occupied the second floor of the old hospital building on the northeast side of Santa Fe. An ancient building with a façade composed of outdated crank-out windows and wooden balconies, it had at one time been a mental institution.

Gilda Humphreys had been head of the division for so long that everyone agreed that her shelf-life had expired years earlier, if indeed she had ever been effective in this position. Well-rounded in the field of Archaeology, she was a chunky woman whose demeanor could be described as irritable by nature. Her matronly sense of fashion made her appear years beyond her actual age of forty. Despite a hefty salary, she shopped at lower-end retail stores. Deep chocolate brown eyes were minimized by mousy hair, which she wore pulled back in an unflattering chignon or secured with a rubber band. Yet, there was something about her you couldn't pin down—perhaps a feeling this was a butterfly waiting to escape its cocoon.

As Chief Archaeologist, Gilda's job was to oversee all aspects of historic preservation in the state, which included filling out forms and doling out federal and state dollars. She was viewed as a tyrant both by investors interested in purchasing historic buildings and by private landowners with archaeological sites on their property. Over the years she had managed to offend almost everyone, including her employees, who avoided unnecessary contact with her.

She was married to George Humphreys, an under-challenged man who chose to stay home and spend his days reading and cooking. He was overqualified for every available job, but the best housekeeper a wife could want.

Gilda's desk typically overflowed with stacks of unread mail. Her assistant of three years, Antoine Nelson, stood at attention by her side as she began the task of clearing the clutter. A newspaper article from the previous month caught her attention. She scanned down the page to learn Tim McCabe, a local gallery owner, had purchased privately owned San Lazaro Pueblo some years earlier and was preparing to undertake excavations. Gilda's cheeks turned beet red.

"How the hell did his happen, Antoine?" she raged. "This makes us look like fools."

"It was all over the local news, Mrs. Humphreys," he said.

"Perhaps you should have called it to my attention."

"I'm sorry. I put the article on your desk some time ago. I assumed you read it. I attached the follow-up article about recent excavations."

"We must have had the opportunity to acquire that site. As usual, our dear Director dropped the ball."

Gilda had frequently been at odds with Tom Rodriguez, the Cultural Affairs Officer. Their contentious relationship provoked Rodriguez into rejecting most of her suggestions, regardless of their feasibility. Gilda had no choice but to go along with his edicts, which caused her to morph into a token employee and limited her duties to educating the public rather than implementing policy. Of Cherokee Indian heritage, she resented that a prehistoric archaeological plot of land would have ever been purchased by a private individual, let alone a white man. Gilda Humphreys was certain of one thing, though: *she would do her darnedest to make Tim McCabe's life miserable.*

"Antoine, get me everything you can find about Tim McCabe, and everything available about the San Lazaro area," she said. "And don't take your sweet time about it."

"Yes, Ma'am. Right away." Antoine left the room. His pace seemed to quicken whenever he left her presence. He returned an hour later, arms laden with files.

Gilda looked at him with distaste. "Is that a new shirt, Antoine? I hear it takes a confident man to wear pink. Valentine's Day was last week."

"It's not pink. It's salmon."

"Ah, salmon. Well, okay then."

"And for your information, Lisa, my fiancée, bought it for me."

"Well, I'm sure Lisa has very good taste." Gilda smirked. "Now keep digging. This can't be everything I need."

○෫

Antoine had become desensitized to the harangues of his boss. At every opportunity she insulted him with cutting remarks ranging from his effeminate mannerisms to his hawk-like nose and curly brown hair. He was aware she referred to him as Tinkerbell because he was tall, lanky and scarecrow thin.

He returned to the file room to search for anything he could find that might appease her, even though he knew it was a waste of time. But, hey, he needed the job. Still, he couldn't help but think, *One of these days that bitch is going to get what's coming to her.*

CHAPTER SEVEN

Twenty miles south of Santa Fe near the village of Cerrillos, the three thousand acre Crawford Ranch lay in the center of a valley bordered by the Ortiz Mountains to the west, and abutting San Lazaro Pueblo ruins to the east. Tim McCabe had lucked into the purchase of the ruins a few years before. When the ranch came on the market, he convinced his wife it would serve as a great get away place from their active life in Santa Fe. While Laura was off on a cruise to Greece with her sisters-in-law, he decided to upgrade the house. She would return before her birthday and he thought the remodeling would be the perfect present.

Laura McCabe was a striking woman in her early sixties. Her curly blond hair, worn in a short bob, was sprinkled with streaks of silver. They had met thirty years ago when he traveled from Idaho to her father's thoroughbred horse ranch in Ruidoso, an upscale town in southern New Mexico. They married and returned to Kooskia, Idaho, where he was Sheriff. After her parents were killed in an accident, she inherited land and a business that were worth millions and convinced her husband to quit law enforcement so they could settle in Santa Fe. Within a few years, they amassed a large collection of Native American and Spanish Colonial art, eventually opening a successful gallery on trendy Canyon Road.

Tim McCabe was in his early sixties, an easy-going almost six-foot tall cowboy with deep blue eyes and graying hair. He was headed to his ranch to dig a little on the ruins and check the progress on the house. On the outskirts of Santa Fe he stopped at the Jack In The Box Drive-In on Cerrillos Road for his favorite meal, a green chili cheeseburger, fries and a Coke. The shrill voice of the plastic clown head directed him to move forward to pick up his order. As he rounded the bend from the main drag onto State Road 14, he munched on the last of the salty fries. He drove past the State Penitentiary, where three decades ago a prison riot garnered the top spot on the evening news. The fire station was off to the right, surrounded by a field of large boulders. A few miles farther he took a left at County Road 55A, a rarely graded washboard road that transformed into a boggy mire of red clay mud every summer during the monsoon season. He steered his Hummer under the railroad trestle and crossed the dry bed of the Galisteo River, which occasionally overflowed its banks and precluded even a Hummer from crossing.

Beyond the last curve at the edge of the property, McCabe opened the gate and drove through, scanning the land he loved so much, its rolling hills peppered with juniper and piñon trees. Parking near the fence, he glanced over at the old windmill that faithfully turned in the gentle breeze. A short time later he was kneeling on a sandstone slab, sifting small piles of dirt, looking for beads and small bone fragments.

The dry heat of the midday sun warmed the sandy soil and added another ten degrees to the temperature, wilting the mountain laurel and miniature daisies. To the north, a cluster of rapidly rising clouds gathered overhead as a thunderstorm loomed. New Mexico was in the throes of a drought and so far Mother Nature had ignored the Cochiti Pueblo rain dancers. McCabe thought it would be a welcome sight to see the creek bubbling across the property.

Lightning flashes and rolling thunder pounded through

the canyon and soon convinced McCabe to head toward the house. The clouds failed to release any moisture, and ten minutes later they moved on. Typical of Santa Fe County, where at any given time the skies fluctuated between dark gray and crystal blue.

As he walked through the door, McCabe saw the contractor had made a lot of progress in the last month. The furniture and phone were in, and the hot tub was ready to bubble. Assured Laura would be impressed, he decided to give the new digs a test run that evening.

The carpenter motioned from the laundry room. "Hey, Tim, glad you stopped by. I need to discuss a few of the finishing touches with you."

"Doing a great job there, Mark. The place is starting to look like home."

"Couple more days and we'll have the exterior wall plastered and the driveway paved. That should be about it. You gonna be around for a while?"

"You bet, happy to say that I am. I need to familiarize myself with that new kitchen. I've been stocking the refrigerator so that when Laura returns from her trip tomorrow I can bring her out here and grill a few steaks."

McCabe set about inspecting the house, jotting down things to discuss with Mark, who had done an incredible job converting the fifties style ranch house into a modern combination of wood and adobe. The Venetian plastered walls reminded him of the ancient church at Las Trampas, an eighteenth century Hispanic settlement in Northern New Mexico where every year in late spring parishioners hand-plastered the walls of San José Catholic Church. Nothing more inviting than the beauty of fresh plaster.

In recent months, discoveries at the ruins adjacent to the ranch had kept McCabe busier than he thought possible. To date, a cluster of nine prehistoric rooms had been excavated, and each bucket of dirt screened for artifacts. The number of relics unearthed boggled the mind. Curiosity over potential historical discoveries served to catapult him to the front page of every newspaper in the Southwest. He was a popular man. Archaeologists from across the nation scoured the Internet, Googling for any scrap of information they could find on McCabe and San Lazaro Pueblo. His post office box and email address overflowed with inquiries, most of which he had little time to answer.

As he walked through the kitchen, McCabe heard the phone ringing. He located the phone tucked in a slot next to the microwave.

"Tim McCabe, here."

"Yes, Mr. McCabe, this is Gilda Humphreys, Archaeologist for the State of New Mexico. We met a few years ago at your gallery."

"I remember. You were looking to confiscate a Zuni fetish that a client had brought into the gallery for appraisal. I don't recall the circumstances to be very pleasant."

"Yes, well, I'm sure I was just doing my job. Now, do you have a moment?"

"Just walked in the door, but let me kick off my boots and I'll be right with you."

Gilda rolled her eyes and waited, impatiently tapping her fingers on the desk. After removing his boots, McCabe sat on the living room couch, stretched out his legs, and picked up the cordless. "All right, Mrs. Humphreys. What can I do for you?"

"I've been reading about current activity at San Lazaro Pueblo, and I must say I am a bit concerned about what might be taking place on sacred ground." Humphreys coughed to clear her throat.

McCabe could see where this conversation was going. "Sacred ground? I don't know what you're referring to. What does sacred ground look like?"

"Mr. McCabe, I don't think you're that naïve."

"Do you understand, Miss—"

"*Mrs.* Humphreys, Mr. McCabe. Gilda Humphreys."

"Thank you. Do you understand that these ruins are on my private ranch, and we are working under the supervision of a professional archaeologist?"

"My concern is not *who* is conducting the excavations, but rather *what* they are excavating."

"And by that you mean what, Ms. Humphreys?" McCabe could feel the muscles in his neck tensing.

"I've heard that there may be unmarked human burials where you are digging. Is that correct?"

"No, Ma'am. That is not correct. We have not encountered any evidence of human remains."

Gilda ignored his response and went on the attack. "Surely you are aware that my office is required to investigate any excavation site where human remains might be interred," she said with an edge to her voice. She stifled another cough.

"Well, Ms. Humphreys, it seems to me that you need to upgrade the quality of your rumor mill. And the idea of you investigating theoretical burial sites on my land is bullshit— but you probably know that."

"No matter. What you people are doing falls under my jurisdiction as State Archaeologist," she continued.

McCabe's Irish temper was about to detonate. "Apparently you are not hearing me, Miss Humphreys. There is no indication whatsoever of anything happening at San Lazaro that requires your attention. I think you would be better served by dealing with informants who know what they're talking about, and in the meantime you might go back and study the law a little more carefully before you attempt to impose yourself in places where you don't belong."

"I beg your pardon?" she said, her voice escalating.

"From where I sit, your office has no authority on my private property or anyone else's."

"You don't seem to be hearing *me,* Mr. McCabe. It's my

job to protect the remains and any appurtenant objects, since anything found with a burial is considered to be a component. I assume you're also aware that any violation of the statute regarding unmarked human burials comes with a pretty stiff felony charge."

"Yes, I've heard everything you've said. Let me put it another way. San Lazaro does not fall under your jurisdiction. It is not on state property."

As if she had not heard a word McCabe said, she continued to stress her point. "You seem to be having difficulty understanding what I'm saying."

"I'll tell you what, lady. If we come across any ancients who are buried, interred, entombed or sepulchered, I'll call your office. Now if you don't mind, I have my supper to think about," McCabe said.

"Nevertheless, I'll need to come out and take a look at what you're doing," she continued, ignoring his effort to end the conversation. "When would be a good time for you?"

"Maybe sometime down the road, but not now. I don't have anyone I can spring loose to show you around. Sorry," he said politely, and hung up. Replacing the phone in its cradle, McCabe smiled and twisted the cap off a pint of Wild Turkey.

What a pain in the ass. But sure as hell don't underestimate that woman.

ॐ

"Damn," Gilda yelled. She slammed the phone down and buzzed her assistant. She hated amateur diggers and this one was now at the top of her list. She put a lozenge in her mouth. *Damn raspy throat.*

"Antoine. Get me the Attorney General on the horn, now."

That SOB doesn't know who he's dealing with. I'll get the AG's office to issue a court order allowing me to investigate the possibility of anyone out there tampering with human remains and then we'll see how fast he changes his attitude. He won't be able to dig for river rock when I get through with him.

CHAPTER EIGHT

Tim McCabe and Foster Burke had met one summer in New York over a decade ago at an auction of Native American art, where they were locked in a bidding war over a century old Chief's Blanket—each determined to have it, no matter what the cost. A well-timed telephone bid by an anonymous bidder left them both with mouths agape. They had been friends ever since.

Foster Burke, almost a mirror image of Tim McCabe, was tall, with sandy brown hair flecked with gray. An easy-going man with an affable temperament, his 185 pounds looked fine on his six-foot frame. Like McCabe, he was an avid collector of American Indian artifacts. He ran a competing gallery on the Paseo and was highly respected in the community for his extensive knowledge of art and artifacts.

Jenny Burke looked younger than sixty-five. She wore her silver hair pulled back and clipped with a sterling feather barrette. She had the porcelain skin of a China doll, and rarely wore more than a touch of lipstick and cheek color. Jenny also had a great sense of humor that registered as a mischievous glint in her topaz blue eyes. Her face expressed the resilience of a long life filled with unexpected challenges, the most recent being her husband's victorious battle against cancer. On their return from an overseas buying trip, Foster called Tim McCabe to set up a lunch date. Tim answered on the third ring.

"Hey, *amigo*. Where you been hiding? I had almost convinced myself I might have to go out and find myself another best friend," Burke said.

"I might say the same about you," said McCabe.

"How are things going on your end of town?"

"Laura sends her love. She's been home since Valentine's Day, but she's still jet-lagging."

"Knowing our wives, I'm sure they've already made plans to meet for lunch. Jenny probably texted her from the plane."

Following a bit of small talk, the two made plans to meet for lunch.

◌

McCabe parked in the lot adjacent to the restaurant. Foster Burke drove up behind him and honked. They walked the short distance to the entrance of The Pink Adobe, or "The Pink," as it was affectionately called. Established in 1944, the restaurant quickly became a favorite watering hole for both locals and tourists. Thick adobe walls and clerestory windows infused pleasant warmth in the three-hundred-year-old building.

The owner greeted them at the door and directed them to a table. "Thanks for coming in, we've missed you two around here," she said.

"I've eaten lunch at least once a week here for years," Burke said, just as a waitress came over to buss him on the cheek. "I like that with the exception of a few *turistas*, most everyone in here is a regular."

"I'm going to enjoy this," McCabe said, pulling the wooden chair out from the table. "I'm partial to their enchilada plate and I haven't had one since last week. I spend so much time out at the ruins, I usually eat at the San Marcos Feed Store on the road to Cerrillos. That's where I buy my baby ducks in the springtime and feed for the horses. The café there is pretty high on everyone's list, too."

Foster sat in the chair next to McCabe. "Since Jenny and I spent the last six months overseas, I wondered about how the excavations at San Lazaro are coming. I gotta say, I really envy you for having those ruins. I could spend the rest of my life working at a place like that."

"Yup. I do consider myself fortunate that this piece of land fell into my lap when the bank foreclosed on the property."

The waitress handed each of them a menu. "I'll give you two a few minutes."

"No need," said McCabe. "I'm a creature of habit, and I'll have the blue corn enchilada plate, please."

"Same here," said Burke, handing the menu back to the waitress.

"So how are things with the State? I read somewhere that they weren't too happy," said Burke.

"When the state archaeologists learned what had transpired, they felt they'd been robbed. Some of those folks feel like they're entitled to every historic site in the state, even the ones on private property."

"Sounds like you came out ahead on that one."

"And since I last saw you, the adjoining ranch came up for sale and Laura and I bought it." McCabe grinned.

"No kidding? That's going to make things more convenient."

"You betcha."

When their food arrived, they paused long enough to eat, but continued to talk between bites.

"I was looking forward to having lunch with you, Foster. It's been a while," said McCabe. "I wanted to catch you up on where things stand. Laura and I recently decided to sell the gallery. It's been a fun business, but we figure it's time to move on."

"Sorry to hear that. We've been competitors for a long

time. Who am I going to do battle with for any historic items that come up? Any particular reason?"

McCabe noticed the room had become crowded and shifted his chair, facing Burke. He lowered his voice.

"We're pretty well off financially. We'd just like to lighten our load while we're still young enough to enjoy retirement. We own the property and most of the inventory and would like to unload it all without too much of a fuss."

"How much stock are we talking about here?"

"About as much as you have in your gallery," McCabe replied, stirring his iced tea thoughtfully. "We've made our living through art, but my love is ethnic antiques and that's where we're heaviest. You can almost name it and we have it. Native pots, baskets, beaded things, weapons. The list goes on. There's also a whole collection of historic New Mexican Colonial Santos, you know, old *retablos, bultos*, along with furniture and tinwork."

The busboy cleared the table and Burke waited until he had moved away to continue.

"I take it you two have given this a lot of thought."

"We've been mulling it over for quite some time now. We have a list of places we haven't traveled to, and disposing of the collection and later the building would open up a whole world of opportunity to do that. If it was just me, I'd be out at the ranch chasing cattle full-time, but Laura's a city girl, likes to be at the hub of things. She's the Neiman-Marcus type while I lean a little closer to Wal-Mart, but we've made it work for all these years, so I guess we're committed. The stuff in the house is staying put. She couldn't live without the old *santo* in the hallway."

"I get the picture."

The restaurant had thinned out considerably. Burke felt more comfortable discussing matters with McCabe.

"Well, there's a couple of ways you can approach this. Considering you are pretty well known, I'm sure you would draw a crowd if you opted for an auction. For that I'd suggest Sotheby's. We both know they have a solid reputation. One word of caution, though. Auctions don't always meet the seller's high expectations."

"I imagine they don't," said McCabe.

"Do you remember about ten years ago a fellow decided to auction his entire collection of antique New Mexican material?" Burke continued. "Sotheby's developed a nice catalog and made the stuff available on the Internet. Generated a lot of interest. But then much of the stuff sold for less than the low estimates. The guy sued them for breach of contract and it turned into a dog fight, which he lost. My point is there's no way to predict what something's going to sell for. On the other hand, to try to piecemeal things out one at a time would take forever and be a waste of your time. I say this only so you can make a sober judgment."

"I would say on a scale of one to ten, ninety-nine percent of our stuff is mostly tens," McCabe said. "I have no doubt they'll command a reasonable price."

"I agree. I've coveted a few of your pieces over the years," Burke chortled.

"Tell you what," McCabe said. "We've been friends for a long time. You can have first dibs on whatever you want."

"I appreciate that, Tim, but first let's figure out the best way to dispose of your collection and get you the most bang for your bucks."

McCabe signed the credit card receipt and handed it to the waitress, who smiled sweetly.

"What's your opinion of a museum as a place for some of my collection?"

"Listen, Tim, I consider donating to a museum a dead end street. My personal experience has been that museum basements are full of someone's prized possessions that rarely see the light of day. Some excellent examples of American Indian art have never been on display to the public," said

Burke. "They're just sitting in storage areas. That's a real shame, and although my wife and I have some very desirable items in our own collection, the last thing I want is for them to be hidden away."

"I hear you. I want all this stuff to be appreciated," said McCabe, checking his pocket to retrieve his keys.

"Now," Burke changed the subject. "Tell me how I'm going to weasel an invitation to hang out with you at the ruins."

"I've been meaning to give you a personal tour, but every time I turn around, you and Jenny are flying off to another exotic location."

"I think I'm all traveled out for a while. My calendar's clear."

"How about later this week, say Thursday at ten o'clock? Bring hiking boots, water, and an open mind. I'll furnish the education."

"I'll be there."

CHAPTER NINE

Tim McCabe drove over the dusty washboard road leading to the ranch with Foster Burke riding shotgun. He pointed out the sandstone formations jutting from the earth, surrounded by rolling hills scattered with cactus, piñon trees and juniper bushes.

"It's pretty peaceful up here. The only thing you have to worry about is running into some of the full-time residents, like rattlers, scorpions and black widows. I make it a point to carry my equalizer." said McCabe, pointing to the pistol secured between the seats.

"This is awesome, Tim. I'm amazed at how the terrain changes once you leave the main road."

"Yes, and when we reach the ruins, you will see six hundred years of history unfold. You can almost visualize a thousand Indians at work making rabbit nets and arrowheads. I find that fascinating."

"The past has always been intriguing," Burke said. "I'm constantly amazed at how often local archaeologists try to change its imprint on the future. You can't build a turkey from a feather and then write an article about it. The past is what it is."

At the mention of archaeologists, Gilda Humphreys and her relentless harangues drifted through McCabe's mind, but just as quickly he pushed the thought aside. "Just another mile or so after this last curve. This is a good time to take a look at the tunnel without the excavation crew around. I like to make my own discoveries before I call them in to continue the dig."

The vehicle fishtailed as the tires caught the ruts in the road, causing Burke to hold on tight.

"Whoa, Nellie," said McCabe, maneuvering the Hummer to a stop a few feet beyond the gate. He stepped onto the running board. "Let me introduce you to Medicine Rock."

"Wow," was Burke's response to an enormous monolith lodged comfortably at the edge of the barbed wire fence. "That must be two stories high."

"Twenty-eight feet, to be exact, with a cave in the center carved by Mother Nature over a thousand summers. Now if you'll grab a couple of lanterns there, I'll get my gear."

The entrance to the tunnel was covered over with piles of cholla cactus and remnants of a pack rat's nest to discourage curious trespassers.

"Now I know how Richard Wetherill felt when he first climbed down into Mesa Verde. How long have you known about this tunnel, Tim?" Burke leaned forward to assist McCabe in moving the debris.

"It was discovered last year quite by accident. I was doing some ground mapping before an excavation, and ended up getting shot. Jemimah Hodge happened to be riding her horse in the area, looking for a shortcut."

"That name sounds familiar."

McCabe unzipped the gear bag, checked the contents and slung it over his shoulder.

"She's now the forensic psychologist for the County. I was bleeding out and probably left for dead. She called an ambulance and it got me to the hospital in time. Sometime later she was out here tying up loose ends on the shooting. She stepped into the cave to get out of the hot sun and sat on a boulder, which moved enough to throw her off balance. She rolled it on its side and exposed the entrance to this tunnel.

We came out a few days later to check things out and by the time we were halfway through, we made a gruesome discovery." McCabe pointed in the direction of the ranch house.

"Yeah, I remember reading about the bodies. Headlines around Santa Fe for months. So what was her reaction to this whole unfolding drama?"

"She was a trooper. I know it must have scared the hell out of her, but if it hadn't been for her finding the tunnel, we'd never have found the bodies. Interesting lady. My wife and I have come to think of her as a daughter."

Burke followed McCabe down the wooden ladder.

"Watch your step there, Burke. I'm not sure I'd be able to haul you up to the top if you slipped."

Halfway into the tunnel, McCabe stopped to shine a light on the wall. "There should be some marks right around here." He pointed to a circular indentation about a foot above the floor, knelt and brushed off a thick layer of silt underneath one of the glyphs to expose a long arrow carved in the rock.

"You think the arrow points to something deeper inside the wall?"

"You've got a good eye, Burke. Hand me that small rock pick from the pack."

McCabe carefully tapped a layer of hardened mud on the surface and exposed a deeper linear recess emanating from the arrow and continuing for a short distance to the right. Burke moved the light along as McCabe patiently chipped away at the mud.

"Hold that light over here, Burke. I think I've found something."

CHAPTER TEN

Jemimah drove into the Coronado Apartment Complex on the south side of Santa Fe. The nondescript compound built in the seventies with units in various states of disrepair had been taken over by the city and converted to public housing. When she knocked on the door of Number 306, Tommy Griego answered. He was thirty-eight, Hispanic, short in stature and rotund.

"Yeah, what do you want?" he said.

Jemimah introduced herself and handed him her card. "Mr. Griego, we spoke on the phone yesterday. I called about your ex-wife, Meribel. I'm sorry for your loss."

"Not my loss, Ma'am. She left me over a year ago."

"May I come in?" Jemimah said.

"Sure. Excuse the mess. My kids don't pick up after themselves." He pulled up a chair at the kitchen table and motioned for her to sit in the other.

Jemimah carefully moved a Coke can to the side and placed her file on the table.

"As you know, we're working on the investigation of this case. Do you mind if I ask you a few questions, which will save you having to come down to the Sheriff's Office?"

Griego looked at her through puffy eyes.

"Can I offer you a glass of water, or a soft drink?"

Jemimah declined. She couldn't tell if Griego had a medical condition or if his ex-wife's murder had affected him more than he was saying.

"Have they figured out who killed her yet?" he asked.

"Unfortunately, no. We don't usually solve cases as quickly as they do on television. How did you and your ex-wife get along?"

He shrugged. "You talking recently or what?"

"Whatever comes to mind. How long were you married?"

"About thirteen years."

"Were those happy years?"

He grimaced. "You point me to someone who can say they have a happy marriage and I'll point out ten who don't. We had three kids, well actually two—the other, she had before we met."

"Was she employed?"

"Part of the time, mostly in retail."

"Had you had any recent contact?" Griego reached for the cat who had climbed on the table and held her in his lap.

"Aside from her texting me and asking for money every so often, no."

"Did you give her money?"

His sweeping gesture took in the modest interior. "Do I look like Donald Trump? I'm living in city housing because we lost our house and everything in it along with our car. Once in a while I would give her a few bucks, but I'm sure she always took it straight to the casino."

Jemimah sensed his frustration. "Did she have a gambling habit?"

"Addiction is a better word. Couldn't keep her out of there. She always had an excuse."

Before Jemimah could ask the next question, the phone rang. "Do you have to answer that?"

"Nah. Probably some damned bill collector. They can stand in line with the rest of them."

"When was the last time you physically saw her?"

"Well, aside from looking at her Facebook page, I hadn't

seen her in months. She promised the kids they could go out for dinner on her birthday, but she never showed up."

"Speaking of Facebook, did you have access to her page?"

He thrummed the table with his short, thick fingers. "Everybody did. She kept her profile as public. She used it to torment me."

"How so?"

Realizing what he was doing, he stopped thrumming and folded his arms across his broad chest. "When she didn't send her nasty photos to me in a text, she posted them all over Facebook for the whole world to see, including our kids."

"By 'nasty,' what do you mean?"

"Suggestive photos with whoever she happened to be screwing at the time, some *chollo* or biker dude, who the hell knows. She had over a thousand friends on that site, mostly guys; every one of them could see her boobs splattered all over the page."

"From all the information we've gathered, it didn't appear that she lived anywhere in particular. Did you have an address for her?"

"No. After we broke up she couldn't stay at a job for long. She was running with a fast crowd, you know—sex, drugs and rock and roll."

"Was she into drugs?"

Griego stood up to check the caller ID on the phone. "I don't know for sure. Every time I saw her, she seemed hyper, but I wouldn't put it past her. Someone said she was stealing jewelry from her employer and selling it at the gold store in Albuquerque. After a while nobody would hire her or take her in. She lived at a motel on Cerrillos Road for a while and then couldn't pay for it anymore so they threw her out and kept all her stuff."

"Mr. Griego, considering everything that has gone on in recent years, how did you feel about her?"

He sat back down in the chair. "Not bad enough to kill

her if that's what you're asking. Yeah, I'm pissed, but there's not a hell of a lot I can do about that. It's taken me this long to start getting over her and now I have to plan a funeral with our kids. That sucks. And who's going to pay for that?"

Jemimah rose to her feet and extended her hand. "Thank you, I think that's all the questions I have. Do you mind if I contact you if I need additional information?"

He shook her hand. "Sure. I'm not going anywhere."

Jemimah walked to her vehicle, making another mental note about her interview with the victim's ex-husband. Griego hadn't been too happy about how his life had turned out, but she didn't think he hated his ex-wife enough to kill her. What's more, she figured he was still carrying a torch for her.

CHAPTER ELEVEN

Detective Chacon had just completed his review of footage from the surveillance tape provided by the casino and was discussing it with Romero. They were in the kitchen of the Cerrillos substation.

"What did you find, Artie?" Romero said.

"Some good and some bad."

"Let me have both. We're overdue for some progress on this case."

They took their mugs of coffee to the conference room, where they made themselves comfortable.

"I had the manager plug the victim's card into their system for the week preceding the discovery of the body. We hit pay dirt on Friday, about ten days ago. The video zeroed in on her coming through the main doors after getting off the shuttle. I might say here that the driver doesn't remember picking her up, but he drives that route ten times a day."

"Go on."

"So she's sitting at a nickel machine, plays for a while, then a male comes into view, sits down next to her."

"Did it look as though she recognized him?"

"No, she ignored him at first, and about thirty minutes later it looks like she stopped playing and started up a conversation with him. Maybe she was out of coins on her machine. They talked for a while and then got up and went into the lounge."

"Anyone able to ID the guy?"

"No, the manager checked and there was no player card in the machine next to hers during that time period."

"Any video in the lounge?" Romero said.

"No, some kind of privacy thing. Only two both pointing in the direction of the bartenders to make sure they don't pocket any of the money. The video in the main part of the casino shows a back view of them walking into the lounge, arm in arm, and sometime after midnight we see her heading out to the parking lot. There's a man going through the doors right after her, but there's also a bunch of other people, and we see mostly the back of their heads."

Romero took a sip of his coffee.

"Don't the videos stretch out into the parking lot?"

"Seems the camera pointing to the main lot wasn't working that night. Within that time frame, the other one shows the side of a pickup truck with two occupants, but there's no way to identify either of them."

"Just our luck," Romero said, slamming his fist on the table and prompting Chacon to grab his mug to keep it from spilling. "This guy could be our killer. See if the casino can find someone who resembles him in any video they've shot as far back as they can go. The FBI oughta have some kind of facial recognition software we can use."

Chacon wagged a finger. "No can do, Boss. That's the bad news. The casino erases surveillance videos every seven days. They don't see a need to keep them beyond that. And remember, they run their own show without interference from the state or the feds."

"Crap." Romero paused, finally adding, "Well, do your best. Somebody's got to know this guy."

"Could be, unless he's an out-of-towner. There weren't any concerts scheduled for that weekend or events at the hotel."

"Maybe someone who was playing on the nearby machines might know him. Have them pull their player cards to see what info you can get and check the hotel surveillance tapes in case our killer might have been registered there, Artie."

Artie stood and finished off his coffee. "Sounds like a long shot. He wouldn't have been parked in the casino parking lot in that case but I'll put Detective Martinez on it."

CHAPTER TWELVE

Down in the tunnel at the Indian ruins, with an experienced hand, McCabe pushed the sediment aside on a section of the lower wall. The surface had the texture of an adobe brick. Working about a foot above floor level he tapped the center lightly, and the surrounding section crumbled.

"Take a look at this, Burke. It looks like some kind of side chamber dug into the wall. I can't tell how deep it is."

"See if you can stick your arm through the hole," Burke said, impatient to discover the possibilities.

"Are you nuts?" McCabe laughed. "I might get a handful of rattler."

Burke had a sheepish grin on his face. "Tell me, what can I do to help, then?"

McCabe motioned him forward. "Just keep pointing that light in this direction. In fact, here, point both lights and maybe that will free me up to move a little faster. It's times like this I wish I was twenty years younger and a lot more foolish."

An hour later McCabe had chipped away most of the hard plaster from around the initial hole. He stood up to stretch his legs. "Here's where being younger comes in handy. These old knees are stiffening up."

"Let me help." Burke handed the lantern to McCabe, knelt and pushed aside the remaining bucket of residue. He dusted off his knees. "It's all yours, Tim."

"You ready for this?" asked McCabe.

"I've been holding my breath for an hour. I think I'm going to pass out," Burke chuckled.

The small alcove was about three feet in diameter. McCabe leaned in and aimed the light toward the center. He panned the area with the light to make sure there were no surprises waiting in the wings, biting or stinging creatures long in residence. A decomposed set of rattlers sat in one corner. "Looks like there's some small pottery bowls and ollas embedded in the dirt. Hand me the whisk broom that's in a side pocket of my backpack."

Burke reached for the broom and pointed his light into the niche-like compartment. "I just remembered I have a camera with me, Tim. I'm sure you need some kind of record here. Let me take a few photos before you get in there."

"Good idea. I'm thinking there's more than what we see on the surface." While Burke steadied the camera, McCabe reached in to extricate the bowls, setting them a few feet ahead in the tunnel. He whisked away the surface dirt on the floor, then stopped. "Jeezus criminy, take a look at this!"

Burke craned his head into the compartment and flashed the light around. Next to a cluster of deer antlers circled by quartz crystals he could make out the shape of a box embedded in the mud floor. "Holy smokes, Tim. I've never seen anything like this. *Ouch*." He bumped his head as he pulled out.

McCabe let out a long, low whistle as he stood up. "We have to go back out to the Hummer. We're going to need better tools to extricate this box without damaging the surface."

"I need a drink," chuckled Burke, shaking the dirt from his trousers.

McCabe turned and froze in mid-step. He motioned to Burke with his hand. "Shhh. I thought I heard someone cough."

They walked cautiously toward the exit and McCabe unholstered his pistol. As they emerged from the tunnel, he noticed fresh footprints leading away from the cave.

"Looks like somebody might have been nosing around up here."

He checked the immediate surroundings. Burke took a look behind Medicine Rock. "Nothing up here but a couple of nosy piñon jays."

Satisfied they were alone, McCabe retrieved a canvas bag and an additional lantern from the Hummer. He handed Burke a bottle of water. "Here's your drink," he smiled. "Let's catch a few breaths. That's hard work for two old codgers."

They sat cross-legged on the floor of the cave, drank from their bottles and gazed out at the peaceful expanse of Del Chorro Creek, watching the slow moving water disappear around the bend. Outwardly, they looked like two well-dressed old prospectors in their cotton shirts and indigo jeans. Deep inside, though, they felt like ten-year-old boys about to embark on an adventure. Off in the distance a covey of quail padded gently on the ground, the mother craning her neck to assure each was following behind her. A big footed roadrunner zipped across the landscape, taking cover in a chamisa bush, the perfect camouflage for its woody coloring.

"Ready?" McCabe said.

"Let's do it," said Burke. They hurried down the ladder into the tunnel. Burke set up some free-standing lights at the base of the entry to the small cavern. McCabe unwrapped the pickaxe and small hoe and rolled out a thick mat on the ground so he could kneel with less discomfort. He reached into the cavern and tapped the axe around the box, using a small hand-rake to push debris to the side. It was a tedious process. The two traded off the task.

"All right. Looks like we're getting a little movement here," McCabe said. The box had begun to separate from the hard rock. "We're going to leave all the dirt there so one of the students can sift it for small objects."

McCabe used a long metal stake to dislodge the box. "This looks like it's made out of some kind of thick hide. If the hole was just a bit wider, I could get a better grasp." Just then the surrounding dirt loosened up enough to allow him to slide it out.

Burke stood anxiously behind him, unable to help in the narrow space.

"Oh, boy, oh boy," laughed McCabe, as he tugged on the box and it fell to the floor with a thud. "If there was enough room in here, I'd dance a jig."

"Do you want to open it down here?" Burke asked.

"Patience, young warrior, let me brush the dust off," said McCabe. "First let's get these tools up the ladder, and then between the two of us we'll see if we can haul it up into the daylight. It's solid, but nothing us two old coots can't handle. Those weekly visits to the gym ought to count for something."

Out in the bright noon-time sun, McCabe was the first one up the ladder. He reached down to carefully lift the box to the surface, while Burke pushed from the third rung of the ladder.

"From the looks of it, the hide's pretty ancient and liable to give at any moment." Burke lifted a corner with his thumb.

"Tell you what," McCabe said. "I'd actually feel a lot more comfortable if we got this box out of here. I hate to be paranoid, but I sure don't want to be seen opening it in case those footprints mean someone's lurking around."

"Okay by me. I'll go down and gather up the rest of the stuff. You back the Hummer up so we can get everything loaded."

"Good idea."

ca

Two hundred yards away, Gilda Humphreys squatted behind a gigantic mudstone, binoculars in hand. The sudden activity outside the cave caught her off guard. Coming from the south end of the ruins, she hadn't seen the Hummer parked behind Medicine Rock. Looking for signs of unlawful excavation, she had snuck down the entrance of the tunnel and barely made it back to her spot when she homed in on the two men climbing up the ladder. She spotted McCabe immediately but didn't recognize his companion. Activating the zoom lens on her camera, she began snapping photos, focusing primarily on the fascinating box the two were carrying toward the vehicle. This was an interesting turn of events.

"So, Mr. McCabe. Let's see how cocky you are when I show up on your doorstep with a document ordering you to turn over any bones or relics that just might be in that box."

CHAPTER THIRTEEN

L ater that afternoon, McCabe pulled the Hummer into the driveway of his upper Canyon Road home. Nestled at the base of the Sangre de Cristo Mountains adjacent to Museum Hill Road, the upper story of his adobe house peeked out from behind a massive eight foot wall. Two energetic Dachshunds greeted the men as they stepped out of the vehicle. McCabe leaned down to stroke their necks, reaching into his pocket for a treat while shushing their joyous yapping.

He directed Burke to the guest bathroom. "There's where you can wash off some of the grime. The housekeeper won't stand for us tracking dirt all over the house. I'll meet you in the studio, which is the door over there."

McCabe's studio consisted of an immense room with high ceilings attached to an equally large four car garage. Burke whistled. "I see you've expanded this side of the property since I was last here. You could house a fleet of helicopters and still have room for a full-sized yacht."

The walls of the side room were lined with cabinets, drawers, shelves and boxes filled with artifacts uncovered from the ruins. Pots, tools, beads, bones and everything else imaginable filled the drawers. Cases with arrowheads, stone weapons and *metates* took up another wall, with a row of massive pots on the top shelf. "I don't know *what* to say, Tim. This is better than being at the Indian Arts Museum. I've never seen so much great material in one spot. Impressive."

"The room tends to have that effect on people. Next time you and Jenny come for dinner, we can open some of those drawers. But for now let's see what mystery inhabits the inside of that box."

He backed the Hummer into the garage, easing it into a space next to the studio. He raised the rear door and they set the box onto a cart, wheeled it in and lifted it onto a long wooden table.

After carefully vacuuming the surface, McCabe inhaled deeply and reached for the metal hasp which moved with little effort. Together he and Burke lifted the lid of the hide box as more layers of dust and dirt fell to the table. Both men gasped in unison, momentarily speechless.

The box was full almost to the brim. Rows of silver coins and gold jewelry set with what at first glance appeared to be emeralds covered the top layer. Egg-sized turquoise discs lined the edges. A large gold cross encrusted with jewels jutted out from a corner. Everything seemed surreal. McCabe carefully dug around the center. "We can't just dump everything out. It's going to take us a while to uncover it all," he said. "Right now it's enough to just stand here and look at it. I can't get over it. My heart's been doing flip-flops. Damn! This is fantastic, isn't it? I can't wait for Laura to see it."

Burke wiped his forehead with a paper towel. "When I told Jenny I was spending some time with you today, she got a great big grin on her face."

"Why was that?" McCabe chuckled.

"She said something about how she and Laura were going to be artifact widows until we got it out of our system."

"Yeah, as if that would ever happen."

"Seriously, any thoughts on where this stuff came from, Tim?"

McCabe cleared the inside of the lid with a small feather duster. "Well, there have always been rumors about such treasures as Coronado's Gold. So it's not too farfetched to believe this might date back a couple of centuries. I read somewhere there's a lot more to the Cibola legend than history has suggested. This stuff looks like it's been underground for a long time. Take a look at the patina on this bronze disc. That didn't just happen overnight. I doubt if we'll ever know the true origins of everything in the box, but we're sure going to have fun speculating. God, this is exciting."

The only Native American object in the box was a medicine bundle with several carved animal fetishes and an assortment of small objects, quartz crystals, arrowheads, painted pottery circles, and a few small bone fragments in a small tanned buckskin bag. McCabe thought it probably belonged to a medicine man over four hundred years ago. He set the item aside to decide later what Pueblo he could give it to. The two men worked in silence until sundown.

∞

To address increased activity on the ruins and purchase of the adjacent ranch property, McCabe had taken a six month sabbatical from his part-time job at the Santa Fe County Sheriff's satellite office in Cerrillos. Decades after he had settled in Santa Fe, his long-time friend, Sheriff Medrano had asked for help on a cabinet full of cold cases and he was hooked again. His full attention was now focused on the hide box discovered at the ruins. He needed more time to get things prioritized. Sitting at his desk in his home office, he dialed Detective Romero, who answered on the first ring.

"Sheriff's Office, Romero here."

"Where's that pretty assistant of yours, Rick? She's got a much nicer voice."

"Hey, Tim. I was beginning to think you'd decided to abandon ship on us. You coming back next week? Clarissa's out shopping for supplies and I'm up to my ears with this latest murder case. Could use a little help."

McCabe leaned back in his chair. "Afraid I'm going to

need another couple of weeks, Rick. Something came up that needs my attention. In addition to dealing with the State Archaeologist tracking every step I take out there, I recently unearthed an interesting find during a dig."

"Anything I can do?"

"No, but thank you. I promise it won't be longer than the end of the month."

"All right, I'll let the Sheriff know. Jemimah's been waiting to discuss a couple of cases with you. She's stumped and needs some of your insightful advice to point her in the right direction."

"How is Jemimah doing? Better still, how are you two doing?"

"I'm happy to report things are moving along pretty well. We've been on a few dates and such. I'll spare you the happy details."

McCabe laughed. "*Sí Señor*, I'm sure I can read between the lines."

"Well don't jinx it by jumping the gun," Romero said. "We're taking it in baby steps. I've been following your sage advice about not spooking her with the wrong kind of attention."

"So how's that working?"

"I'll tell you one thing. She's sure a lot more receptive than she was a year ago around this time."

"Sounds like things are moving in the right direction. Give her our love and tell her I'm looking forward to spending some time with her. Knowing her, though, she'll probably have those cases solved by the time I step in."

"Will do, my friend. I'll keep you posted on any new developments, if you know what I mean."

"We want only the best for you two, Rick. Maybe I need to drop in to the Cathedral downtown and light a candle to St. Anthony. Isn't he the one who helps people out when they need a little nudge in a relationship?"

"I'm sure he'd spread it around Heaven that an old Episcopalian like you stopped by for a chat."

"Can't hurt," McCabe said, smiling on his end of the conversation. "Laura talks to that old *santo* on the table in the hallway all the time and I'm sure he listens to her."

"Thanks, Tim. We're missing you around here, so get your business done and we'll catch up over breakfast."

McCabe hung up, dialed Burke's number and invited him to lunch. He had a lot on his mind.

C&

The afternoon was hot and sultry, unusual for Santa Fe this time of year. McCabe was in a pensive mood as he and Foster Burke sat across from each other in their favorite restaurant. The waitress chitchatted and took their order. McCabe leaned back in the booth.

"Something going on, Tim? You seem a little distracted."

McCabe looked around him to make sure no one was in listening distance. Just the same, he kept his voice low. "You know, I've been doing a lot of thinking about that box we discovered and its contents. I imagine it was probably buried for a couple of centuries. None of these items appear to be sacred other than the medicine bundle, and I'll figure out how to deal with that."

"In what way, might I ask?"

He smiled and thanked the waitress when she brought their drinks and food, then waited for her to leave before continuing. The place wasn't too busy, and the other patrons seemed fully absorbed in their own conversations, but you could never be too careful. McCabe knew the sound of voices carried in these small adobe rooms. "There's been a lot of palaver lately from the government about making sure any significant items unearthed in archaeological digs are returned to the original Pueblos. We have a different situation here. None of this is Native American material. The Spanish had missions at both San Lazaro and San Marcos Pueblos, and after they came under attack during the Pueblo revolt in 1680, the Tano Indians became refugees, assimilating into other Pueblos, some as far away as Arizona. We're going to have to assume they might have gathered these things from nearby Spanish missions and holed them up to keep the marauding Indians from getting to them. Maybe they had the stuff hidden even before that."

Burke whistled. "I had no idea. That sure puts a different light on things. What do you think should be done with this material, Tim? I know donating it to a museum is out of the question."

"I'm glad we agree on that. Here's a thought. What about us partnering up and deciding what to do with this booty? I've been feeling my age a little these days and I'd sure like your help in putting this together."

"Hah, I'm no spring chicken myself, but if you're offering, hell, I'd be thrilled to be in on it."

"So far only our wives have seen the contents. I'd like to keep it that way for a while."

"What do you have in mind?"

McCabe leaned in closer to Burke. "How about maybe we take it all and bury it somewhere?"

"You mean back at the ruins? What purpose would that serve?"

"No, not at the ruins. Somewhere in the mountains. I don't know. I haven't thought it through, yet."

Burke narrowed his eyes, his head forward. "Are you serious? You do know how much this stuff is worth?" His voice was almost a whisper.

"Sure. I have a pretty good idea, no doubt about it, but that's not the issue here."

"What is the issue, then?"

"Look, Foster. We've both lived long and prosperous lives. You could even say they've been charmed. I know we've worked hard to get where we are today, but maybe it's about time we give something back. Just what would I accomplish by selling the stuff in the box? Uncle Sam would find a way to get his pound of flesh. I sure as heck don't need any more money, and my family's well taken care of. You understand what I'm saying?"

After waiting for the waitress to clear their plates, Burke said, "Yeah, I do. But how would we go about setting something like this in motion? It would be one hell of an undertaking."

McCabe grinned. "You know that feeling of chasing down something you're dying to have in your collection? You attend all the ethno shows, hang out at all the auctions, whether around here or maybe somewhere back East, flying all over the countryside to be the first one to have a whack at some great object, some rare effigy or Kachina. Maybe even a Chief's Blanket like the one we were battling over when we met?"

Burke slapped his thigh in his enthusiasm, then both men took a moment to cast about, ensuring that he hadn't called attention to them. People still seemed to be minding their own business. When he spoke again, Burke made a special effort not to speak too loudly. "Yes, sir. I can honestly say I've done that on more occasions than I care to remember. Missed out on my fiftieth birthday party just to hop on the red eye to San Francisco. I've probably logged a million frequent flyer miles chasing rainbows."

"Then you know what it's all about," McCabe said. "So you travel to the ends of the earth to get your hands on this elusive object, no matter what the cost, then when you finally have it in your hot little hands, somewhere along the line you suddenly realize that it was the chase you were after. It was much more exciting searching for it than actually finding it."

"I can't tell you how many times I've had those exact same feelings, my friend."

"At the end of the day, it had nothing to do with the object itself. It was all about the thrill of the chase and the people you met along the way."

"You're right on all accounts, Tim."

"Say, Burke, let's get out of here and continue this somewhere else. I don't want to seem paranoid, but you never know when the walls have ears in these places."

They moved the conversation out to the parking lot, sitting in McCabe's Hummer.

"So you're talking about a treasure hunt, Tim?" Burke took a moment to absorb the prospect. "I've got a vault-full of some pretty impressive stuff myself that I'd be willing to include."

"Me, too. I've stashed a couple of handfuls of American eagles and double eagles, along with a few placer nuggets from the Alaskan Gold Rush. We can even throw in some other gold jewelry. I have a Peruvian gold bracelet with a row of rare gems that's been sitting in a case waiting for someone with a big enough bank account to buy it."

"Well, then, I'll do you one better," Burke chuckled. "I'll throw in a 1742 half *escudo* Spanish gold necklace. It's got eight pure gold doubloons. Fancy and impressive."

"Think about it. Another thing, with such an extraordinary array of material, we can't hide a treasure in that old hide box. It would deteriorate before anyone could start the hunt. The side lacing's already started to fray. I sent a small sample to the anthropology lab and they suspect it might be at least three hundred years old."

"So what can we use, maybe have someone build a box?"

"No, I have a better idea. Thirty years ago I made a trade with another dealer for a miniature bronze dowry chest from Gaul. I think it just might fill the bill. It's pretty rare and dates to about 250 A.D."

"Let's take a look. I'll gather my stuff and bring it over."

McCabe looked over at Burke. "Here's another thought.

I've been working on a memoir about my life for a couple of years now. I'm thinking maybe I should include a few chapters about the treasure hunt."

"That's a great idea, Tim. How far along are you?"

"It's basically ready to go to press, cover and all. If I add a few chapters, that just changes the size of the spine. Our family owns a small publishing house that's printed all my previous books and any profit goes to charity. I don't have to jump through any hoops dealing with a big publisher who wants things done their way and gets half the profits in the end."

"I'd say that would be a perfect place to mention a treasure hunt," said Burke. "So now all we have to do is formulate a plan."

"It's going to require complete confidentiality; not even our families can know all the details. This would be the legacy each of us leaves. Can you imagine the ramifications of this idea?"

"I'm beginning to," said Burke. "I'm feeling as giddy as a perennial wallflower who's just been invited to the prom."

CHAPTER FOURTEEN

By the end of the week, McCabe and Burke had worked out the kinks in their plan to hide a treasure. McCabe placed an autobiography inside a small glass jar sealed with wax, with details regarding the origin of the treasure and the individuals connected to it. He also fine-tuned the final stages of his memoir and included several chapters on the history of the treasure that would be up for grabs once the book was released. Interspersed throughout the pages were clues which, if deciphered correctly, would ultimately lead to the right spot.

That evening after cocktails, their wives waited at the McCabe home for the arrival of a limo. Both women were polished and sophisticated. They wore casual clothing *à la Santa Fe*, long cotton skirts and custom made boots, their wrists and necks adorned with turquoise and silver jewelry designed exclusively for them. They were headed to the Santa Fe Opera, without their spouses, who were far more interested in discussing buried treasure than listening to Italian soprano Nicola Beller Carbone perform in her American operatic debut. They waved as the men drove off in Burke's Lexus, headed for dinner.

As the limo pulled onto the gated brick driveway to take the women to the opera, the sun slowly dipped into the Jemez Mountains. It jutted from the horizon as a huge coral disk, soaking the surrounding clouds with a sherbet hue.

The men arrived at Santacafé, where the hostess escorted them to a private dining room. McCabe leaned back on the cushion of the leather chairs. "I'm glad our wives get along so well," he said. "Otherwise they'd be on our cases to join in some of this upper crust entertainment they like to partake of. Give me an old John Wayne movie or a good Michael McGarrity thriller and a bottle of beer, and that's my idea of a few hours well spent."

"Yeah, I think they enjoy themselves more when we're not hanging around. Just like a couple of teenage girls." He looked around the room. "I think this is my new favorite restaurant. Nice of them to accommodate your request for a private room."

"They do aim to please. So, Foster, it looks as though everything is falling into place. My memoir's off to the printer and it should hit the bookstores in a couple of weeks. About that time, we should be well on our way. I have a publicist working on getting the word out to the media."

"Something's been bothering me, Tim. I've been thinking that maybe the clues scattered throughout the chapters might be a little too complicated for the average person to decipher. I'm no dummy and after reading the galleys, I was lost."

"Well, you and I aren't the ones who are going to be out there looking for it, so you might say we have the upper hand."

Burke tapped the palms of his hands together. "Yes, but we do want it to be found eventually, not buried in a place so obscure it will never be discovered."

"That's the point, Foster. We *do* want it to be found, but there's no point in making it too easy. What purpose would it serve for someone to find it a few days after the book is released? If that's the case, we might as well drop it off in the middle of San Francisco Street in front of the Cathedral. Whoever wants that treasure is going to have to work for it.

That's a hell of a lot of money there. It's going to take intelligence and stamina and a couple of pair of good boots."

"So you're saying there's a possibility *we* might never know when it's found?"

"Right. We might already have gone off to see our maker, for that matter. That's part of the reality of being our age. But that's not to say we won't be watching all the action from some heavenly perch."

"You've given this a lot of thought, haven't you?" Burke smiled.

"I have indeed, and you signed on as a partner in crime, so to speak. Someone to dot the I's and cross the T's."

"That would be me," laughed Burke, as they clicked their bottles of Corona. He had gained a lot of respect for this guy in recent months. He exuded a certain down-to-earth quality that was lacking in any of Burke's other friends, who were more interested in the kill, not the chase.

CHAPTER FIFTEEN

March disappeared into April, blowing in an unexpected heat wave. Spring was masquerading as summer, with days uncomfortably warm and nights still cool and breezy. The morning was inching toward another scorcher. For the past decade in Santa Fe it had become more the norm for daytime temperatures to hit the mid-nineties earlier than in previous years. The Channel Thirteen weatherman blamed the changes on either *El Niño* or *La Niña,* as he wiped the sweat from his brow.

Bart Wolfe was a seedy character who spent most of his days hanging around the Village of Cerrillos, hoping to score a sale or buy the street drug of the week from some loser in straits direr than his. About five foot eight, he wore his straight brown hair loose or tied at the neck. His usual wardrobe consisted of Wrangler jeans, cowboy boots, and the least soiled white t-shirt from the hamper topped with a long-sleeved cowboy shirt. His favorite hand-tooled leather belt and round silver buckle circled his thin waist.

Bart was feeling the heat a lot these days. He lived alone in a trailer park on the south edge of Highway 14 and the 599 Bypass, about three miles north of the State Prison, a place where he had been a guest in previous years on drug related charges. His trailer home was equipped with nothing but a couple of cooling fans to circulate the air. Scattered throughout the living room were dirty socks, beer cans and pizza cartons. Ashtrays overflowed with cigarette butts. A dust-covered glass bong sat in the corner on top of another load of smelly laundry. It was doubtful he would ever win a *Good Housekeeping* Award, or any other award, for that matter.

By current relationship standards, Bart was no prize. Most women wouldn't want to bring him home to Momma, even if he had money, which he didn't. He bathed and shaved only when he had a hankering for female companionship. Most times, when he hung around the bar, he only managed to get lucky when the vision of both parties was clouded by alcohol.

Spinning his wheels around the house that morning, Bart was channel surfing between puffs on a cigarette, watching nothing in particular on TV. He crumpled the empty pack of Camels, tossed it in the basket and was pausing to reach for a beer when a news program caught his eye. Tim McCabe sat on a couch next to Foster Burke, both Santa Fe art gallery owners. The two were being interviewed on *Good Morning America* by a drop-dead gorgeous blonde wearing a bright red dress and spike heels.

The men were both Robert Redford handsome; young-looking for their ages. These two cowboys were about to turn the national news scene on its side. The blonde with the automatic smile was bubbling over about a recently released book. Bart's ears caught the words *Santa Fe* and *hidden treasure* and punched the remote volume to high.

"Well, gentlemen. Tell me a little about your book and the treasure itself. Is there a treasure map with a big red X on it to accompany the book?" the news anchor asked, her turquoise blue eyes directed toward Camera One.

"No map. The clues are all scattered throughout the book," Tim McCabe said. "Not even our own families know the exact spot where it's buried. Burke here is a former Air Force pilot and you couldn't waterboard the location out of him."

"What on earth prompted this whole idea? Were you two just sitting around brainstorming about something interesting to do?" Here came that engaging smile again.

"We've been friends for a long time, and stemming from our good fortune in life we both figured that we had something we wanted to share with others," said Burke.

"And what do your wives think about all this treasure talk?"

"Our wives are both loving, understanding women. They'd have to be, to put up with the likes of us all these years. I can tell you they're excited at the prospect," said Burke.

"I second that," said McCabe. "My wife deserves to be on top of that pedestal where I placed her. She's the one who's provided the solid foundation our life has been based on."

"Sounds like you two are pretty lucky."

"Lucky isn't the word for it. Fortunate, blessed, all of the above."

"Now let's get back to the treasure. What exactly is in that chest? Can you give us an idea? It's hard to believe something this incredible would be out there for the taking," the newscaster said.

"Let us assure you it is a *real* treasure. Not a figment of someone's imagination," offered Burke.

The blonde smiled, revealing a perfect set of teeth. "I'm sure there are viewers in our audience who are going to think this is just a publicity stunt, don't you think?"

"They can think what they want," McCabe responded. "Neither of us has any need for publicity."

"Let me ask you this," she continued. "Why didn't you just donate the money to charity? I'm sure there are many organizations out there that could use this kind of windfall."

"I'm sure there are, but in our lifetimes, we have both supported many charities with generous donations and continue to do so," said McCabe. "The proceeds from all my book sales go directly to charity."

"You could make it a guessing contest and whoever guessed right would win a prize and the rest of the proceeds would go to charity," she said.

"What? And deprive a whole bunch of people the chance of finding a real treasure and experiencing the thrill of the chase?" said McCabe, grinning to deflect her accusatory tone.

"That's the title of your book, isn't it? *The Thrill of the Chase*?" she said dramatically.

"Yes, and that's exactly what it's all about. The thrill of the chase," McCabe repeated. "We're giving ordinary, every-day people out there an opportunity to experience the adventure of a lifetime. To go out and find an honest to goodness buried treasure. How often does a chance like this come up, and you don't even have to buy a lottery ticket? Imagine how many people will abandon their computers and television sets to embark on a hunt which will bring them closer to their family and friends."

"Well, all I can say is that you two must have pretty deep pockets, gentlemen," she said.

"We've worked hard all our lives and invested wisely," Burke answered. "Both of us in art and McCabe here in cattle ranching."

"So what have you packed this incredible chest with, if I might ask?" she said, glancing at her watch. "We have about three minutes and I'm sure our audience is on the edge of their seats."

"Well," Burke said. "There are plenty of gold and silver coins, a few platinum trinkets."

"There's also some pre-Columbian gold animal figures and ancient Chinese amulets carved from jade," added McCabe. "Along with that, there's a Spanish seventeenth century gold bracelet with a large ruby, and a 1742 half *escudo* Spanish gold necklace that probably belonged to Queen Isabella."

"Forgive me if I drool. It sounds like a king's ransom from where I sit," she laughed.

"Pretty much," said Burke.

"And you say you're preparing to bury it somewhere in the U.S.?"

"Yes, Ma'am. That's the plan," smiled McCabe.

"And the clues can be found in your book?" She held the book up for the camera.

"That they are," said McCabe.

"One more question. Do either of you think the treasure will be found? Or is it like searching for a needle in a haystack?"

"It might take a year or ten or even a hundred years, but someone's going to find it," said McCabe. "Someday. We can almost guarantee it."

Bart flicked off the TV. He had already decided to head over to Collected Works Bookstore in Santa Fe and buy himself a copy of McCabe's book. Hell, he figured he had just as much chance as anyone else. He'd spent a lot of time wallowing in misery. Maybe it was time to get out there and live a little. A big old treasure like that would sure make life easier for a cowpoke like him.

CHAPTER SIXTEEN

Sheriff Medrano was on the phone with Detective Romero. "How the hell did this casino case go cold so quickly? Your detectives dragging their feet?"

"We've all been working it, Sheriff. There's just not enough evidence to put the pieces of the puzzle together. It's been almost two months and we haven't had one single lead," Romero said.

"There's gotta be something, someone. This isn't our first barbecue. Get your people out into the bushes to stir things up."

"I have a meeting with Dr. Hodge to see if she's been able to come up with anything," Romero said.

"Well get on it. Maybe she'll show you guys how it's done. I might just have to give her a raise if she solves this one."

Romero hung up the phone as his assistant, Clarissa tapped on his door.

"Sorry to be late, Boss. Traffic's backed up to the interstate," she said.

"So I heard. Sheriff Medrano couldn't make it all the way out here, so he called instead."

"I take it you were the first target of the day?"

"Looked like it. Give me a buzz when Dr. Hodge gets here."

"That should brighten up your day," she said, her eyebrows raised.

"Don't you have some calls to make?" he said, shooing her out of his office. "I'm sure that new boyfriend of yours has already left a few messages."

Clarissa was thirty-nine and recently divorced. She had worked for Romero since he was promoted to lieutenant and appointed to run the Cerrillos satellite office several years back. A secretary at the Sheriff's Department almost as long as Romero had been a detective, she jumped at the chance to be his assistant. He had been a friend of her husband's and was like a brother to her.

∝

Jemimah parked on the gravel driveway, threw the keys in her purse and glanced in the mirror. She looked forward to meeting with Detective Romero, even though the subject was murder. Clarissa greeted her enthusiastically.

"He's in his office," she said. "Waiting with open arms, I'm sure."

Jemimah laughed. "Strictly business," she said. She couldn't help but notice how accommodating Clarissa was whenever she stopped in to see Rick. Did she suspect they were seeing each other?

Detective Romero came out of his office to greet her. He reached for her arm and escorted her into his office, closing the door on a smiling Clarissa.

"Have a seat. Can I get you some coffee? I really would like to kiss you, but I'll control myself," he said, stroking her hair as he walked by.

"I could quote from the County's handbook regarding inter-office relationships, but I won't," she smiled.

"So I guess we'll just have to get down to business," Romero said, sitting at his desk. "Have you come up with anything new on the casino murder? Sheriff's about to ream us a new one for not making any progress."

"Unfortunately I have very little to report. Detectives

Chacon and Martinez both said they were at a standstill with the casino. It's not that they're not cooperating, they just don't have anything more to offer."

Romero thumbed through the file. "Chacon's report states that the casino informed him all the surveillance tapes had been erased or taped over. So did somebody look through every tape throughout the casino, including the food bar, to see if anyone recognized the guy she was with?"

"Yes, and came up with nothing. You know, Rick, just because she sat next to him and then accompanied him to the lounge doesn't make him the killer. Maybe they both headed in different directions after they went out the door."

"Were you able to get the names of any previous husbands, boyfriends, coworkers, anything?"

"I interviewed her ex-husband, who stated without reservation that she had left him and their kids over a year ago after suffering some kind of meltdown," Jemimah said. "I gathered she turned a full one hundred eighty degrees after the divorce."

Romero leaned forward. "How so?"

"Running around with every guy she met, drinking, partying, and maybe even doing drugs. Hard to say. The guy sounds pretty bitter and didn't have any kind words to say about her, even though they'd been together for about thirteen years."

"Any chance he could be a suspect? You know how some guys never get over being left holding the bag."

She shook her head. "My impression was that he was confused, bitter and angry, mostly because she was able to just up and walk off without a word, without taking anyone into consideration except herself. But the children had already lost their mother once and he said they were devastated. He didn't seem to be the type who would put a double whammy on their kids, not with his Catholic upbringing. Co-worker of his said he's done an admirable job of keeping the family together in spite of losing their home and their mother."

"How about her family, employment history and all that?"

Jemimah folded her long legs. "The most I could determine was that because of a gambling habit she had acquired over the years, her family had washed their hands of her. Her sister said she could never tell when Amy was telling the truth and when she wasn't. Her excuses for borrowing money ran the gamut until everyone got wise and figured she was taking it to the casino."

"What about her employers?"

"She had a couple of good jobs in retail, working for some of the high end jewelry stores on the Plaza. She even worked for your friend, Davey. He said he had to let her go when things started going missing. She denied it but he had it on tape. After that she bounced from job to job, never lasting more than a month."

"Looks like this case is going to spend some time in the back of the file cabinet. Maybe something will come up."

"Seems that way." She shrugged apologetically. "Sorry I wasn't much help, but you can't knit a blanket if you haven't any yarn."

CHAPTER SEVENTEEN

Northern New Mexico's spectacular landscape is abundant with an unbelievable array of arroyos and ravines, perfect for stashing a treasure or hiding a body. There are river beds and jagged mountain tops, abandoned mines and shafts, caverns and caves, any number of places where something can be hidden from view. In addition, there are unscrupulous individuals who would stop at nothing to find such a treasure if they had the means. State Archaeologist Gilda Humphreys fit that profile. She had scrutinized McCabe's memoir a hundred times, charting the different possibilities gleaned from the clues in the book. As a public official she was precluded from participating in any activity that might bring unwelcome publicity to a State agency. How would it appear if one of their overpaid employees embarked on a treasure hunt? She could already hear the gossip mill humming.

No, she would come up with another solution.

Gilda stood in line at Albertson's grocery store waiting for the soccer mom in front of her to pay for an overflowing basket of junk food. The man directly behind her tapped his foot impatiently, a carton of Camel cigarettes in his hand.

"Do you mind if I go in front of you, lady? This is all I've got, and I'm dying for a smoke," he said.

"Excuse me? You can wait your turn like the rest of us," Gilda retorted.

"Don't get your ovaries in an uproar. It don't mean shit

to me. I can open up a pack right here and light one up."

Gilda pointed to the area above the customer service desk. "Don't you see that NO Smoking sign?"

"Rules aren't something I pay a lot of attention to. You look like you probably follow every one of them."

Gilda ignored the man's rudeness and began to unload her cart. He leaned in again.

"If you don't mind my saying so, that's a pretty interesting necklace you're wearing," he said. His tone shifted to one of unabashed interest in the turquoise and silver jewelry around her neck.

Caught off-guard, she rethought her initial reaction to the man. Maybe he wasn't such a boor. "Well, thank you. It's one of my favorites," she said. "I purchased it from a silversmith in Ganado, Arizona, some years ago."

"Looks like the turquoise came out of the Bisbee Mine. Nice looking stone and pretty rare to boot," he said.

"Sounds like you know a bit about turquoise. Are you a dealer?"

"No, I'm what they call a picker. I've sifted through almost every square inch of the Cerrillos area looking for turquoise nuggets, beads and the like. I assemble them into necklaces and sell them mostly to the trading post."

"Do you have a card?"

Bart stifled a laugh. "I fly by the seat of my pants, lady. You can always find me in Cerrillos. Bart Wolfe's the name."

Gilda turned to reply but the cashier waved at her impatiently. By the time she loaded the groceries into her car, Bart Wolfe was already blazing down the highway, cigarette smoke tailing out the driver's side window.

❧

The next afternoon, Gilda drove out to the Indian ruins. Even though she had no authority on private property, she was determined to catch McCabe in the act of unearthing illegal artifacts. She would deal with the legalities when the occasion arose. She was also very curious about the box she saw them carry out of the tunnel.

Following a leisurely drive, she found the main gate locked and no apparent excavations under way. Undaunted, she wound her way around the back road to the ruins and remained out of sight, hoping to videotape any shenanigans she was sure he was involved in. There was nobody around.

On the return drive to Santa Fe Gilda followed an impulse and took the turnoff to Cerrillos. She parked in front of the general store, where a panhandler was working a group of tourists.

She hollered out her window. "Excuse me, there, do you know Bart Wolfe?"

"Bart? Yeah, saw him a while ago. He's probably inside taking a leak." The panhandler flashed his bogus *I'm homeless and need money* sign at her. She handed him a dollar.

"Gee, thanks. Are you sure you can spare it?" he said.

Gilda parked next to the horse trough and walked along the weathered deck in front of the store. She was almost to the entrance when she spotted Bart trudging across the street from Mary's Bar. She could smell the alcohol on his breath as he stood within a foot of her.

"You looking for me?" he said, and although he didn't seem to recognize her, his demeanor was relaxed.

"Yes, Mr. Wolfe. I don't know if you remember me. We were in line a while back at the grocery store."

"Oh, yeah, I do. Did you come out here just to see me? Don't like women chasing me down. Bad for my reputation."

"I'm in a bit of a rush, but if you have some time later this week, I'd like to sit down and have a discussion with you."

"Discussion, like in *can we talk*?"

"I think I can use a man of your talents."

Bart stuck his chest out. "I got plenty of those, 'specially between the sheets," he grunted. Gilda disregarded his lowbrow remark.

"I have a proposition for you, but as I said, I'm in a hurry. I have to be in southern Colorado for the next few days, but on my return trip, maybe we could meet somewhere along the road?"

"Depends on how far along the road."

"I was thinking of having lunch at the Embudo Station on Wednesday. Maybe we could meet there after?"

"Geez, lady. That's quite a ways out from here. Almost halfway to Taos." Bart hesitated for a moment. "But I guess that would be all right. Ain't nothin' on my schedule that's so important I can't take a ride."

"Good. I'll see you there around two."

"Can I buy you a drink? The bar's right over there. I just came out to get some air."

"No. No thanks. So I'll see you at the restaurant on Wednesday?"

"Yeah, sure. No problem."

℅

Bart watched as Gilda's car pulled out onto the highway. Two minutes later he was sitting at the bar, trying to put the make on a woman who looked to be about twice his age. She winked and leaned forward, accentuating her ample cleavage. That was a sufficient invitation for Bart.

CHAPTER EIGHTEEN

What was there not to love about Santa Fe? The people, the weather, the architecture. It was a cultural melting pot, a subtle blend of *Gringo, Indio y Hispano*. In the early years of the twentieth century, the *Raza* outnumbered them all, but over the decades, tourists who came to visit and decided to stay tilted the numbers in favor of the *Anglos*. Since the 1960s, the city had almost doubled in size, and it slowly became Aspenized. The family businesses on the Plaza had all been replaced by upscale galleries and gift shops. Designer clothing parlors for well-to-do tourists looking for a wardrobe of broom skirts, vests and squash blossom necklaces rounded out the offerings. There was no place to hide.

It was a typical Santa Fe Friday night in early May. The street was alive with dozens of gallery openings and music blaring from the speakers on the plaza bandstand. Hundreds of people milled about like ants, some wearing shorts and t-shirts and others in their lets-go-do-some-tequila-shots party clothes.

A few miles from the Plaza, in McCabe's studio, Tim McCabe and Foster Burke were surveying the bronze chest they would fill with artifacts. It was perfect. The hide box had been dusted off, wrapped in protective paper and relegated to a shelf. They sifted through the contents one last time. Every item was carefully set in place, with each layer sparkling like a mountain of diamonds. At first glance, the least valuable might have been the silver dollars, dwarfed by the number of gold coins. At a recent auction, a 1933 Saint-Gaudens double eagle twenty dollar gold coin garnered a price of seven and a half million. The twenty troy pounds of gold in the chest would make just about anyone salivate; it was worth about three hundred thousand in the present market. Virtually everything they chose epitomized the phrase *wildest dreams*. This was going to be a hundred times more exciting than winning the lottery. They carefully closed the lid and carried the chest into the living room in preparation for its final destination.

The room had a twenty-foot ceiling, with large beams set in thick adobe walls. The walls were covered with hand-woven Indian rugs and ceremonial wear. Wooden shelves filled with historic pottery ran across one side. An old crucifix hung from the center of the kiva fireplace in the corner. McCabe retrieved a couple of beers from the wet bar in the corner and handed one to Burke.

He sat on the couch with his feet propped up on a worn leather ottoman and made a broad, sweeping gesture. "Wouldn't this make a great exhibit at the Smithsonian? Imagine it on a polished ebony pedestal surrounded by lasers. Everyone could partake of its magnificence."

"Having second thoughts there, *amigo*?" said Burke.

"No, just imagining different scenarios. I like to do that, you know."

"Hey, anyone who can come up with this treasure idea definitely has a fertile mind." Burke checked off the items on his tablet. "Looks like everything is taken care of."

"I can guarantee that this treasure hunt is going to draw a lot of people out of the woodwork. They're going to be stumbling all over each other," said McCabe.

Burke scratched his head as he marveled at the display. "Maybe at the beginning, but only the serious contenders will stay with it. Not everyone will have the stamina to keep up the chase."

"You're probably right, Foster." He hefted himself to this feet and walked over to touch a few of the coins and turn them over in his hands. "But whoever finds it not only has to be ambitious, but cunning and determined, to boot. This isn't for the faint of heart or the weekend warriors. I'm sure we'll be plowed under with requests ranging from the ridiculous to the sublime." McCabe shook his head and backed away from the pile. "There's so much Twittering and Facebooking that I can't keep up with it all. I finally had to program my phone to go direct to message. The number of calls I've been receiving is mindboggling."

McCabe grinned. The whole business was making him giddy, almost high. He sat in the chair next to Burke. "With so much publicity out there, the potential for something going amiss is minimized by the fact that whoever finds it probably won't be able to keep it a secret. Someone's going to be enjoying their fifteen minutes of fame and we'll be hearing about it on the evening news. Gonna have to work hard to keep our heads from swelling to double their size. My wife, for one, would never allow it."

He pointed to his laptop. "In addition, there's an article about us in the *Huffington Post*. There's going to be a lot of sweat expended in looking for the treasure—someone just has to decipher the clues. Take a look, they published the poem from the book."

Burke reached for the laptop and read out loud.

There's a treasure in the mountains
Gently hidden in the night
Where coyotes howl and barn owls hoot
And leaves covered with blight.
Take heed of what I tell you
And wander the canyons down
Walk by as waters run fast and high
And the trout wears a crown

There are no roads to find
But borders edge the brown
Keep your eyes on the horizon
Your head on your shoulders
Blaze along the path and to the right
A long trail of boulders.
Move forward through the dark and
Paddle the creek for an hour
Where springs abound
Raise the board along the edge
And take the booty with a sledge.
Why do I do this you ask?
To give you a daunting task
If you are strong and bold
Hear me all and listen well,
You alone will find the gold
Or return again to hell.

Burke smiled and tapped his brow in a deliberate fashion. "Anybody ever tell you that underneath that slightly wrinkled exterior lies a mind filled with pure genius?"

"You just did."

"One thought, *amigo*," Burke said. "You ever see *The Treasure of the Sierra Madre*?"

"Long time ago," McCabe said. "Bogart movie, right?"

"Well, there are a lot of books and movies about the pursuit of treasure and what it does to people. You're not worried about greed?"

"This is reality, Foster, not a movie."

"Hmm, but every time you pick up a newspaper there are so many unhappy stories about lottery winners and the effect of their newfound wealth on friends and relatives ..."

McCabe sat back in his easy chair, a thoughtful look on his face. "I prefer to think the best of human nature, Foster," he said. "There are just as many lottery stories that end happily as there are cautionary tales. I read somewhere that the owner of a small company set up retirement funds for all his employees. Here's hoping the winner is deserving of his or her bounty."

They both raised their glasses of beer.

After weeks of preparation, the word was officially out. Early the following morning, the rented SUV was all packed up and ready to go, its destination a secret shared only by the two. They laughed as McCabe repeated the clue he gave a pushy reporter. "All I can tell you is that the treasure is buried four hundred miles due west of Chicago." As a lawman, McCabe was aware that their cellphones could be tracked to within a few feet of their destination. He made sure theirs remained at home and purchased a disposable phone for emergency use. A vehicle switch would occur somewhere down the road to assure they weren't being followed or tracked by GPS.

McCabe drove out of the driveway onto Old Santa Fe Trail and made his way toward the Interstate. By late afternoon the following day they would be headed home.

BOOK TWO –
METAMORPHOSIS

CHAPTER NINETEEN

Forty miles north of Santa Fe on Highway 68, the Embudo Station is a historic narrow gauge train station dating from the mid-1800s. Dubbed the Chile Line, it served the railroad between Colorado and Santa Fe. Use of the trains began to wane in the 1950s.

In recent years, the abandoned station had been converted into a popular restaurant in the middle of a grove of cottonwood trees shading the riverfront patio. Gilda Humphreys preferred to eat inside the restaurant, where there was less chance of being bombarded by pesky mosquitoes and yellow jackets.

As she waited for Bart Wolfe to arrive, she surveyed the furnishings of the room. Every stick of furniture including the bar was constructed from roughhewn wood. It resembled a saloon on a western movie set. She directed her gaze toward the ceiling, expecting to see stuffed animal trophies hanging on the walls. The décor was not to her taste, but the food was excellent. She was annoyed that Bart hadn't arrived yet and was about to leave when she saw his white van pull into a handicapped space.

ൟ

Bart switched off the ignition and popped a couple of Xanax into his mouth, washing them down with a swallow of beer. He had awoken in a state of anxiety that morning and hoped the drugs would bring him into focus. His experience was that in the right quantity, Xanax was like that—a blue goddess with the ability to produce a feeling of mild euphoria. It would take about fifteen minutes, but he would get there. He engaged the parking brake and inhaled deeply.

"You're late," Gilda said as Bart sauntered toward her.

"Well, good afternoon to you, too, Ma'am," he said, checking his watch. It was barely five minutes after the hour.

"Sit down. I don't have all day. And for Christ's sake, button your shirt. Nothing more unsightly than exposed greasy chest hair."

Bart felt like reaching across the table and rubbing his chest hair in her face. "Yes, Ma'am. I understand. My schedule is pretty tight, too," he said as he pulled out a chair making a loud scraping sound. Truth was, Bart spent most of his time sitting at the bar in Madrid. He wasn't sure what kind of proposition this woman wanted to pitch at him, but he knew for damned sure it wasn't *sexual*, at least he wasn't picking up any vibes in that direction.

Gilda snapped at the waitress. "Can we have some service here? I'd like to order dessert." She requested a cup of coffee and an apricot scone. She looked at Bart, who would have preferred a beer, but she ordered a glass of iced tea for him.

"Let's get down to business here, Mr. Wolfe. I'll get right to the point. I'm looking for someone to do a little job and I'm willing to pay a reasonable fee to get it taken care of."

"As long as I don't have to kill anybody off, lady, I'm pretty much open to anything," he said, a grimy smirk on his face.

"This is a serious matter, Mr. Wolfe, no need to make light of it."

"Okay, okay. I was just trying to inject some humor into the situation, not even guessing what it is you're getting at. So tell me what you want and I'll tell you whether or not I want to do it."

Gilda moved her head, almost touching Bart's nose. "All right. Now please listen carefully. I don't want to have to repeat this. What I'd like you to do doesn't involve breaking any laws. You would just keep an eye on someone, perhaps follow him around for a short time."

"Are you looking for something in particular?" said Bart.

"Yes, actually I am. I'm interested in a map or drawing that this man might have in his possession. Frankly, I want you to get it for me when you see he's not in the area."

"Do you want me to hurt 'im?" He could feel his pupils starting to dilate from the pills he'd popped earlier. "That would cost you extra."

"No, no. Not that. That's out of the question. I'd like to get my hands on this drawing to see what is on it." She cleared her raspy throat. "I'll provide you with a digital camera to take a picture. There's no need to steal anything."

Bart crossed his arms. "Sometimes I'm a little slow figuring out people's motives and I want to be clear about exactly what I'm being hired on to do. Looks to me like you're after some kind of treasure map. You know, like some of them old rich guys who go out looking for stuff with metal detectors." Bart believed he had a knack for finding buried things, even if others might not agree.

"You are a very perceptive man, Mr. Wolfe. Initially what I want from you is your pledge of confidentiality. Do I have that?"

Jeezus. Maybe she wants me to write my name in blood. "Yes, Ma'am. I swear on a stack of Bibles."

"There's no need to be condescending. A simple yes or no will do." Gilda explained to Bart that she wanted him to keep an eye on Tim McCabe and Foster Burke when they were out digging at the ruins, which she knew they did a couple of times a week. Once they headed back to town, he was to enter the ranch house and search for anything resembling a map or drawing. She had practically memorized the clues in McCabe's memoir, but she needed more information. The clues were bathed in a veil of mystery that wouldn't make them easy to solve, and she suspected there had to be a map or drawing that would make finding the treasure quite a bit quicker. No way could McCabe and Burke just pick out a random spot to hide their treasure without putting it down on paper, *somewhere.* That would be counterproductive. At least that's what she would have done.

Bart had been drumming his fingers on the table as she spoke, but now he stopped and cocked his head. "Tim McCabe?" he said. "You talking about the guy who owns the Indian ruins next to the Crawford Ranch in Cerrillos?"

"Yes, and keep your voice down." She looked around, worried that they might have been overheard. McCabe was well known in this area. "He recently purchased the ranch property and has been doing some remodeling," she continued in a lower voice.

"I didn't know that, but yes, I do know him. He can be a pretty good shot with a rifle when he finds a trespasser nosing around." On the sly, Bart had helped himself to a number of small artifacts from the ruins long before McCabe came into the picture. He started drumming on the table again but stopped when the woman put her hand on his to still it. Once again, there was nothing sexual in the gesture, just a determination to make him behave.

"Normally," she said, removing her hand gingerly as if worried about what plague she might have exposed herself to, "he splits his day between the Sheriff's Office and on the ruins and doesn't return to Santa Fe until late afternoon, but I believe he's still on leave from the Department. I haven't seen his vehicle there recently and I don't think he's spending time at the ranch itself, either. There's been a lot of construction going on at the house and the archaeological crews haven't been excavating the ruins for weeks."

Wolfe folded his arms high across his greasy chest.

"Sounds like you've been doing a little checking on your own. What's this paper supposed to look like?"

"I'm not sure. I assume it's a hand-drawn map of sorts." She cleared her throat once more, reaching for a glass of water. With that raspy cough and the way her neck craned, she reminded Bart of a goose, in more ways than one. "Can you do this?"

"Sure I can. But it ain't gonna be easy. I could be arrested or land up with a pound of buckshot in my behind, you know. Who the hell is going to help me then?"

She took a long sip of coffee and avoided his eyes. "I'm assuming you have enough sense to be careful. I'm not asking you to risk your life. You can determine if McCabe is in Santa Fe or at the ruins. If he's at one, he's certainly not going to be at the other."

"Well, answer me this. You said you weren't asking me to do something illegal. Doesn't breaking into a house and taking something fall under that category?"

Gilda sighed. "There's a difference between photographing something and removing that item from the premises."

"I'd say that's mincing words. Pretty convenient if you don't mind my saying," Bart said.

"If you don't think you can do this, say so. I'll find somebody else."

"Well, good luck on that, lady."

She reached for her purse and stood up. "So what's it going to be, Bart?"

"Okay, I'm in. How do I get a hold of you when I find this so-called map?"

"Here's my card. Don't call me at the office. Just leave a message on my cell. Here's the camera. Very simple to operate. Even an idiot can figure it out. The instructions are on the side." She returned to finishing off her coffee.

Bart wondered which idiot she was referring to. "Will do,

Ma'am. I'll be in touch," he said, pushing out the wooden chair. He walked to the cooler and picked up a six-pack of Bud, paid for it and whistled a tune on the way to the parking lot.

Talk about a golden goose. If I play my cards right, this crazy lady might just provide me with a nice little nest egg.

Sitting in his van guzzling down a beer, he used his own camera to take a photo of Gilda Humphreys as she got into the State car. One never knew when something might come in handy.

I might look stupid, but I'm nobody's fool.

CHAPTER TWENTY

Bart Wolfe wasn't surprised to find the patio door unlocked at McCabe's new digs. He'd worked construction and knew workers hardly ever remembered to lock the doors, especially out in that area. He did think it uncommon, though, that a cop could be so careless. He appeased the dog with a rib bone taken from the trash bin behind the restaurant and walked into the house. Bart knew that same dog would alert him if anyone drove up while he was checking things out.

The ranch house had been completely remodeled since the last time he was there. The kitchen was modern and fancy. Everything about the place appeared to be different, not like when his friend Charlie Cooper was the caretaker a couple of years back and grew a huge crop of Marijuana in the sunroom. Bart's itchy fingers were tempted to snag something to sell later but thought he'd better resist that temptation. Stealing from a cop wasn't a smart thing to do, although what *was* he doing there if it wasn't exactly that?

He searched down the hall for an office. Within seconds he was rifling through papers on the desk. He pulled out the top drawer of the file cabinet and found a file labeled *Book Galleys*. He thumbed through that and then tried the second drawer. He spotted a manila folder labeled *Miscellaneous*. Jackpot! Between two files he found a crude drawing neatly tucked inside another folder. This might be what goose lady was looking for. He took a couple of photos using her camera, and a couple more with his own.

In another drawer he found a letter dating from the 1970s from an inmate who was soon to be released from prison in Arizona. It had a rough drawing attached to it. The handwritten letter requested McCabe foot the bill so he could search for the lost Taos Brink's truck robbery treasure, hidden since 1972, after three robbers were arrested following a chase down the highway into the Taos Canyon. The strongbox taken from the Brink's truck was never recovered. There was a handwritten notation across the top of the letter that merely said *Bullshit*. Bart took a photo of both for himself only. He carefully replaced the folders, wound his way back through the house, closed the door tightly behind him, and tossed another treat at the dog.

Bart had parked his van behind a grove of salt cedars next to Medicine Rock. It took him ten minutes to hustle along the fence line, keeping an eye out to make sure nobody drove up. He jumped in the van and drove toward Santa Fe, confident he was now holding all the high cards in the deck and a bonus to boot. He didn't know exactly what Gilda was after, but he could tell she was a schemer. Being a con man himself, he didn't feel too uncomfortable dealing with her. He tucked the camera in the glove box next to his pistol. He called to tell Gilda he had found a rough drawing, but it was going to be difficult to decipher. He added that it didn't look much like a map to him.

"It doesn't matter what it looks like to you," she snapped. "Drop the camera by my office. How long will it take you to get here?"

"Don't get your panties in a twist. I'm on the bypass right now. It will take me half an hour to get all the way across town. I still gotta stop for gas, which, by the way, lady, I'm expecting to be reimbursed for."

By the time Bart reached Gilda's office the parking lot

was empty. She unlocked the main door and directed him down the hall. Once there, she yanked the camera from his hands. He watched as she inserted the memory stick into her computer and brought up the photos on the screen. Bart smirked as he sat in the easy chair. He figured she would go ballistic if she knew he'd already stopped by the Wal-Mart photo center to run off a few copies for himself.

"Aha," Gilda smiled. "This looks very promising." She printed a copy and directed Bart to the chair next to her desk. "Take a look at this. Don't you think it looks like the Taos area?"

Bart studied the paper as if for the first time. "Well, I'm pretty familiar with Taos Canyon, and it *might* have something to do with that area, hard to tell. This is a pretty rough drawing. You can make out a river and a canyon of sorts, not much else. There's sure as hell no recognizable landmarks that would convince me."

Gilda placed the paper neatly into a folder. "McCabe's memoir has an assortment of clues interspersed throughout the pages and if we can put those clues together, we might have a starting point. I seem to remember him mentioning something about Taos."

"Pretty strange to put clues right out there in a book for everyone to see. I don't get it."

"A little out of the ordinary, perhaps, but not everyone has the intelligence to decipher the clues or the guts to chase them. These are fairly ambiguous references. It's going to take a genius to figure them out."

"Ambigawhat?" Bart said, scratching his head. "I don't think I know that word."

"Ambiguous, unclear, cryptic, vague."

&

Gilda coughed loudly. She had forgotten she was dealing with an uneducated man, someone with the brain of a

Neanderthal. He wouldn't be difficult to control. She might have to lead him by the hand but she didn't have to worry about him blabbing everything all over the place. At least she hoped that was the case. Gilda considered herself to be a fairly good judge of character.

"Oh, yeah, I get it," Bart lied. So where do we go from here?"

"As I mentioned at the restaurant, I'll front you whatever it takes, within reason, to get you started on the search. I want you to find the exact location shown on this map and then I'll go up there with you to start digging. Will five hundred be enough?" She reached into her purse and pulled out a wad of bills.

Bart almost let out a whoop. "Er, yes, Ma'am. That would be okay for right now."

"Bear in mind I expect you to keep in contact with me on a regular basis. And stop repeating that annoying ma'am bullshit. I'm not your great aunt. Coming from you it sounds insincere."

This guy's a real piece of work. I'm going to have to be whipping his ass at every turn.

"Oh, yes, *Ma'am*. I will be in touch," Bart said, rising to his feet.

"You have my number. Now, please, I have work to get back to." She waved him toward the door, her head already turned away.

08

Did she prefer he said, *Yes, bitch*?

But Bart was too excited to waste much energy on Gilda's snooty attitude. His enthusiasm propelled him down the steps of the building. He nearly cart-wheeled out to the parking lot. He had been down to his last few dollars. The present lull in the economy precluded him from selling his last batch of weed, which was sitting in a bag at the bottom of the clothes hamper in the laundry room. But things were sure looking up. First, he was going to the bank to crack a hundred, and then home to sleep off the hangover he'd been nursing for days. In the morning, he would take a quick exploratory ride along the highway to Taos, to check out that second map he'd stolen from McCabe. Gilda didn't know it, but she was going to finance *his* treasure hunt. At least it wasn't as far-fetched as her idea. He had little to lose except time, and he had an abundance of that.

Late the next afternoon near Taos Canyon, Bart hiked alongside a spring surrounded by the remains of an old Indian settlement deep in the mountains of the Orilla Verde, where the Rio Pueblo and the Rio Grande joined waters. He stumbled across Petaca, a small 19th century Spanish community south of Taos, where life all but stood still. Abandoned *acequias* were overgrown with dry gourds, unlike in other areas of the north where the *mayordomos* had already begun the annual cleaning of the ditches to make way for planting.

In a canyon near an old campsite he stumbled onto a hidden crevice in the cliff wall. The entrance opened into a narrow, zigzag ravine. Bart glanced at the map but couldn't find any reference to that, and walked on toward the mouth of the canyon. Off in the distance he could hear a coyote wailing. He put a hand up to shield his eyes from the setting sun. From this vantage point he could see a lush green valley with a stream meandering through the center. Surrounded by the Carson National Forest, the grass was thick and deep. He scouted the area for another hour, wishing he had brought another beer, and decided to call it a day.

On the return drive to Santa Fe, he stopped at the travel store for a topographical map of the Taos Valley. He planned to study it closely and then return to do some serious poking around. But foremost on his mind, he was going to pull up a barstool and have a drink at his favorite watering hole in Madrid.

CHAPTER TWENTY-ONE

As Jemimah unlocked her front door, she was greeted by her energetic Border Collie's tail wag and the ringing of her phone. It was Detective Romero.

"Hey, Sweet Cheeks. You sound winded. Did I catch you at a bad time?"

"Just walked in the door. About to hug the dog, fill her bowl, kick my shoes off and spend the rest of the night watching a click flick," she said.

"Well, don't watch Channel Seven. They're doing a special report on unsolved murders in New Mexico and our casino case is at the top of the news. Reporter's taking the Sheriff to task for not solving the case."

"Nothing new?"

"Nope, and it's been a long day. Too long. Sheriff Medrano kept my butt nailed to the wall all afternoon, shuffling interviews with the media and unraveling tips that dead-ended. Everything he didn't want to deal with."

Jemimah laughed. "Poor thing. I feel your pain."

"You don't sound very sympathetic, there."

"Listen, I can remember Medrano picking on me for a solid month when I first signed on. Had me close to tears a couple of times."

"Yeah, but with you his bark was worse than his bite. He didn't know how to deal with a woman of your caliber. You had him stumped. Brains and beauty is a fierce combination."

"Awww, thank you. Are we needing a little sympathy,

Detective? I could grab a few things and be at your place in half an hour. We've been going in opposite directions for a couple of weeks now and I, for one, am missing you."

Romero was about to take her up on the offer when his call-waiting clicked. "Hold that thought, Jem, I've got another call coming in. I'll get back to you."

It was the crime lab. "You working overtime, Harold?" Romero said.

"My usual. I'm up to my *chongos* in reports. About the only time I can get to them is after hours when the switchboard's shut down."

"What you got for me?" Romero said.

"Nothing you're going to like. That pistol the State Police confiscated last week isn't the one used to kill that woman from the casino. Not even close. Striations on the slug didn't match," he said.

Damn. Another barrier in the road. "Thanks for cranking that out. I appreciate it."

Romero clicked the receiver and dialed Jemimah. Her phone went directly to voicemail, indicating she was probably down for the count. He left her a message about meeting for lunch the following day and called it a night.

❧

Shortly after noon, the couple was seated at a table at Jambo Café, a new African restaurant located in a strip mall on the south side of Santa Fe. A first of its kind in an area most comfortable with anything red chili, the establishment specialized in exotic African and Caribbean cuisine, and had become an overnight sensation.

"Even though this has to be a working lunch and not a date, I thought we might try this place. See anything you like?" Romero said.

"I'm torn between the coconut kabobs and the curried crab cakes," Jemimah said.

"Well, I'm having the goat stew. I heard it's great. And not only that, there was a Billy goat that harassed me all through my childhood, butting me around every chance he got, so I'd like to imagine I'm finally getting even," Romero said.

Jemimah laughed. "I'm not even going to try to psychoanalyze that one."

After they had finished eating, Romero brought Jemimah up to date on the case. "I got a call from the crime lab last night. It wasn't what we were hoping."

"I assume the bullets from the gun recovered by State Police weren't a match."

"No, and we've been dead-ending for a few months now. I hate to say this, but unless something breaks, we're done for a while," he said.

"I haven't had much success, either. I've interviewed the ex-husband, her mother and her family. Most of her friends had written her off over a year ago, so none of them had contact other than an occasional sighting at Wal-Mart or the casino."

"You said earlier she had been banned from the casino. What was that about?"

"Everyone I interviewed said she was a feisty woman, sometimes a little too feisty. She wouldn't let anyone intimidate her and if they looked at her cross-eyed, she would go after them. Sounded a little passive aggressive to me," she said.

"How old did you say she was?"

"Forty or so."

"A little old to be engaged in catfights, don't you think?" he said.

"Happened right there on the casino floor. Security guards had to break the two women up. Before they arrested her, she told the guard the other woman was 'talking shit' about her family. No telling what that was."

"Speaking of the casino," Romero said, "we're at a standstill there also. Without surveillance tapes there's no way we can determine if the guy she was talking to had been in there before. From the looks of it, he sat down to play the machine next to her, they started up a conversation, hit the bar and possibly left together. And nothing about that scenario says he's our killer. She could have walked out the door, hitched a ride with someone in the parking lot, and that was the end of it."

"But she didn't own a car. She had to leave with him."

"The sad part about it is that you would think that with as much money as the casinos rake in—and there are about seven of them just on that sixty mile stretch between Santa Fe and Taos—they would have better security to protect their patrons," Jemimah said.

"I talked to a security guard who's worked several of the casinos in the area, and he said most of them are diligent about keeping parking lot security in working order. There's been a couple of assaults and rapes in the past and the last thing they need is anything that discourages people from going there and spending their money. What's your gut tell you about this case, Jem?"

"I can't see any logic to this killing. If he just met her, didn't know anything about her other than she was fairly nice-looking and apparently friendly, what could have happened? From the tapes, it appeared they were hitting it off."

"Maybe she pushed one of his buttons after they left. Hard to say. It's all speculation at this stage, and we have nobody to tell us anything different," Romero said.

"Why would he shoot her after he strangled her?"

"Probably needed to make sure she was dead. Otherwise she could identify him. Coroner said that the rocks placed over the body made it almost impossible to distinguish if there were any defensive wounds," he said.

"I've also wondered why he didn't just dump her body somewhere instead of half-ass burying her and taking the time to cover it with rocks. Don't you think he would have been afraid of somebody spotting him?"

"Not in that part of the county," Romero said. "He either was familiar enough with the area to know that, or was cocky enough to take the chance of being pulled over in the middle of the night with a body in the trunk. Anyway, we haven't been able to determine if he killed her there and found it convenient to dump the body. I'm sure he never expected someone to be in the same place gathering rocks a couple of days later."

"I spoke with Detective Martinez, who checked all the pending cases in the adjoining states, and there's nothing similar there either. No attempted strangulation finished off by a bullet to the head."

"I'm afraid, sweetness, that we've hit a major brick wall. It's annoying as hell to strike out before we've even gotten to first base. Let's get out of here." He stood up and laid down money for the check. "Clarissa's going to be tracking me down if I don't get back to that pile of work sitting on my desk."

CHAPTER TWENTY-TWO

At eight o'clock on Monday morning, Bart loaded up his van with a backpack, camp shovel and a twelve-pack of beer. There was a line at the Giant station and a ten minute wait to gas up and replenish his cigarette supply before he took off toward Taos. He had spent the weekend poring through the references in Tim McCabe's memoir and every map of Northern New Mexico he could get his hands on and decided that was all a waste of time. McCabe was a lot smarter than Gilda was giving him credit for. What would be the point of burying his bronze box so close to home? That was when Bart decided he wasn't going to rely on the drawing he gave Gilda—the one she was certain was the map to McCabe's treasure. He thought that was too far-fetched. But he had carefully studied the map attached to the letter to McCabe from the Arizona inmate who alleged he was part of the group connected to the Brinks robbery. That made a lot more sense. At least there were a couple of landmarks indicated that might just lead him to something interesting.

Driving through the canyon, Bart couldn't help but notice that the waters of the Rio Grande ran much slower through the communities of Velarde and Rinconada, compared to their rapid and torturous journey through the twisting canyons closer to Taos. One of the clues in McCabe's book mentioned something about slow water. Maybe he would look around there sometime later. He figured he owed

Gilda that much. After all, she was financing a hell of a lot more than she was aware of.

He parked the van at the scenic overlook near Pilar, took a long puff on his cigarette and finished off the beer he'd poured into a McDonald's soda cup. He grabbed his backpack and slung it over his shoulders and pulled a .38 pistol out of the door flap and slipped it into the side pouch. A pint of Jim Beam rounded out his provisions. He looked across the expanse of hills and chose a long narrow trail northwest of the overlook. He could see Wheeler Peak off in the distance. Walking in the stillness of early morning, he was infused with the excitement of the possibilities of becoming a rich man, primarily because he had the sense to dig deeper into McCabe's files and find a map for a real treasure. Those convicts must have known what they were doing.

Bart was not a thinking man, but it struck him that Gilda must be nuts. She needed to understand that there weren't going to be visible clues on these trails to lead to McCabe's treasure, short of Wiley Coyote standing next to a big arrow pointing to a *dig here* sign. It was obvious no-one had been on the trail he was on for some time. She was going to be searching in the wrong area. Hell, for all he knew she could be a thousand miles off. After an hour of walking through brush along the Rio Hondo, he reached the point where the river met with the Rio Grande. The noise was deafening. Bart tossed his backpack under a tree and stopped to have a smoke. He was stretched out with his back against the trunk of an old cottonwood when he felt the first raindrops. The rain began as a slow drizzle and then pelted the area for what seemed like hours. The sky was dark and foreboding, with a dense fog obscuring his vision. The trees offered little protection. Within minutes Bart's clothing was sopping wet. A thunderous bolt of lightning cracked around him, raising the hair on his arms. He wasn't dumb enough to try finding his way back to his vehicle. As the deluge slowed to a sprinkle, the clouds dissipated and the sun came blazing through. After a while, aside from the ground being damp, you couldn't tell it had rained at all. *Typical.*

Bart gathered his stuff and took off walking again. He spotted a cave a few hundred yards to his left. *That would be too easy.* The cave faced east and the noonday sun was shining directly into it. No matter. It was a good a place as any to take a leak. He stumbled over and peered inside. Even with the bright sunlight, it was too dark inside to make anything out. He pulled out his flashlight and ran it against the cave wall. There were ancient petroglyphs carved in the walls along with initials of visitors to the cave. Off in the brush somewhere the wail of a coyote pierced the silence. Bart shuddered. It reminded him of the many times he was at San Lazaro scrounging around for arrowheads when a pack of coyotes started wailing around him. That always managed to scare him shitless. He made his way up a narrow trail, looking for anything that might resemble the notations on the map.

After spending the afternoon trekking through the brush and tiptoeing through rows of blooming cactus, Bart secured his gear and headed back to town. He planned to hook up with a nice-looking chick that night at the bar, and didn't want to pass up the possibility of an easy score. The already elusive treasure was going to have to wait. He had just enough time to shower, shave, and slap on some lady-pleasing cologne.

That night Bart's wishes were fulfilled. He didn't get home until noon the next day.

CHAPTER TWENTY-THREE

On his next trip out, Bart was in a hurry to get back on his hunt. He had no problem locating the spot where he left off. He didn't care if he was just chasing rainbows. The inmate's map had a notation about the Taos Canyon area, so he decided to move downriver. Undaunted and fueled by an eighty-proof liquid breakfast, Bart spread out and took another look at the quad map of Northern New Mexico. In previous years, he had fished almost the entire area from Capulin to La Sombra. Along with Las Petacas, these were the favored campgrounds, which for obvious reasons he wanted to avoid.

By late afternoon, he was feeling the effects of the higher altitude. The heavy backpack and belly full of whiskey didn't help matters much. After a couple of beers, he hiked up a seldom used trail in an isolated wooded section near the gorge to find a place to relieve himself. The notation on the inmate's map indicated a clearing next to a grove of salt cedars. This looked promising, so he dropped his gear and knelt in the middle of a small patch of Indian rice grass. The spot was as close to the drawing as anywhere had been so far. He plotted out a couple of square feet on the dirt and began to dig in the center. At about two feet deep, the camping shovel made a loud clank. His heart rate accelerated. It had to be metal. No rock was going to make that kind of sound.

With renewed energy, Bart scraped the dirt from the sides of the hole with his hands. He used the shovel to loosen the soil. He was digging like a dervish, heaving dirt as fast as his arms could move. A corner of what appeared to be a metal box emerged. He pushed against it with all his weight, but it wouldn't budge. He scoured around the area for a stick to use as a fulcrum. It still wouldn't move. Near exhaustion, he stopped to light a cigarette, sat on the ground and leaned up against a tree.

What the hell am I in such a hurry for? he mused. *I've got all the time in the world. Nobody else is hanging around these parts digging for treasure, but oh man, this could be it!* He untied the bandana from his neck and wiped his brow.

Bart snuffed out the cigarette and resumed shoveling dirt. Inch by inch as he dug deeper, the ground became harder. He cursed when it didn't take long to exhaust himself again. *Shit, this is getting me nowhere.* He searched in his backpack for a rope. He tied one end around the top of the metal box and wrapped the remainder around the trunk of a nearby tree. He gave the rope a few hard yanks. *Nothing.* He continued to shove and pull to no avail. The box might as well be embedded in cement. Bart kept pulling, his dogged perseverance fueled by the alcohol he had consumed. He was damned and determined to see what was in the box. Frustrated, he knelt down and continued to scrape dirt from around the sides, hoping to loosen it enough to unearth it. Damned if it wasn't looking more like a strongbox with every ounce of dirt he removed.

As he chipped away at the ground, a thought crossed his mind. *How was he going to get this box back to the van once he dug it out?* He was more than a couple of miles from where he had parked. Paranoid to begin with, he'd read too many stories of hunters encountering gold mines and buried treasure and then losing their way when they went back to retrieve it. If he got it open, maybe he could fill his backpack with everything he could carry and then rebury the box. His mind was reeling, his heart was doing flip-flops. He peered down at the hole. *Oh, man, looks like I might have to dig all the way down to hell. This damned box better start loosening up. It's getting late.* But what the hell? He had come this far and he was going to go for it. There was no law that said he'd have to tell anyone about his good fortune, especially Gilda. She could go off looking for McCabe's treasure on her own, and his gut told him that wasn't anywhere around these parts.

He heard the crackling of branches and then footsteps directly behind him. *Son of a bitch.* His pistol was in the backpack next to his knee. Without so much as a blink, he slowly leaned forward, cocked the gun and spun around. An eight point buck fixated on him, turned its head and gracefully bounded off. His whole body trembling, Bart exhaled deeply and leaned back on the tree trunk. The sun was turning a darker shade of orange. A gray pall covered the sky. It wouldn't be long before he was engulfed in pitch black darkness.

Bart had no choice but to replace all the dirt into the hole and return the next day to finish unearthing the box. No point in spending the night, since the temperature could easily drop into the forties and he had no plans to bed down in the van. He was fairly confident he could find the place again. To make sure, he pulled off the turquoise blue shirt he was wearing and cut it into strips with his pocket knife. He painstakingly tied the strips to the branches hanging over the spot, making sure they wouldn't come loose with the wind. Then, at frequent intervals on his way down the canyon, he left a ribbon dangling wherever he could. By the time he reached the van, he was stumbling in the dark. He couldn't tell if the spot he marked was two miles or ten from where he was standing.

CHAPTER TWENTY-FOUR

Bathed in sunlight ninety percent of the time, juniper trees dotted the hills around Madrid. Everything appeared tranquil, the peaceful serenity of this June morning broken only by the occasional whirring of a helicopter off in the distance, or an eighteen wheeler chugging through on its way to catch Interstate 40 some miles south. The town, twenty-five miles south of Santa Fe, had a colorful history that began in the early days of mining.

Most people said *Mad-rid*, while others said *Muh-drid*, but no matter how it was pronounced, the town was a study in contradictions. On the one hand, it was an artsy craftsy place filled to saturation with garish shops featuring blown glass, pottery, weavings, folk art and run of the mill everything else. On the other hand, occasional strong undercurrents indicated the presence of an overwhelming number of marijuana crops being grown illegally within the village boundaries; thus the need for the occasional foray into the area by County Sheriff helicopters searching for visible crops in secluded fields and near private residences.

Gilda Humphreys slammed her cellphone shut for the fifth time. She had been trying to reach Bart Wolfe, whom she had spotted some weeks before making out like a horny teenager in a corner booth at the tavern in Madrid. She drove into the parking lot in hopes of catching him there again. She noticed the barrel-chested bartender out in the parking lot and beckoned him. He sauntered over to her vehicle.

"Excuse me; I'm looking for Bart Wolfe. Have you seen him recently?"

"You a cop?"

"Certainly not," she huffed. "Has he been around?"

"Bart is always around, at one time or another."

"Well, has he been here lately?"

"Nah, not for a while. Saw him last weekend and he was taking off somewhere to go camping."

Gilda gritted her teeth. Getting information from this man was like peeling an artichoke. "By chance did he say where he was going?"

"Up north, somewhere in the mountains. Didn't say specifically. Maybe Taos."

She reached out the window and handed him her card and a twenty dollar bill. "Listen, I'd appreciate it if you could do me a favor and call me if he comes by?"

"You a friend of his?"

"Yes, you could say that."

The guy smiled broadly and winked. He shoved the twenty in his side pocket. "Sure, I can do that. Old Bart never misses a chance to have a cold one most evenings."

The next afternoon, Gilda's cellphone rang as she was leaving work. The bartender made good on his promise. She jumped in her car and drove to Madrid. From the door of the tavern, she could see Bart sitting at the bar along with the rest of the regulars, his back turned to her. They all looked alike from that position. The bartender jabbed him on the shoulder and motioned toward the door. Bart squinted his eyes to look at Gilda as she walked toward him.

"What the hell are you doing here?"

"I need to talk to you, Bart."

"Well, I'm a little busy right now."

"Yes, I can see how important it is to secure your place at the bar."

"I'd rather discuss this later."

Gilda stood her ground. "No, we'll do this right now. I have an extremely low tolerance for bullshit, Bart, so you need to quit avoiding me and afford me the courtesy of returning my damn calls."

"All right, all right. Don't get your knickers in a twist."

Bart slid off the stool, balanced the drink in his hand and ambled across the sawdust-covered floor toward her. "I didn't sign up for no drama, lady. Besides, half the time my phone ain't working. I'll give you a call tomorrow."

He turned around to return to the bar. Gilda grabbed his sleeve and pulled him toward a table.

"Sit down, dammit. I paid you good money to get something done for me, and I want action." Gilda motioned the waitress for a drink. "Make it a double vodka gimlet, easy on the ice, and bring him another beer."

Bart was having a problem looking her straight in the eyes. It was clear that he wasn't used to women acting like they were boss.

"There wasn't any need for you to track me down. I was going to let you in on what I've been doing," Bart said.

"And just when did you plan on doing that? It appears to me that you've been pretty damned secretive. Every time I've called or stopped by your place, you've been conveniently unavailable. I don't like playing games, Bart."

Bart glared at her. "You got no call to be checking on my every move. I told you I'd be in touch."

"Well, up to this point, you haven't told me a damn thing. I've been sitting in the dark for weeks. I paid you for some answers and you've come up with zilch." Gilda took a big swallow of her drink, waiting for Bart to continue.

"I've just been doing a little preliminary exploring, that's all," he lied. "I've been up to Taos a couple of times, looking for places that someone might just pick to bury something. I haven't found a thing, and didn't see any need to call and check in every day. That's a lot of damned territory to cover.

It's not as though there's a big sign out there or something."

Bart ordered another round of drinks. It had been a while since he had a real woman sitting next to him. Most of the ones he picked up were barflies too drunk to walk and who usually hung around the bar hoping to score free drinks or drugs, whatever happened to be on the menu that night.

Gilda cleared her throat, emitting the recognizable raspy sound. She found herself oddly attracted to this gruff, sometimes seedy looking man. What a difference a good haircut and shave would make. There was more to it than that. Whatever it was, being this close to Bart produced an awareness she couldn't deny. Her sex life with her husband had become non-existent over the years and she had given up pondering the reason. She was certain of one thing, though. George Humphreys had become old before his time. Sitting at a table with Bart, she was feeling young and sexy.

◌

After a few drinks, Bart had to admit that once she loosened up, Gilda wasn't as bad as he first imagined. *I'd like to get her good and laid.* The band was playing a few belly rubbing country songs. He pulled her up by the hand to dance.

Gilda pretended to protest and then laughed as they stepped onto the dance floor. He moved closer and leaned forward, her head resting on his shoulder. He planted a wet kiss on her lips. He was pleasantly surprised that she didn't bolt. Bart smiled to himself. *This is going to be a touchdown.* By the time midnight came around, they were stretched out in the back of his van.

He pulled her close, feeling her breath hot on his cheek. This was going to be a different kind of experience for Bart. He was partial to blondes, leggy ones if he could get them, but this woman had an earthy quality that really turned him on. Besides, he was too horny to back out now. He was going for it and she was willing to go along for the ride.

"C'mere, woman," he said, his voice as coarse as sandpaper.

There was no question that Bart had his hands full. Gilda was relentless in pleasuring him in more ways than he could remember. When he caught his breath an hour later, Bart whistled. "Damn, lady, how long you been holding that in?"

Gilda smiled. "I told you. I'm very thorough at everything I do."

"I'll say."

⚜

It had been a long time since Gilda had been physically intimate. Her face felt hot as she pulled her clothes on. Bart walked her to her car while he fumbled with the zipper on his pants. He gave her a long kiss and stumbled back to his van.

When she arrived home long after midnight, she felt her way through the darkness. The sound of snoring coming from his bedroom told her George was fast asleep. The next morning he was scrambling eggs as she slipped into the bathroom and ran cold water over her face. He didn't notice the renewed color in her cheeks.

⚜

Bart, on the other hand, rolled over on his arm. The sun wasn't up yet, but there was enough light in the room to get around. His mouth felt like he'd eaten a pound of feathers. No denying he was hung over. He vaguely remembered the previous night's coupling.

Christ. I need to learn to keep it in my pants.

CHAPTER TWENTY-FIVE

Following her unexpected liaison with Bart Wolfe, Gilda acted like a love-struck teenager experiencing a long forgotten first bout of puppy love. Employees whispered behind her back about the sudden change in her behavior. It was uncharacteristic of her to be so civil.

"Maybe she went out and got laid," said one.

"Yeah, by someone other than her husband," snickered another. They all knew George Humphreys was no George Clooney. There was reason to speculate. Their boss was acting like a human being, for a change, and nobody wanted to rock the proverbial boat. Just as obvious was the fact that these days she seemed to be paying a little more attention to her wardrobe. Gilda was starting to come to life.

Gilda Humphreys had never done a thing wrong in her life, until she met Bart Wolfe. She was at a loss for words to explain, even to herself, what she was doing getting involved with such a felonious character. She wondered if maybe she was going through menopause. Nope, too young. She was barely in her early forties. *Maybe I'm just no good.*

The following week Bart called her to report his progress, a glowing account embellished with pipe dreams and wishful thinking. The reality was, he was no closer to finding McCabe's treasure than he was to winning the lottery. Fact was, he wasn't even looking for it.

Gilda's voice was friendly and flirtatious, but Bart made no mention of their night together. She bit her lip to keep from appearing too needy. As days passed, the calls became less frequent, and Gilda was back to leaving messages. The rejection she felt brought on a flood of emotions as she sat in the parking lot of the Madrid tavern hoping to catch him as he stopped in for a beer. After waiting an hour, she drove onto the highway. By the time she reached the Cerrillos turnoff, she was in tears. *What a damned fool I am.* She pulled her car to the side of the road next to the Garden of the Gods. She sobbed even louder at the irony of being surrounded by such magnificent scenery and experiencing such a wave of despair. Spent, she leaned back on the headrest and closed her eyes.

Secrets. Secrets. Always the secrets. What was it he had said? Don't tell anyone our secret. I'll bring you a brand new dolly, just for you.

In the remote areas of 1970s Northern New Mexico, a store-bought doll was a rare commodity for a child, and more so for an orphan. Gilda was the product of a liaison between her Cherokee mother and a cowboy she had met at the rodeo. Gilda's mother had run off, leaving her with her grandmother, an elderly woman barely equipped to care for herself, let alone a small child. Without hesitation, she gave the two-year-old-little girl with long brown pigtails to the farm couple down the road. Unable to have children of their own, the grandmother assured herself they would take good care of the child. After all, they looked nice enough.

Six years later Gilda wished herself invisible as she ran down the path from the barn, across the alfalfa field and through the yard. The pitched roof adobe house stood alone in the middle of all that acreage. There were high mountain peaks surrounding the valley, almost close enough to touch. The spring thaw had not yet begun and the indigo blue mountain tops were glazed with layers of white vanilla. Thank God the window of her bedroom was still open. She pulled herself through with effort, panting as if she had just run a two minute mile. She had, and now she was safe. For the moment.

The small bedroom was sparse, lacking in everything a young girl should have. The blankets covering the single bed were homemade from scraps of used clothing. There was a small wooden dresser to hold the few dresses and sweaters purchased for her from the Goodwill Store in nearby Española. By the time she heard the farm truck winding its way up the drive the sun had set and her room was dark. Gilda had been sitting in the corner, her arms wrapped tight around her knees, her body crunched up as small as she could make it. She would no longer be invisible. She cringed as the doors to the truck slammed shut. Out in the yard she heard the man shouting instructions to the Mexican day workers. As the couple entered through the kitchen, the man continued shouting at his wife, who looked up at him with the most evil of looks, but said nothing.

"Gilda!" he hollered. "Get your ass in here and help your aunt fix supper."

She felt the lump in her throat and swallowed hard as she walked down the hallway toward the kitchen. "Coming," she said.

"Happy Birthday to you, Happy Birthday to you. Happy Birthday Dear Gilda. Happy Birthday to you," they sang in off-key unison as she reached the archway to the kitchen.

She was flabbergasted. She hadn't realized it was her birthday. The couple stood next to the wooden kitchen table, he in his blue denim dungarees, she in her faded paisley housedress. A small chocolate frosted cake sat in the center of the table, eight bright blue candles blazing.

"Blow them out, Gilda, and make a wish," her aunt said.

Gilda was so taken aback she barely had enough breath, but she blew toward the candles and broke into twitters of muted laughter.

Her foster uncle handed her a box wrapped with tan

paper and a bright red ribbon. "Open it," he said. "It's for you."

Inside the box was the most beautiful doll she had ever seen. It was just as he had promised. Their secret was safe.

CHAPTER TWENTY-SIX

Every day that week, Bart anticipated a trip back up to Taos canyon. Over the previous weekend he had blown the tranny on the van. The mechanic couldn't promise it would be ready until later in the week. He hadn't slept for a couple of nights, anxious to return to the mountains to finish digging up the strongbox. Finally, at the end of the week, he was ready to go. He thought he'd better pack enough provisions for an overnight stay. No telling how long it was going to take this time, and there was no use driving back and forth from Taos to Santa Fe. The cost of repairing the van and several tanks of gas was taking a heavy toll as he dipped into his dwindling bankroll, and he didn't dare ask Gilda for any more money. Instead, he drove to the pawn shop and hocked his rifle.

Bart never relished the idea of being on the road to Taos, no matter what the reason. A few summers back, a gigantic basalt boulder had become dislodged during a heavy rainstorm and lurched down the mountain toward the highway. It struck a commercial bus, killing five people and injuring a slew of others. Bart had been tailgating behind the bus when the accident occurred. As the rock pummeled the bus, it veered to the left, causing Bart's truck to smash into the barrier fence fifty feet above the raging river. He was hanging by a prayer when the highway patrol rescued him. He survived with just a few scratches. Good thing he'd been drunk.

He loaded the van and drove the distance to Taos, smoking all the way. He was a consummate chain smoker, and the ashtray overflowed with foul-smelling cigarette butts. The radio blasted a string of Waylon Jennings songs as Bart pulled into the RKO Park and paid the fee for two days in advance. A heavily tattooed wannabe biker with spiked hair took his money, popped it into the cash register and handed him a receipt. Bart let it drop to the floor.

"Goin' hiking?" he small talked.

"Yeah, got a few days off so I'm gonna spend some time in the mountains," Bart lied. "Probably hike over to the Gorge."

"That's a damned long hike from here. You might want to consider parking up at the next camp outside of Tres Piedras. That will get you a lot closer to the gorge."

"Yep, that's what I hear," Bart said. "This is just fine with me." He pulled the backpack over his shoulders and headed across the highway, dodging an eighteen wheeler that came barreling around the bend.

The clerk turned to his girlfriend. "If that guy's a hiker, I'm Miss America. He's not going to get too far in those ratty-ass cowboy boots."

Bart crossed over the Rio Grande at a small bridge past the general store in Pilar. About a mile upriver, he stopped and lit a cigarette and took a look at the drawing he quickly sketched when he left the mountains last week. He made notes of everything he could recall about the place where he discovered the metal box which he was sure was the stolen money from the Brinks robbery. But even if it wasn't, there had to be something of value in that box. Someone went to a lot of trouble to bury it out there, and he hoped it was the three convicts.

The day was pleasantly cool, but Bart was sweating like a camp cook. He pulled off his jacket and secured it around his waist. He scanned down the page of notes as he walked toward the hills adjacent to the river. The water thrashed noisily against the rocks in a deafening roar. After a while it became a steady drone. It reminded Bart of the time the area was plagued by a similar sound. *Taos Hum* was the name given by New Mexico natives to a humming sound which in 1993 became so acute that Taos residents demanded a full investigation from the government. Nobody ever found the source of the sound, but most figured it was the military conducting their usual secret missions, which Bart suspected was probably true. Look what had gone on in Roswell. *No aliens, my ass.*

A cool shroud fell on the side of the mountains as the sun dropped below the horizon. Bart shuddered and zipped up his hoodie. The sky had quickly slipped into darkness. The temperature had started to plummet. He stumbled onto a grassy knoll against a rocky ledge and unloaded his gear. Stretching out his legs, he leaned back on the tree trunk and took a gulp of whiskey from his stash of miniatures. He shuddered as he heard the eerie screech of a hoot owl somewhere in the distance.

Bad luck omen if he ever heard one.

Bart began to mull over all the different possibilities. Might as well make myself comfortable. *I should have brought a damned pack horse. How am I going to haul the box out when I get back to it? Should have planned things a little better. Oh, maybe I won't have to drag the box out. If it's all paper money, I can carry it out in my backpack.* He took another swallow of whiskey. A long-eared jackrabbit scooted across the river's edge, stopping in mid-hop to give him the eye before bouncing off into the thicket. He liked being out in the fresh air. Sure was different from the smoke-filled bars he spent most of his leisure time in.

Bart was a loner. He liked women, but only for one night at a time. His last relationship had ended suddenly when his longtime girlfriend became the victim in a bizarre series of murders that were featured in the local headlines for months. Bart hadn't been the same since. So he kicked himself for starting an affair with the archaeologist. Well, he couldn't really call it an affair. They'd only been in the sack once and he was determined not to let it happen again, although she sure seemed receptive to continuing. Besides, she was married. In the past, Bart had been on the receiving end of another man's ire and went out of his way to avoid a repeat performance.

Nothing like staring down the barrel of a shotgun held by an irate husband. No thanks.

The next morning, snuggled up in an army blanket, he awoke as the sun peered over the mountains. His bones ached as he pulled himself upright. He munched on a bag of chips, drank a Coke and then took off up the side of a hill. He stopped to check the notes scribbled on a scrap of paper. He hadn't yet spotted any of the bright blue strips of cloth he'd left tied to the branches to direct him back to the spot, but he just knew that the clearing had to be around here somewhere.

Wandering up the various trails, Bart was dumbfounded. He wasn't having any luck at all. *Dammit, I've got to be close. I remember walking off the trail to take a leak. Where the hell is it?* He traced his route back down the path, found his original starting point and decided to give it another try. Leaning against an old cottonwood, he lit a cigarette and fortified his nerves with a shot of whiskey. His ears perked up at the sound of someone nearby. A young boy came skipping down the trail, singing at the top of his lungs. He smiled and waved a big hello to Bart and continued to belt out a song from some Nickelodeon music video. As he came into view, Bart noticed that as he traipsed along he was waving a banner of long strips of blue cloth fastened to a stick.

Bart gasped and hollered after him. "Hey, kid, where'd you get those rags?"

"Way back there tied to a bunch of trees. I think I got them all. I hope so. I don't know what they're for, but they're cool. *Bzzzzz.* See how they move in the wind? Just like an airplane." And off he went, skipping on his way, pulling the makeshift banner alongside, the morning breeze blowing in his wake.

Bart almost blacked out from the shock. His heart jumped and he felt like vomiting. By the time he recovered, the kid was already a mile down the road. He gathered his gear and sprinted up the trail, checking to see if there were any footprints. Everything looked different. Heavy rains had changed the configuration of the terrain and now the ground was dry. Without the markers, there was no way in hell Bart was ever going to find the box he had almost dug up the week before. His mind was in a stupor as he drove back into town. He was out of cigarettes. He was out of whiskey. And he was shit out of luck.

☙

Following a twelve hour binge at the tavern in Madrid, Bart Wolfe didn't want to even think about what he was going to do next. He shoved aside the thought that he needed to develop a conscience. He sure as hell didn't feel compelled to share this misadventure with Gilda. She already believed he was incompetent.

CHAPTER TWENTY-SEVEN

Gilda hadn't been able to sleep lately. She was having problems at work. Tom Rodriguez, Director of the agency, had been constantly on her case about everything and nothing. She cleared her desk early, grabbed her purse and headed out to the parking lot. She reached into her pocket for the keys and, as she pressed the door lock, looked up to see Bart Wolfe leaning against the hood of her car, smoking a cigarette. Irritated at his lackadaisical attitude and his refusal to keep in touch with her, she wasn't sure how to react. She also didn't want to appear as though she gave a damn. After all, it had been several weeks since they frolicked in the back of his van and quite honestly, she had been looking forward to a repeat performance. Except for one thing: he hadn't called.

Gilda spoke first. "I believe I told you not to show up at my office unannounced, Bart. What do you want?"

"Been meaning to call you, but been busy."

"I prefer not to talk here. Let's go somewhere else. I don't want to call attention to myself. These people already talk up a storm about me and I don't need to add more fuel to their gossip."

Bart figured that was just her prissy way. She didn't want to be seen with him anywhere, period.

"You mind taking a drive out to Madrid? We can go separately or leave your car here," he said. "I know it's a ways out, but if you ain't doin' nothing …"

"Let me park my car at the Roadrunner stop off 599. It's halfway, but you're going to have to drive me back there," she said. She knew they could just as well talk right there, but whatever was motivating her at that moment erased all her self-confidence and common sense. As she drove to their meeting point, she chided herself for not walking away.

As Gilda parked near the back lot next to the train tracks and waited for Bart to round the corner, she could feel the perspiration forming on the palms of her hands. He drove up next to her and reached across the seat to unlock the door. It didn't escape her that he wasn't enough of a gentleman to get out of his car and open the door for her.

"You sure you don't mind taking a ride? You look a little pissed."

Gilda noticed he hadn't once yet called her by name. "That's putting it mildly, Bart."

A few miles out on Highway 14, Gilda confronted him. "Just what the hell kind of game have you been playing, Bart? You promised to call me regularly and I haven't heard from you in weeks."

"I told you. I've been busy. Man's got to earn a living, you know. I don't get a fat paycheck for sitting on my ass at a desk or driving around country roads chasing down Indian relics."

The setting sun was blazing through the windshield. Gilda fiddled with the visor. "Are you saying you have a job?"

"I'm saying I've always had one job or another. Doesn't necessarily mean I work nine to five."

"Exactly what is it you do?"

"A lot of things."

"Specifically?"

Bart turned to face her. "Shit, not that it's any of your business, but I've been cultivating a crop of Mary Jane. It's just about ready to harvest."

"Keep your eyes on the road. I don't care if you've been

growing potatoes. I thought we had an arrangement. I told you I would pay you to help me narrow down the location of the treasure and I was serious, but you don't seem to be able to hold up your end of the agreement."

"Maybe you should be the one out there looking for it. So far I haven't been able to put my finger on anything." Bart wasn't about to admit he'd actively been looking for over a month, but not for *her* treasure.

"You know I can't do that. It might put my job in jeopardy."

"Sounds like a crock to me. Whatever you do with your free time has nothing to do with your job. I'm not that stupid." He drove into the parking lot of the tavern and screeched into a parking space.

As they walked into the dimly lit bar, Bart put his hand on the small of her back, directing her to a corner table. "This looks like a good spot. Sit yourself down. I'll get us a couple of beers."

"I prefer vodka," she said. "Very little ice."

Bart returned to the table and plunked the drinks on a napkin, spilling a little of her drink. "Sorry, I ain't no barmaid." He sat down next to her.

"So, let's cut the small talk. Last time we spoke, you were going to take a trip to Taos to check the area out," she said, taking a big gulp of her drink. She needed that, considering the day she'd had, and Bart wasn't making it any easier. "Have you made any real progress?"

Bart nervously twisted the napkin. "Nothing. It's like looking for piñon nuts in a pile of rabbit dung. Do you realize how much ground Taos Canyon covers? There ain't no way you can figure out if something's buried out there."

"I don't believe it's that much of a long shot. I can feel it in my gut. They must have buried the chest out there. It's the only logical place. Who's going to be out looking in another state? That doesn't make sense. McCabe took up roots around here and they go pretty deep. Neither of them has strong ties to other areas. It has to be here in New Mexico."

"Well, what makes sense to you just might not make sense to anyone else," Bart said, signaling to the bartender. "I think you might want to consider going out there yourself. Then you'll see how complicated this whole thing is. You need to just pick an area. I can't be scouring the whole damn canyon looking for some damned clue that doesn't exist. Those guys are pulling your leg. There ain't no brown houses up in that area," Bart said, referring to one of the clues in the book, *borders edge the brown.* Bart knew he wasn't at the top of any class, but he had enough intelligence to make it this far in life. The way he was feeling right now, he didn't give a blue tinker's damn about anybody's treasure. He had just lost what was probably his only chance of ever having money in the bank.

Gilda sighed. "You can't take things too literally, Bart. That could mean anything. It could mean a brown house, a pool of brown trout, or maybe somebody out there named Brown. Who knows what these two were thinking? Even a headstone in a cemetery could be part of the puzzle."

"That's my point exactly. I don't think two intelligent men would bury anything in a place that was too obvious. You're probably about a thousand miles off. Yellowstone is mentioned a bunch of times. There's no reason why it couldn't be buried there."

"I think you're wrong, Bart, but I'm not paying you for advice."

The band started to set up in the corner. Bart pulled his chair closer to Gilda's. "For all we know, McCabe and Burke could have buried the treasure on the moon. I don't believe a word of it and they've sent everyone on a chase wilder than any goose I know."

Gilda was silent. She had a lot to think about. Had she made a mistake bringing Bart on board? Now wasn't the time to make a decision of what she was going to do next. The band started their first number, making conversation difficult over the din. The place was starting to get crowded. She decided it was time for her to leave, but Bart insisted.

After another round of drinks, Bart's overall tone changed. He found Gilda to be more interesting by the minute. Oh, not for the technical stuff she rattled on about, but the sexy demeanor he hadn't noticed. There was a deeper layer beneath the crust hardened by a loveless marriage. He could feel himself becoming excited.

As if reading Bart's mind, Gilda viewed him with anticipation. She too was at a loss to explain her fascination with this man. God knows she had been sexually deprived for the last five years. She couldn't recall the last time her husband had even consented to sex. The memory had already faded from her mind. In the titillation of the moment sitting close to Bart, she let down her guard, allowing herself to be pulled into her own home-grown fantasy about love and romance. Her cheeks flushed as he put his hand on her thigh.

"What you thinking, there, lady?" Bart smirked. He could read a willing woman like a book. She was looking at him all googly-eyed. A few more drinks and he knew where this was headed. The same place as last time. The foam mattress in his van. He grinned like a barracuda as they found their way toward the exit, all thought of treasure hunts having taken a seat at the back of the bus.

CHAPTER TWENTY-EIGHT

Staring out the kitchen window, Gilda watched as her long-unemployed husband mowed the front lawn with a gusto she found annoying. Following her graduation from the University of New Mexico, she had held down one position or another with the State, working part-time jobs while she cracked the books toward a doctorate in archaeology and moved up the ladder until she was hired in her current position.

Then everything came to a halt. Within a month of the unprecedented election of New Mexico's first female governor, changes started trickling down the pike. Less qualified but more politically oriented employees were being promoted to jobs she could only dream about. With her extensive background, she could have easily been head of the department. She blamed all this on the fact that the department's current director, Tom Rodriguez, was one of the Governor's first political appointees. Not only that, he was an influential member of the powerful Public Regulation Commission, which oversaw not only utilities but motor carriers and the insurance industry as well. Rumor was that he had shady dealings under the table, something Gilda wished she knew more about. She'd like to have a nice tidbit to hang him with.

She couldn't stand to be in the same room with Rodriguez. He had blocked every chance she had of a promotion, citing insignificant incidents in her personnel file as his reasoning. Fortunately Gilda was in an exempt position and couldn't be terminated, but Rodriguez could sure make life difficult enough for her to throw in the towel. That's why having a chance to find McCabe's treasure was so important to her. Pipe dream or not, it would secure her future.

Gilda hadn't planned to go out and look for the treasure, but it didn't take much of a stretch to convince herself that she was entitled to it as she watched the price of gold and silver skyrocket upward. After all, Burke and McCabe had opened a Pandora's Box by publishing a book on their proposed treasure hunt. With all the recent publicity, she knew it wouldn't be long before the whole damn world got wind of it and whoever found the treasure would be rolling in money. The point was that she was going to have a head start if things went her way. After all, she had something nobody else had. A map.

She couldn't understand why Bart Wolfe had given up so easily. According to him, it was just too freakin' hard to wander around the mountains without direction. Well, *she* wouldn't have that problem. Gilda was dead certain the treasure had to be in the Taos area. She felt it in her bones. Besides, she had long been proficient at reading maps and the drawing she had from McCabe's house had several landmarks on it that looked familiar.

What the hell did Bart know? He hadn't consulted her at all. Just went off half-cocked on his own. SHE was an expert on dirt. She knew all the ways one could tell if the ground had been disturbed, a month ago or a hundred years ago. After all, that's what she did for a living.

Gilda took a few days off from work and didn't bother to tell her husband. She took a trip to Taos to check out exactly where Bart said he had been. He had given her the maps where the trails he explored were delineated. From the looks of it, he hadn't been anywhere near where she told him to go. Mid-morning she arrived at the Rio Grande Gorge, parked at the visitor center and wandered around for most of the day, looking beyond the hilltops. Resting in a grassy nook, she stopped to drink from her canteen. For miles across the arroyos beyond where the chamisa and mountain laurels were blooming, she could see the snow covered peaks of a dark mountain range reaching up toward the sky. In his book McCabe had mentioned that a good friend of his had left him instructions to spread her ashes around Taos Mountain after her death.

Years ago, as a member of a search team, Gilda had flown across the sacred mountain, its landscape thick with ponderosa and aspen groves. But finding a lost hiker in the dense mountain range proved to be futile, much like hunting for treasure. Maybe she would drive closer in to Taos and check out that mountainous area. It abutted Taos Pueblo and she'd never had a problem with the elders. She could easily convince them she was there on official business.

She went back to her car and drove to the KOA campground where Bart said he usually parked. She went inside and waited while a customer paid the attendant for his purchases.

"Can I help you, Ma'am? The campground's a little full right now, but I might be able to squeeze you in if you don't mind parking in the unpaved lot."

"Thank you, but not today," Gilda said. "I'm just looking for information about a friend who might have been here."

"Lots of people park here, Ma'am. I couldn't pick one of them out of a lineup if I had to."

"Nothing that extreme. This person is about five-ten, a little on the thin side, always wears cowboy boots and drives a white van with a peace sign on the back door."

"Oh, yeah, sure. That guy's been out here half a dozen times or so in the last couple of months. Not too talkative. Parks his car and pays the fee for the day. Says he's just hiking around, but he doesn't seem like the hiking type. Never has anything with him other than his boots and a backpack, probably filled with beer."

"Did you happen to notice what area he seemed to focus on?"

"Let me see. He usually took off across the highway. From the looks of it, he trekked past the usual campgrounds up in that area there and up a ways. He's usually gone for the whole day. Last time he was here he looked like he'd been run through a wheat thrasher. Bounded down the mountain cussing up a blue streak as he got into his van, then tore out of here like a maniac."

"Did he say anything to you?

"Nah, I just happened to be out there cleaning up a mess near where he parked and heard him bitching to himself about something or other. I wasn't really listening."

"One more question. Did he ever have anyone else with him?"

"You his wife or something?"

"No, not hardly."

"Yeah, I think one time he had some chick with him. They didn't walk very far. She wasn't the hiking type, considering what she was wearing, high heels and all. Wasn't long before they were back in the van. Sounded like they were having a party in there, if you know what I mean." He smiled a knowing smile.

"No, I don't, and I don't need you to explain it to me," Gilda huffed. "That sounds like a story you just concocted. Only an idiot would wear high heels to the mountains."

"Well, excuse me all to hell, lady. You asked and I told you."

"I'm sorry. I didn't mean to be so abrupt. Thank you," she said, turning on her heels toward the exit.

Gilda yanked the door open and almost pulled it off the hinges. She stormed toward her vehicle and sat in the parking lot for a few minutes to calm down before pulling out onto the highway. She went in the direction of Taos and up to the Pueblo. As she drove near the edge below the mountains, she decided the treasure couldn't be buried around there. These Pueblo Indians weren't going to allow anybody, even Tim McCabe, to trespass on their sacred ground. And more importantly, nobody would be allowed anywhere on the property to go searching for it.

As she wound her way down the highway past Pilar, she glanced toward the parking lot where she had stopped a few hours before. *So that son-of-a-bitch has been out here half a dozen times, and maybe not always by himself. No wonder I could never catch him.* She reached into her purse for her cell and speed-dialed Bart's number. No answer. She tossed the phone on the seat and headed back to Santa Fe.

CHAPTER TWENTY-NINE

Gilda sped into her driveway, barely missing the trash cans laid out like sentries on the edge of the sidewalk. The screen door slammed shut as she burst through the kitchen. "That mangy son-of-a-bitch," she muttered.

"What's going on, Gilda?" her husband asked, looking up from his newspaper, concerned he might be the reason for her ire.

"Bart Wolfe. That worthless do-nothing I paid to obtain information for me. I've called him fifty times and he hasn't returned any of my calls."

"Who is this person and what does he have to do with anything? Some second-class citizen you dug up on one of your travels?"

"I had an arrangement with him to locate some papers that have valuable information on them, and once he did, it turns out he's been using the information to conduct his own search."

"Are you still going on about that so-called treasure? I thought you gave up on that idea."

"Look, George." She poured herself a glass of water, drank half the glass, and wiped her mouth with the back of her hand. "Finding something like that would enhance our lives considerably. We could retire to the Bahamas somewhere and never have to put up with this weather. We'd have nothing to worry about. I'm sick and tired of working my butt off while everyone else gets promoted. At this rate,

I'll have to work until I'm seventy just to make it worth my while." She put the glass in the sink with a loud bang. It was a wonder it didn't break.

"Everyone and their mother's going to be looking for that imaginary treasure. I read today that after those two appeared on *Good Morning America*, the book sold out the first run in less than a month. Bunch of suckers spending forty bucks a pop to read about some fairy tale conjured up by two con men."

She sat down next to him at the kitchen table. "I don't think so. I believe I would have a head start from the map Wolfe found."

"What makes you think it's a map of the treasure? It could be a map of almost anything."

She popped two aspirin into her mouth and swallowed. "Well I'm convinced it has something to do with the treasure, I just don't know what."

George folded the newspaper and set it aside."I told you *I* would help you in any way, but no, you obviously preferred a stranger who seems to have screwed you over. What did you expect? From the looks of it, he sounds like a pretty shady character. I gave you credit for having more sense than that, Gilda. You've got as much chance of finding that treasure as I have of getting a job at the White House or you getting promoted."

"What?" She stood again and started to pace. She was trying to keep her voice from rising. "Let me tell you something, George. I have worked damned hard"—she slapped the table for emphasis—"to get us where we are, and right now we'd be getting pretty close to the poorhouse if it wasn't for my paycheck. Some of those so-called investments you made took a big chunk out of our savings, and you certainly haven't been pounding the pavement looking for a job to help out."

He heaved a sigh and threw up his hands. "Here we go

again. I told you there are no jobs out there, unless you want me working at Wal-Mart, and I'm sure that would play havoc with your social status. You're the one who insisted I stay home and take care of the house and water your precious plants in the greenhouse. Just because your 401K took a dive with the market crash doesn't mean it won't ever build back up. Chrissake, woman, this recession didn't happen just to you. I wish to hell you'd make up your mind." George Humphreys also wished *he* could find a buried treasure somewhere. He'd use it to get the hell away from her.

"I know, I know. It just angers me that Wolfe couldn't follow a simple request."

"And that simple request was what, to lead you to the treasure?"

"No, I asked him to locate a map for me," she blurted. "Which he did, and then I wanted him to scout around the Taos area to see what he could find."

George was aghast. "Oh, for cryin' out loud, Gilda. Surely you don't believe the story concocted by those two dealers? Don't you get it? It's all a damn publicity stunt. What makes you so sure they buried a *real* treasure for every lunatic to go out searching for? Get a grip. That doesn't even make sense."

She busied herself making a fresh pot of coffee. "As much television as you watch," she said, filling the machine with water and fitting the filter in the basket, "you'd think you would have noticed how often they've been interviewed. In that memoir Tim McCabe wrote, he talks about burying a treasure somewhere in the mountains." She tried to clear her voice, but it didn't help. She was hoarse again. "It's all right there in that book on the table." She suddenly erupted into coughing spasms.

"Why don't you do something about that annoying cough?" he interrupted. "Go see a damned ENT."

Ignoring his remark, she continued. "You wait and see.

It's not as far-fetched as you might think."

"Has anyone else on this green earth seen this so-called treasure, besides on the cover of his book?"

"I saw it with my own eyes, George. I took some photos with a powerful zoom lens when he and another guy were coming out of a tunnel on his property. Here, look at this if you don't believe me." She slid a sheaf of prints under his face.

George took a few minutes to examine them. Finally he pushed them away and said, "All I see here is two guys carrying a box that looks like it's about to collapse. Where do you get the idea that there's a treasure inside?"

"Because it's too much of a coincidence that a couple of weeks after I shot these photos, these two introduce a treasure hunt to the world."

George took a closer look and had a sudden change of heart. Maybe his wife wasn't so far out in left field. "You just might have stumbled onto something. So how would you go about finding something like this once it's buried?"

"The chest they put all the stuff in is by itself worth a small fortune. McCabe describes it as a miniature bronze dowry box from Gaul, dating to about 250 A.D. I looked it up on the Internet, and it is so rare that every museum in the country would like to have one in their collection. It's almost identical to the one in the Getty Museum," she said, clearing her throat. "I can't imagine him being dumb enough to part with something that valuable, but I must admit it adds a good spin to the prospect of searching for it. Not only that, each of them added some fairly valuable items from their own collections."

"Let me see that drawing again. Maybe I'd like to embark on a little treasure hunting myself."

"*You*?" she snorted. "You've never been ten miles away from home, let alone out in the mountains. You'd probably be eaten by a pack of coyotes."

"*I should be so lucky*," George muttered under his breath.

BOOK THREE –
LIGHTS OUT

CHAPTER THIRTY

The tangerine glow brushed the mountain tops in the final moments of the sunset. Gilda had been tapping markers into the trees for over an hour to document her progress in the canyon. She leaned over to pick up her backpack. The crackling of leaves startled her. She could make out the silhouette of a man moving toward her. A look of anguish spread over her face as he came within a foot of her. She frantically reached for her cellphone.

He pulled a guitar wire from his inside pocket.

She gasped. "What ..."

Inches from her she stared into the blank look in the deep wells of darkness that were his eyes. His breath was rank and heavy.

Her voice trembled. "Please. Don't hurt me."

He pushed his face into hers. "Nobody's going to hear you."

Gilda lurched forward. He grabbed her arm and pulled her back, knocking her to her knees. He squeezed the cord around her neck as she struggled to get free. He reached under his coat. The bullet shattered her head. A cloud of smoke filled the air around her as her lifeless body dropped to the ground.

He dragged her to the edge of the river and rolled her over the embankment, waiting for the splash. Looking over the ledge, he discovered she had fallen into a boat tangled in the bushes and roared with laughter.

"Would you look at that? Perfect three point landing."

The stranger retrieved his gear, clicked on his flashlight and made his way down the hill where his car was parked behind a clump of chamisa. He was in no hurry. The job was done.

A blast of cold air brushed against his neck as he dumped his pack in the trunk. He sat in the driver's seat, started the engine and fiddled with the radio. *Nothing but static.* Not yet ready to take off, he lit a cigarette and eased back on the headrest and closed his eyes. He stretched to relax his back.

His body suddenly jerked. He must have dozed off. Time to get back to town. A long drive ahead. Forgetting the engine was running, he cursed at the loud screech it emitted as he turned the key. He shifted into gear, pulled out onto the highway and disappeared into the darkness.

By the time Gilda's body was discovered, he'd be long gone. A grin crept over his sunburned face. He congratulated himself for having committed a perfect crime in an imperfect world.

CHAPTER THIRTY-ONE

Joseph Stibbe was on a sorely needed vacation from his job as an emergency medical technician for Santa Fe County. He was hankering to do some trout fishing, and the upper Rio Grande River near Taos was the perfect setting to indulge his passion. Romantically unattached and in his late forties, Stibbe was retired after twenty years on the force with the New Mexico Game and Fish Department.

Not one to stay idle, he sharpened his skills as an EMT and landed a job with the County. His sandy brown hair was peppered with gray streaks of recent vintage, and his piercing green eyes were framed by squint wrinkles from trekking in the New Mexico sun for most of his life. A lean yet muscular physique stemmed from being an avid hiker.

He traversed U.S. Highway 285, the road to Taos, and stopped at the Rancho Casados Diner in Española to order black coffee and a breakfast burrito smothered with green chili. Although he was a *Gringo*, he had been baptized by fire when introduced to a meal of northern New Mexican red and green chili. Most of the restaurants in his old stomping grounds a few miles from Cerrillos served the tongue-searing food for which he had developed an addiction.

Back on the road, he was exhilarated by the pastoral tranquility of early morning as the highway merged into State Road 68. He was looking forward to bagging several cutthroat trout or northern pike in a secluded corner of the river.

About fifteen miles south of Taos, he paid the fee and

parked at the campground. Gathering up his fly-fishing gear and the empty creel, he headed across the pavement to Orilla Verde, his favorite spot, where the blue-green water eddied behind a car-sized boulder. It was the perfect day for fishing, or anything else for that matter.

The sun crawled its way up from the horizon into an alluring Georgia O'Keeffe blue sky. The air was crisp and cool, its piney smell mixed with wildflowers. Twigs and pinecones snapped as he walked. A red-tailed hawk soared overhead. Stibbe knew it wouldn't be long before groups of rafters would be skimming down the river, their shrieks piercing the morning air. The wide river was a deep shade of indigo, with tufts of whitewater splashing over dark boulders as it undulated downstream. He surveyed the area then started to hike up the canyon, where there would be fewer distractions.

Within seconds of his first cast, he felt a strike. Under the shadow of a cottonwood grove, with the Poundmeister fly tied securely to a three pound test leader, it wasn't long before he bagged his limit, all wiggling on the pillow of grass at the bottom of the creel. His catch included a sixteen-inch brown trout.

He gathered his gear and walked a half-mile upstream, where he crossed a rickety makeshift bridge. His mouth watered as he envisioned the big trout simmering in a cast-iron skillet on the stove, its succulent insides stuffed with chili seasoned bread crumbs and piñon nuts.

Stibbe whistled a tune as he trekked down the narrow canyon and stopped to prepare to cast his line one last time. He looked over the riverbank to see if there were any bushes below where he might get tangled up. He spotted a small boat sloshing back and forth in an eddy at the water's edge. It was caught in a zig in the water, noisily knocking against the jagged rocks in a heavily shaded nook. An arm dangled over the side of the boat. He moved toward the bank and lowered himself into the fast-moving icy water to get a closer look.

What he saw next made him jump back in horror, his heart pounding like a jackhammer. His stomach lurched. It wasn't the first time he had seen a corpse, but the shock was no less severe. He forced himself to look again.

A woman's body with a gaping hole where her left ear had been lay in the bottom of the boat. Her lifeless hand seemed to be reaching for the cellphone next to it.

CHAPTER THIRTY-TWO

Just below the widest point of the river, where it meandered along swishing up against the rocky shore, trees and bushes meshed together to form the perfect backdrop for hiking or fishing. Wary trout swam in pools near the craggy rocks, hoping to lunge out and score a tasty morsel offered by way of a metal hook. It was a waiting game.

The small boat thrashed noisily against the V-shaped embankment, bobbing in the shadows of a dense clump of trees. Filtered sunlight streamed through the branches, casting an ominous light around the small craft. The crime scene techs edged closer, wearing rubber diving pants, their feet sliding on the mossy rocks below the water. One tech reached for the rope and untied it, pulling the boat closer to the shore. Even in the fresh air, the cloying smell of decomposition filled the space. There was never enough exposure to prepare one human being to see another's dead body. They donned face masks as they approached the scene. The area was cordoned off with yellow tape and carefully photographed as they waited for the medical examiner for Taos County to work his way down the grade.

The M.E. was annoyed that he had been called out to a crime scene during his wife's dinner party. "Okay, boys, get the boat or the body up here so I can have a better look," he grumbled.

The techs looked at him in disbelief. "Normally, we'd have to wait for a winch, but it's going to be near impossible to get a truck through these narrow trails," said one.

"I can't see how we're going to pull the boat out of the water," said the other. "The ledge is about three feet high. There's no way we can accomplish that."

"Well, do what you have to do. Improvise. Gonna have to drag that gurney all the way back to the van, so it's not going to make much difference how you get the body up here so I can take a look," he said. "I'm not going into that ass-freezing water. You two might just want to get in the boat and go downriver for a couple of miles until you can bring it to shore. If not, figure it out."

"There's no way to tell if the boat would even make it downstream without sinking," the tech replied. "Then we'd be in a bigger mess."

"Not my problem. Just get it done."

Both up to their waists in fast moving water, the techs attempted to maneuver a tarp under the boat and secure the corners with rope. After a few tries, they were able to pull it up onto the flat ground. The M.E., who had been pacing back and forth along the shore and checking his watch, conducted a quick inspection, took a few notes, and snapped his briefcase shut.

"Homicide by strangulation and gunshot wound," he said. "All right. We're done here. Give me a buzz after you get the body back to the morgue. I'll get the autopsy scheduled."

The techs placed the victim in the body bag, secured her to the gurney and began the arduous task of winding their way down the path to the parking lot. By the time they finished, their boss was already home enjoying his party.

CHAPTER THIRTY-THREE

Romero began his day in the usual fashion, jogging around the State Capitol complex, across Old Santa Fe Trail and over to the grounds of St. Francis Cathedral, his boyhood church in downtown Santa Fe. He sprinted the last mile, running along the side of the Public Employees Retirement Association building and then in the direction of his house. Each time he passed this particular government building, he sensed an eerie stillness. As a child, his Grandma Benita told him the building was haunted because it was built over a centuries old cemetery. Her niece had worked there for years as a custodian, and swore that she heard voices in the halls each night as she gathered trash. Romero didn't doubt it for one minute. You didn't have to be psychic to pick up on that. He could practically see shadows of ghosts peering out from behind the blue spruce trees, which reached out like tentacles into the morning sky.

At six o'clock he stepped into his front yard, breathless and panting. In the kitchen, he spooned coffee into the coffee maker, flicked it on and rummaged through the refrigerator for breakfast staples. He settled for a day-old croissant, which he stuffed with a scrambled egg, a piece of ham, and a slice of cheese. A couple of spoons of chopped green chili added a little zest. Before he could take his first bite, the phone rang.

On the other end was Pat Tenorio, a Taos Pueblo Indian detective who had been on the force with Romero before he transferred to Taos.

"Do you know what time it is, Pat?" Romero said.

"Yeah, buddy, same time as here. Indian time," Tenorio said. "People around here get up when the first rooster crows."

"My office doesn't open until eight," Romero said.

"Good thing I had your cell number, then, huh?"

"What do you want?" Romero said, his stomach growling with anticipation of his well-earned breakfast.

"Jeez, Rick. You one of them people who can't function until they've siphoned two cups of coffee down their tank?"

"Something like that. I was just about to have breakfast. But for your information, I've been up before that first rooster." He set the plate back on the counter and stirred cream and sugar into his coffee. "What's going on that can't wait until the sun comes up?" Romero said.

"I need your help out here, Rick. Some guy fishing in the area found a body in a small boat caught up in the rapids. Woman shot through the head."

"Ouch. Who's the vic—anyone of importance?" Romero said.

"Yeah, seems to be. Some state official from Santa Fe. State police is trying to get in touch with her family. She was in the morgue for forty-eight hours before we located her car. Purse and other belongings were in the trunk. Nothing amiss surrounding the vehicle. No prints other than her own."

"So what do you need from me?"

"Well, seeing that the victim's from Santa Fe and I'm pretty short-handed out here—"

"Yeah, I read in the paper about three of your deputies being suspended without pay for selling county property on eBay. One of my guys bought himself a nice Kevlar vest for forty-five bucks," Romero said.

"Don't rub it in. You wouldn't think an officer of the law could be so stupid."

"More like greedy, I think. From what the local paper

reported, they had a whole list of law enforcement issue equipment stored in one of those monthly storage units."

"Yeah. They sold everything they could get their grubby hands on. Now the media's trying to implicate the Sheriff, saying he was aware of the shenanigans going on. We're up to our ears in caca right about now."

"Hate to interrupt, but where do I come in?" Romero said, salivating at the sight of his quickly cooling breakfast.

"First I'd like you to drive up to Taos, maybe we can walk through the crime scene. Get a fresh perspective from Santa Fe's leading detective. I can sign you on as a special investigative officer or *hell*, maybe even transfer the case down to your jurisdiction. Your guys in Santa Fe have better access to state records than we do. We're lucky if our computers boot up every morning. Can you see if your people can handle it? Better you than State Police. Last time I worked a case with them I had to kiss somebody's ass every time I needed an update."

"All right," said Romero. "Give me a little time here. I'll clear it with Sheriff Medrano and get back to you. I don't foresee any problem on this end, but I can't make any promises."

◌੪

By ten o'clock, Romero had been on the job for three hours. The Sheriff gave him the go-ahead to determine how they could help on Tenorio's case. The drive to Taos took him well over an hour. He stopped at a drive-through in Española for a second cup of coffee and then a few miles down the road in Velarde to gas up. Before he reached Taos Canyon, the traffic began to pick up where the highway narrowed to a two lane road with curves marked at forty-five mph. He met up with Detective Tenorio at the gas station in Pilar.

"Hey, Rick, how's things?" Tenorio slapped Romero's back with one hand and shook his hand with the other.

"Can't complain. I was bitching about what I paid for gas in Velarde, but now I'm glad I fueled up there."

"Tourist season, Rick. You know how they like to sock it to all them Texans. Goes up like clockwork as soon as the weather shifts to balmy. It's as predictable as termites in an old log."

"Guess it's the same in Santa Fe, but we're still way lower than here."

"Maybe you need to find yourself one of those rich Texas oil women."

"No thanks."

"Anyway, I see by your badge you made Lieutenant. Congrats. Should I bow or kiss your ring?"

"You could kiss my butt, but a simple curtsy will be sufficient."

Tenorio gave him a friendly punch in the shoulder. "Come on. We'll drive up in my car. Hope you brought your hiking boots. We'll need to walk a little."

They reached the bridge over the Rio Grande at Pilar and circled back for about a mile. As they worked their way down an incline to the edge of the river, Romero could see the yellow tape wrapped around the trees and bushes.

Tenorio pointed to a spot just beyond the river bank. "Here's where the guy discovered the dinghy, tangled up in the willows down there in that eddy."

"What's the story on him?" Romero knelt to take a look at a small scrap of paper. It was nothing.

"Joseph Stibbe? He's clean. We checked him out. He's a paramedic, retired game warden. He was out here taking a few days off to get some fishing time in. He's not on our suspect list. Just a good Samaritan doing his duty by calling nine-one-one."

"Name sounds familiar."

"He used to be stationed outside of Cerrillos when he was with Game and Fish."

Romero stood up, shaking the dirt from his jeans. "This is a long shot, but were your techs able to come up with any prints?"

"Nah. Not even his. He got in the water to get a closer look, but once he saw the body, he didn't touch anything. He was too freaked out, paramedic or not. Forensics scoured the immediate surroundings, but you know how popular the area around here is. Between the hikers, fishermen and rafters, there's always something going on."

"Nobody saw or heard anything?"

"Nothing. Nobody heard shots, but that's not unusual. There's traffic twenty four-seven up and down the canyon. We don't have even a vague idea about who killed this woman. Don't know whether it was random or if she was the intended target." The two detectives walked a few feet up the ridge.

"How did you say she was killed?" Romero said.

"More like overkill. Whoever did it tried to strangle her first and then shot her through the head. Coroner hasn't said if she was already dead when the shot was fired."

"What's the story on the boat?" Romero said.

"Apparently it either broke free from its mooring a few miles upriver, or someone stole it beforehand for a joyride down the whitewater. No way to tell if the boat floated down the river with the corpse or if it was already caught up in the corner here when the killer tossed the body in it. There's blood but no spatter or anything else in the boat. If she was shot where we're standing, surely there would be spatter on the trees, but we've had a heck of a lot of rain lately and this is kind of an open area. She could have also bled out somewhere else."

"Pretty strange place to dump a body, but convenient," said Detective Romero.

"Yeah, I've never seen anything like it. The elders of the Pueblo are concerned that the body might have floated through the Pueblo waters and down to the mouth of the river."

"Why the concern?"

Tenorio leaned up against a tree. "Spirit contamination, I imagine. Most Indian tribes have specific beliefs about death. Having a body float along the edges of the Pueblo doesn't set well with the spirits, particularly since there was nothing natural about the death."

"And there's no way of determining where the boat got into the water?"

"Not really. The rafting company where the boat was originally moored rents a wooded section near the river that runs through the tip of Pueblo land. All the rafts are stored there and then hauled down in a trailer at the beginning of the season. They have a small office at Pilar and the paid trips begin about a mile below that. We're getting conflicting information as to whether anyone noticed that the boat was missing."

"Looks like nobody kept track of it."

"Exactly. It would be different if it had some value, but it's just a utilitarian vehicle. Probably wasn't used but twice a year, if that, and nobody can remember the last time it was taken out. The way it was edged into that corner, you couldn't spot it from the bank. The only reason the guy saw it was because he was about to cast his line in and wanted to make sure there weren't a lot of rocks and debris to get tangled up in."

Romero and Tenorio spent another hour looking around. The techs had been there twice and combed the area. They found nothing of value along the ledge above where the boat had been.

Romero squatted and gazed over the ledge. Finally he said, "It might be that the crime took place here, in this area, then the killer tossed her in the water and by some freak occurrence the boat just happened to be caught up in that corner of the water."

"Sounds crazy enough to be true," said Tenorio.

"What did you say the victim's name was?"

"Didn't. But it's Gilda Humphreys. State Archaeologist. Her offices are near the State Capitol. Did you talk to Sheriff Medrano about helping us out?"

"You know," Romero said. "It's unusual for one jurisdiction to transfer a case to another, but it's not unheard of. Under the circumstances, all I can say is that we can take a shot at it, but bear in mind the case might find its way back into your lap."

Tenorio slapped him on the back. "I owe you one, buddy."

Flinching, Romero replied, "You might owe me more than that if this turns out to be a hornet's nest."

Having promised to fax all the information to Romero, Detective Tenorio breathed a sigh of relief as they returned to their vehicles. That was one less case he'd have to deal with. He was already up to his neck in backed-up cases.

CHAPTER THIRTY-FOUR

Over the weekend, Romero was in the mood to do some home cooking. He invited McCabe, who asked if Foster Burke could come along. Their wives were in Flagstaff on another docent tour sponsored by the museum. Jemimah completed the foursome.

The small group was just perfect for his cozy two bedroom adobe house in the South Capitol area of Santa Fe, about a mile from downtown.

Raised on a diet of authentic New Mexican cuisine, Romero was no stranger to the kitchen. His Grandma Benita had cooked the family Sunday dinners for as long as he could remember. Her table overflowed with serving bowls of beans, chili, *posolé* and platters of freshly baked tortillas. Romero loved to cook, although his work schedule precluded him from engaging in the pastime very often. He spent the afternoon navigating between the kitchen and the living room, where a soccer match semi-final blared from the television.

Because his guests ended up arriving within minutes of one another, Romero stood at the door to greet them. McCabe handed him a copy of his book. When they were all seated in the living room, Romero took a twelve-pack of Corona out of the refrigerator and offered a cold bottle to each, along with a small plate filled with triangular sections of lime.

The friends shared conversation and bowls of hot salsa,

guacamole, and tortilla chips. The timer rang and Romero retrieved a hot casserole from the oven, placing it ceremoniously in the center of the kitchen table.

"Help yourselves, people. There's red and green enchiladas, beans and *posolé*. Something for everyone." He laughed as he spooned an ample portion of enchilada onto his plate. "I just realized I'm the only beaner in the room."

"Don't kid yourself, Rick. We've all become beaners by osmosis," said McCabe. "I could probably build a six-foot wall with all the tortillas I've eaten since I moved to Santa Fe."

"You're quite a cook, Rick," Burke added. "This is every bit as tasty as the food they serve at the Pink Adobe. Maybe you should consider opening a restaurant."

Romero chuckled. "At least we'd have lots of customers. Every cop in town would stop by for their chili fix."

After dinner, the group relaxed out on the patio. There was an iridescent moon overhead and a slight breeze moving the scent of lilacs through the air. Romero leaned back on a lawn chair. McCabe plopped himself on the adjacent lounger. Burke and Jemimah were on the other end of the yard deeply engaged in conversation.

"Hate to talk shop here, Tim," Romero said, "but do you think you could come by the office tomorrow? I need to ask a few questions about your experience with Gilda Humphreys, the State Archaeologist. I understand you had a few run-ins with her."

"Sure," said McCabe, "but I can tell you beforehand that I have nothing good to say about that woman. She was no Mother Teresa. Not by a long shot."

"You know they fished her body out of a boat on the Rio Grande up near Taos?" Romero said.

"Yeah, I read about it in the morning paper. I meant to call you but Burke and I have been deluged with calls about promoting my book and the treasure hunt. Hardly had time to breathe lately."

"How bad was the situation with Gilda Humphreys, Tim?"

"Well, I know she did everything she could to block any move I made, and on my own property, at that."

"When was the last time you interacted with her?"

McCabe sat up. "Hey, Rick. I don't like where this conversation is going. It sounds more like an interrogation than a friendly chat. Am I going to have to lawyer up?"

"I'm sorry, Tim," Romero said. "I was out of line. Didn't mean to throw a wet blanket over the evening."

"I can come by on Monday and answer any questions you have, Rick. Right now I'd sure like a bite of that apricot cobbler you baked up."

Grateful for the segue, the two headed for the kitchen. Romero motioned to Burke and Jemimah to join them. "Dessert's on. There's some piñon ice cream to go with it."

The group returned to the patio, McCabe balancing a double scoop over the hefty serving of cobbler on his plate. Romero unwrapped the book Tim had given him and thumbed through the pages.

"I've been hearing some interesting things about your treasure hunt, Tim. Where on earth did you two come up with the idea?" said Jemimah.

McCabe explained the process, with Foster adding details.

"Speaking of which, what are the chances of an underpaid sheriff's deputy finding that treasure?"

McCabe grinned. "About as good a chance as anybody's, I figure. It's not rocket science. You just gotta read the book I gave you, so you can use your years of experience as a detective to start deciphering the clues. We've also set up a blog on the Internet to throw a few more clues into the mix every chance we get."

"I'll see if I can fit it into my crazy schedule," Romero

said. "Hope you signed it. I want to be able to say I knew you two before you were famous."

The Chinese lanterns strung along the portal added a cozy atmosphere. Romero was glad he had taken the opportunity to invite friends over to share an evening filled with good food, interesting conversation, and cold beer.

After McCabe and Burke left, Jemimah said, "You know, I can't help thinking that there wasn't another side to the Humphreys woman. Of course Tim just sees her as an evil, possibly corrupt government official out to make his life difficult out of pure orneriness. But I bet she was very unhappy. We all have hopes and dreams, and no matter what men think, life has special challenges for women, especially someone like that who was succeeding in what is often considered a man's profession. Who knows what her home life was like?"

Romero gave her a squeeze. "I wouldn't waste too much pity on her."

"Someone has to," Jemimah said with a smile. She gave him a soft kiss.

They both slept like babies that night, enveloped in each other's arms.

CHAPTER THIRTY-FIVE

On Monday morning at the substation, Clarissa greeted McCabe with an enthusiastic embrace.

"Are you coming back to work? That's so great," she said with an engaging smile.

"Not just yet, Clarissa, although I sure have missed seeing you. Got a few more loose ends to tie up."

"Related to that exciting treasure hunt, I assume?"

"You're right on that score."

"So if you're not coming back to work, what brings you all the way out here? Are you on the way to the ruins?"

"Actually the boss wants to see me. Would you tell him I'm here?"

Clarissa looked puzzled as she returned to her desk and buzzed Detective Romero. "Tim McCabe here to see you."

"Send him in, please," Romero said.

Romero greeted his friend at the door. "Mornin' McCabe, I see you survived the weekend. Guess my cooking passed muster. Let's go to the conference room."

As they walked down the hallway, McCabe said, "Sure did. Enjoyed seeing you and Jemimah in a social setting for a change."

"Yeah, it gets a little tiring having to pretend nothing's going on when we're working together."

"I'm sure Sheriff Medrano has a pretty good idea, though."

"You're right on that score. He winks at me anytime she

comes into the room."

They entered the conference room and settled in the two chairs next to the window. There was an awkward moment of silence as Romero shifted gears. "Tim," he finally said, "thanks for coming in. I'm sure this is as uncomfortable for you as it is for me."

"It is. Let's get it over with," said McCabe.

Romero poured coffee into Styrofoam cups and handed one to McCabe.

"I'm sure you know it's standard practice to record interviews related to an investigation. Is that all right with you?"

"Sure."

Romero spoke into the mike. "This is an interview with Tim McCabe, associate deputy for Santa Fe County regarding Case. No. 2812, Gilda Humphreys.

"All right. How well did you know the victim, Mrs. Humphreys?"

"I only met her once, face to face, some years ago. Our next contact was by phone, although I had heard about her from other people in my situation."

"What situation is that?"

"Owning an Indian ruin on private property, it being out of the jurisdiction of the State of New Mexico or the federal government."

"When did you first meet her?"

"A couple of years ago she stormed into our gallery with two state police detectives and an armload of papers."

"What was that about?"

"My gallery had purchased a Zuni fetish from a client who picked it up at the flea market and brought it by for an appraisal and to see if we were interested. Mrs. Humphreys insisted that we needed to turn it over to her office and accused us of stealing a sacred object from a Native American tribe. She had twisted the facts to meet her purpose."

"What happened after that?"

"We returned the item to the fellow who brought it to us and let him deal with. We didn't have any of that information."

"You mentioned a phone conversation. When was that?"

"It was late February of this year." McCabe recounted their conversation and Mrs. Humphreys' demand to be allowed on the property.

"So what was your impression of her based on that conversation?"

"I don't have anything nice to say about that woman. She was determined to run me through the wringer."

"In what way?"

"After that heated discussion and my refusal to allow her free access on my property, every time I turned around, one of her people was standing at my door with a legal document containing another trumped-up charge about excavating human remains. She was relentless."

"Sounds as though she wasn't too happy with you," said Romero.

"Me, herself, the world. Pick one. It's unfortunate she died under those circumstances," McCabe said.

Romero shuffled through the file folder. "On another note, do you think maybe she was in the Taos area looking for your treasure?"

"I have no way of knowing. That subject never came up, but if that's the case, she was about five hundred miles off."

"Do you have any idea why she would be looking around Taos?"

"Not at all. That sounds pretty far-fetched to me. As I said, we never had a conversation about anything more than her belief that I was up to no good unearthing sacred relics on our excavations."

"Did you ever hear from anyone else that she was interested in going after the treasure?"

"No, but I don't think there was anything to preclude her from joining about a thousand other people doing the same."

"So you have no idea why she would be looking in the Taos area."

"I've said it before. The chest is buried more than four hundred miles west of Chicago. That's my story, and I'm sticking to it," McCabe chuckled. "In all seriousness, Rick, I'm sorry for the woman and her family, but it's not easy to forget what a bitch she was."

"Sounds like she was determined to get to you one way or the other."

"She had some personal vendetta against me. I disliked her from the very first conversation we had, and even more when she accused me of covering up the fact that we were unearthing human remains."

"Where did she come up with that story?"

"I think she was so pissed off that the State of New Mexico and her department in particular never had the chance to purchase San Lazaro and make it a state-owned entity where they could conduct their own private digs or let it sit there untouched for another century."

"So you think that she was dogging you out of jealousy?"

McCabe considered a moment before answering. "I'm sure if they had bought the property and actually excavated it themselves, there would have been a lot of publicity and patting of shoulders going on. Based on my knowledge of state-owned archaeological sites, I'm sure they would have just put a wall around it and let it sit there for another century."

"One more question, Tim. Was she aware of all the discoveries you've made?"

"I'm sure she was. There have been a couple of books published, with photos and all. It's mind-boggling what has been found out there. And listen, if this opportunity hadn't fallen in my lap, all the important discoveries we've made in recent months would never have surfaced. I've had the good sense to document every minute we've spent out there. She could have asked for my records and I would have gladly provided them, but she never did."

"Thank you, Tim. I think we've covered everything for the moment," Romero said, clicking off the recorder.

"Listen, Rick, as far as the death of this poor woman is concerned, I don't want to even consider that the treasure hunt was an indirect reason for her murder. There have to be some extenuating circumstances that the police haven't discovered yet."

"We're trying to get to the bottom of it."

McCabe stood and faced Romero. "I'm sure you are. Now it's my turn to get out there and do what I do best—lunch."

CHAPTER THIRTY-SIX

Just as Jemimah had begun to formulate a profile on the casino murder, she was handed the file for the murder of Gilda Humphreys. After visiting both crime scenes, she concluded that whoever killed these women had to be strong enough to move the bodies. Gilda's husband didn't fit that profile, neither did Amy's husband. They were each at the end of a spectrum where she doubted either had ever participated in regular exercise. George Humphreys kept up with the housecleaning and yard chores, and Tommy Griego attended classes at the community college and played video games with his kids. Even if the men were stronger than they looked, neither would have been able to pick up the dead weight of a good-sized adult female body, transport it to a vehicle, and then bury it or toss it over a ledge.

Jemimah noted that both murders took place in remote areas but in different parts of the county. In fact, Gilda Humphreys was murdered in an adjacent county, almost a hundred miles away from the other, and that crime had to have taken place near the river's edge, to preclude the killer being seen dragging the body through the bushes. Because that area was covered with dense overgrowth, she wondered whether the crime occurred in the dark of night, unless a full moon provided sufficient light as it reflected off the water. So far no one had come forward with any viable information on either case. Detectives had followed every lead and examined everything there was to look at. What was Gilda doing out there so late? Had she found something?

There had been no personal belongings scattered about in the casino case. They could have been tossed miles from the crime scene or disposed of in some unknown manner. Jemimah rechecked the list of the contents of Gilda Humphreys' black leather purse found in the trunk of her car. Nothing out of the ordinary. Lipstick, glasses, daybook, pen, a few receipts from Borders, Target and Albertsons, along with an unopened bag of pistachio nuts. Stuffed in the side pockets were an assortment of business cards. She set aside the one with a handwritten phone number on the back. An opened pack of condoms was tucked in the small flap of the change purse. Six were missing.

Humphreys' cellphone was found next to her in the boat. After the crime lab processed it, the tech printed out a copy of a partial record of recent calls provided by the cellular company. The printout gave Jemimah an idea of who had been in communication with Humphreys for the weeks leading up to her death. She went down the list and noted a particular number Humphreys had dialed several times a few weeks before her body was found. She found that the number written on the back of the card also appeared on the printout. Each of the calls lasted for only a few seconds, so Jemimah assumed there had been no answer and no message had been recorded. She emailed the evidence tech to inquire if there were messages Humphreys had not deleted. The tech indicated the cellular provider had been contacted for a log of all activity, including deleted voice and text messages, and that should be forthcoming. The last numbers came in as *private,* making them more difficult to track. If any calls were to or from a phone in a government facility, it would be next to impossible to trace; all calls were channeled through the main switchboard, which handled thousands of calls each day.

CHAPTER THIRTY-SEVEN

While the investigation on the casino case screeched to a halt, Detective Romero obtained a warrant to seize Gilda Humphreys' home and office computers and conduct a search of the residence. Fairly nondescript and located on a cul-de-sac in a middle-class neighborhood off Rodeo Road, the house was a Pueblo style knockoff.

Gilda's husband refused to be interviewed downtown but agreed to answer questions while detectives checked the residence. As Jemimah drove through the neighborhood, she wondered how residents found their way home. Every house looked as though cut by the same cookie cutter. She parked on the street behind the police cruiser and walked up the well-manicured entryway. As she rang the doorbell, she heard the persistent yapping of a small dog. A meek-looking man with large eyes and an outdated crew-cut answered the door. The deputies had already served a copy of the warrant on George Humphreys and were in the midst of their search.

"Mr. Humphreys, I'm Jemimah Hodge. I work for the County Sheriff's office." She handed him her card. "I believe you agreed I could come by at this time to spare you the inconvenience of coming downtown to answer a few questions."

"Yes, I did. Although I didn't realize they'd be taking the house apart," he said abruptly.

Humphreys invited her in and directed her to the living room. The room was neat and uncluttered. A ceiling fan hummed overhead. A large picture window looked out into the carefully landscaped yard. He reached for the TV remote, muted the sound and stood facing her.

"Do you mind if I sit down?" Jemimah said.

"Yes, of course. Anywhere you feel comfortable."

Jemimah sat on the straight-backed chair facing Humphreys. "I can't tell you how sorry I am about your loss. I can't imagine what you're going through."

"Thank you," he said. Jemimah noticed a half-empty glass and bottle of bourbon on the counter. "I'm trying to absorb it all myself."

"You understand that as part of our investigation we are required to interview family members, neighbors and associates, and that this will be just a preliminary statement?"

"Yes, I understand."

"I'll try to be brief. What can you tell me about your wife's activities early last week—anything unusual or out of character?"

"Someone said she was wearing hiking boots when they found her. I didn't know she owned such a thing, although she did have several pairs of sturdy walking shoes. She usually dressed up for work and didn't care to participate in 'casual day' when everyone could wear whatever they wanted. She pretty much adhered to all the dress codes and figured everyone else should, too. She was a stickler for following the rules."

"Maybe she purchased the boots recently?" Jemimah said.

"I won't know until the credit card bills come in at the end of the month. She never carried much cash."

"Did she say anything to you that might indicate something was off kilter?"

"None other than her usual bellyaching about people in her department. She said they were an incompetent bunch."

"Was she having any problems at work that you know

of? Was there anyone she mentioned who might have it in for her?"

Humphreys grunted. "My wife *always* had problems at work. She made sure everyone did what they were paid to do. Bunch of lazy people on the State payroll. Not one of them pulled their weight. Believe me, I've worked as a government employee. I know the drill. The halls are populated with a bunch of cigarette-smoking, coffee-drinking, gossip-mongering suck-asses who have glommed on to these jobs hoping to work just long enough to earn a fat retirement check."

Jemimah noticed Humphreys' face was flushed from his rant. "Was there anyone in particular she complained about on a regular basis? Someone who was aggressive or intimidating toward her?"

"My wife could be pretty aggressive and intimidating herself, Miss Hodge. She never took any BS from anyone, no matter how high up on the ladder they were."

"So you don't think there was anyone in particular who was giving her a hard time?"

"Not really. I was under the impression nobody liked her. If you lined them all up in a row, not a damned one of them would say they gave a hoot one way or the other about her, and if they did, they'd be lying. When I went to pick up some of her stuff from her office, the janitor said, 'There's a joke going around here that five hundred people are under suspicion of murder.' That shows you how disrespectful that bunch is."

"Were you aware she hadn't showed up at work for several days?" Jemimah asked. "I understand she had called in sick."

"No, I wasn't. When she left here the previous Monday morning, I assumed she was going to work, like always. I had no reason to believe otherwise. She looked just fine to me. I fixed her a little breakfast, pancakes and eggs, and she ate well. If she was wearing boots, I sure would have noticed. She was very particular about how she dressed, and she never wore fancy high-heeled shoes or anything like that. She was no fashion queen, by any means, but her clothes were always clean and tailored."

"When she went out in the field, how did she dress?"

"As far as I know she kept a pair of jeans, coveralls, shirt and walking shoes in a bag in the trunk of her car. That way she could change if the necessity arose."

Jemimah checked her notes. "Just a few more questions, Mr. Humphreys. I know this isn't easy. Did your wife ever mention someone by the name of Bart Wolfe?"

"No, not that I can recall," he lied. "Did he work for the State?"

"No, he didn't. Just a name that's come up during our ongoing investigation."

"Have the cops set their sights on anyone in particular? Nobody's telling me anything. I only know what I read in the in the local news, and they sensationalize everything just to sell papers."

"Not at this time. Law enforcement is doing everything it can to find the person who is responsible for this terrible tragedy, Mr. Humphreys."

"I just hope they hurry up. I don't think I can take much more of this."

Jemimah stood. "I think I'm done here. You have my card. If you think of anything you can add to our conversation, please give me a call. My cell number's on the back. Now if you don't mind, I have to speak to one of the detectives before I leave."

"No, not at all. They're in the back, down that hallway," he said.

Detective Martinez informed her that a cursory inspection of the residence had yielded nothing of substance, other than the fact that she and her husband occupied separate bedrooms. Jemimah did notice a copy of Tim McCabe's memoir on the desk next to the computer. There were a number of yellow Post-its sticking out from the pages. Jemimah placed the book in an evidence bag along with three canvas-bound record books.

The techs processed the bedroom walls and carpet with Luminol to make sure there hadn't been a chemical cleanup. Their efforts revealed nothing. It was taking a long time to move from point A to point B.

"We're about to wrap it up here, Doctor Hodge," said Martinez. "I'll get you a copy of my report."

"Thank you," she said. "I'm on my way back to the office myself."

George Humphreys didn't acknowledge Jemimah leaving. Drink in hand, he stared at the blank television set.

As she drove out on the highway, Jemimah had a gnawing feeling that George Humphreys knew a lot more than he was letting on. He wasn't the typical husband in mourning. This whole thing appeared to be just an annoyance, having to make arrangements to bury someone. Most husbands would have shed at least *one* tear.

CHAPTER THIRTY-EIGHT

Holed up in the back room of her office, Jemimah slipped on her honorary detective hat and again flipped through the business cards in Gilda's purse. She dialed the number on the back of one card and waited while the phone rang and then went to message.

> You have reached the celestial abode of Sister Rita, psychic consultant and clairvoyant. I've been waiting to hear from you, my friend. Allow my skills to lead you to the answers you seek by leaving your name and number.

Caught off guard by the cryptic greeting, she hesitated for a few seconds and then left a message that she was interested in meeting to discuss a police matter. The psychic returned her call late that afternoon and scheduled an appointment for the following day.

Halfway up St. Francis Drive Jemimah pulled onto a narrow dirt road across the railroad tracks on the west side of Santa Fe, a part of the city infamous for shady inhabitants and drug deals. In the 1950s, the area was populated by the Southsiders, one of the better known of the *pachuco* gangs. The neighborhood had undergone a recent transformation, becoming a fertile area for speculators to invest and sell small fixer-uppers. They hoped to cash in on the resurgence prompted by the beautification of the nearby rail yard.

The road wound its way behind a cemetery populated with granite mausoleums shaded by giant Siberian elm trees. Many of the *Anglo* entrepreneurs who cultivated the retail aspect of Santa Fe beginning in the 1800s were buried in this exclusive plot of prime real estate. She thought the location was an eerie setting for a palm reader. She parked her vehicle, made sure it was locked, and headed toward a set of decrepit wooden steps. Dozens of wind chimes tinkled above her head. At the front door, a sign read, *No need to knock. Enter quietly. Your destiny awaits.*

She entered through the wrought-iron screen door and when her eyes adjusted to the dimly lit interior, she saw that every available inch of the room was covered with glass votive candles, framed pictures of saints, crosses, icons and crystals. The walls were lined with an assortment of silver and tin *Milagros* and medicine bundles. Books of spells and incantations filled the shelves next to rows of glass jars chock full of herbs and tinctures. Bright blue ceramic eyeballs to ward off *el mal ojo* hung from the ceiling and swayed in the breeze of the ceiling fan, adding to the somewhat macabre setting.

A Victorian couch, two old blue chairs and a round table covered with a lace tablecloth were the only furniture in the room. Sister Rita wafted through a doorway, causing long strings of colorful beads to sway with the movement. She was a slight, dark-haired woman with a smooth complexion and pale brown eyes the color of cinnamon. Jemimah couldn't tell her age. Her makeup had been applied with a heavy hand, eyelids thick with aqua-blue eye shadow, clumpy mascaraed lashes and ruby red lips traced beyond the lip line.

A flowered bandana was wrapped around her head, oversized gold hoops hung from each ear, and dozens of multi-colored bangles adorned her wrists. An embroidered peasant blouse and three-tiered ruffled skirt completed the classic image of a gypsy fortuneteller who might have run her business out of a brightly lit carnival tent in the 1950s.

Jemimah didn't know the difference between a medium and a psychic, and she wasn't sure she wanted to find out. Her only interest was learning why Gilda had come to see this woman. She was surprised to hear the authority in the small woman's voice.

"Sit down, please," she said, "and remove your shoes."

Jemimah sat in one of the chairs and removed her flats. She folded her hands in her lap and did not relax against the chair back, keeping her back very straight.

"Excuse me for a moment," Sister Rita said, and disappeared into the adjoining room. She returned holding a small basket. Jewelry jangled as she placed the basket on the table, adjusting the position of the egg in the center. Jemimah's eyes widened as she watched Rita walk in a circle around her chair and make the sign of the cross over her head with the egg. She gasped, realizing she had just been the recipient of a ritualistic Catholic blessing. Although she had been excommunicated from the Mormon church over twenty years ago, aspects of the religion were still ingrained in her mind. She thought it might be a bad thing for a Mormon to receive a Catholic ritual. However, she was also an avid believer that what didn't kill you potentially made you stronger, and since she hadn't been struck by lightning after being blessed, she must be all right.

Sister Rita continued to make wide sweeping motions around Jemimah with the egg still in her hands.

"May I ask what the significance of the egg is?" Jemimah said.

"There's a bit of negativity surrounding your aura. This will move it swiftly out," she said.

In the large mirror on the wall, Jemimah observed the woman dancing around her like a whirling dervish, drawing crosses in the air space with the egg. She hated to admit it, but as the cleansing process continued she was beginning to feel more relaxed. It hadn't been her intent to get a reading for herself—she didn't believe in spiritualism—but she was willing to go along with Sister Rita's eccentricity to get the information she needed. It appeared that Rita was determined to do whatever was necessary to make all the conditions agreeable. As Jemimah closed her eyes and further relaxed in the chair, she felt a light pressure on the palms of her hands and then on the soles of her bare feet, where Rita continued to work with the egg.

The grandmother clock in the corner pealed in dulcet tones. Jemimah opened her eyes. An entire hour had elapsed since she felt the hard shell of the egg on her hands. In momentary disbelief, she glanced at her watch to confirm the time. *Yes, an entire hour.*

"Now that you're completely relaxed, my dear, we can continue," Rita said.

"I must say I'm feeling less anxious and stressed than when I came in," Jemimah said, "but I would much rather stop and discuss the reason I'm here."

"We're only at the halfway point," Rita said, ignoring Jemimah as she cracked the egg and dropped its contents into a bowl of water. "Now we can access the information you're seeking." Within minutes, the yolk separated and floated to the top, while the white sank to the bottom and formed a lacy design. Rita deftly gathered the yolk and flushed it down the drain.

CHAPTER THIRTY-NINE

Jemimah yawned, briefly forgetting she had come to interview Sister Rita but had instead been subjected to a series of chants and incantations. For a while the setting seemed surreal. Sister Rita motioned her to move her chair closer to the table.

"The purpose of that ritual, my dear, was to flush negativity from your life," said Sister Rita, studying the design left by the egg at the bottom of the glass bowl. "Ah," she looked intently at Jemimah, who sat without blinking. "I see that for some time you've been struggling with an internal crisis involving many aspects of your existence—family, romance, career. Much of this will be resolved in the coming year. I see you have a guardian angel who hovers over you."

"I'm not Catholic. I don't believe in angels," Jemimah said.

"Angels aren't necessarily Catholic," Rita chided. "They are intelligent beings who can materialize from the spiritual world or just be someone who enters our lives. For instance, the man who loves you. I see he has saved your life more than once."

Jemimah assumed she was referring to Detective Romero. "Yes, I guess you could say that."

Sister Rita closed her eyes and inhaled deeply. "I'm ready now. Ask your questions."

"I'm sure you've read the newspapers recently about the body of a woman found in the mountains near Taos?"

"I rarely read the news. It plays havoc with my energy field."

"Your phone number was on a card found in the victim's purse. Her name was Gilda Humphreys. I believe her appointment was sometime around the middle of last month. Do you keep a record of your clients?"

"I never write names in my book. But maybe if you describe her ... I rarely forget a face."

"I can do better than that. I have a photo." Jemimah reached into her satchel and retrieved a folder.

The psychic opened her eyes. "Ah, yes. The archaeologist. The woman was impatient and determined to have a special reading. Most women come here searching for romance or in pursuit of a tall, dark and handsome man. She was different."

"Do you remember what you discussed?"

"Absolutely. It was one of the most bizarre readings I've ever conducted. I used a special deck of Tarot cards with astrological references. I set out five cards to represent the past, present, future, here and now. I shuddered as I turned each card, which ranged from the Ten of Swords to the Judgment card. The Tower Card, the Four of Wands followed, ending with the Hanged Man card. That card represented deeply rooted judgments in her subconscious and indicated she would have nine days to regain her spiritual self. That woman was so emotionally caught up in her situation that she couldn't move outside that realm. She was too selfish to take advantage of any bridges she might cross to get to a better space."

Rita looked at Jemimah, who had a blank look on her face. "I'm sure this doesn't make any sense to you, hearing it second hand," she said.

"I must admit it doesn't. I don't know a Tarot card from a bingo card," Jemimah smiled.

"What I couldn't get her to understand was that the

cards reflect choices, not inevitabilities, but she was already conditioned to believe the worst."

"What did she say that made you believe that about her? Most people described her as stubborn, but realistic most of the time."

"Oh, I'm sure it wasn't a mindset she was aware of. And if she was, she would never acknowledge it. The cards revealed that about her. She came searching for clues about a treasure. She believed a reading would point her directly to it, but that's not my function. Convinced that this treasure was hidden in a particular area, she just wanted validation of her thoughts, even if it came from another realm."

"What area was she talking about?"

"Taos Canyon."

"Did she say how she came up with that idea?"

"She had a hand-drawn map or drawing containing certain elements that made her believe a treasure was buried there. I got the impression that the map didn't specifically say Taos Canyon anywhere on it, but she indicated she knew the area like the back of her hand."

"Did you agree with her ideas?"

"Whether I agreed or not wasn't an issue. I saw dark ripples forming around water and she needed to be extremely careful. Danger lurked around her and I suggested she not underestimate or trivialize the motives of those with whom she came in contact. The choices she was considering were about to catapult her into a series of dark events unless she paid attention to her surroundings and abandoned this quest."

"How did your meeting with her end?"

The bracelets on Sister Rita's wrist jangled as she motioned with her hand. "She refused to process any of it. I couldn't convince her these are impressions that come up during a reading and in many cases can be an accurate indication of the direction a person is headed."

"So she wasn't willing to listen?"

"No. She harrumphed a few times, threw a wad of bills on the table, and stormed out to the parking lot. People come to me for different reasons. The cards didn't reveal what she wanted to see, so she was dissatisfied. I didn't expect to hear from her again."

Jemimah thanked Sister Rita and offered to pay for her time. Sister Rita smiled and showed her to the door. "Wonderful things will be coming into your life. Pay attention."

Jemimah stepped out into the sunlight. Although the "reading" had confirmed Gilda's obsession with finding a treasure, it didn't offer much in the way of evidence. On the positive side, she couldn't help but notice her mind was clear and her step was lighter. She hummed all the way to her office.

CHAPTER FORTY

By the end of the week, Detective Romero had logged plenty of hours working the investigation of the Taos murder and tending to matters in his own jurisdiction. He was baffled by State Archaeologist Gilda Humphreys' lack of connection to anything in the Taos area. None of her office files indicated she had been summoned there by any of the nearby communities or the Pueblo. In fact he learned that Humphreys had long been an unpopular person in tribal circles. Her antagonistic demeanor intimidated and alienated the Indians who had lived close to the earth for centuries. On several occasions, she had been called to task before Tom Rodriguez, the director of her department, for attempting to enforce state and federal legislation that didn't apply to sovereign Pueblos or private owners. Jemimah assumed that was what she had been trying to do to McCabe. She could see why they had locked horns.

How long Humphreys' body had been in the boat was anyone's guess. Icy cold mountain runoff lingered at a cool forty degree temperature. Dense undergrowth provided additional cover. Was it a coincidence she was in the area? The coroner's report indicated she was wearing a pair of light hiking boots, far afield from the low-heel pumps the detectives had found in her bedroom closet.

Romero was almost at the end of a not-a-damn-thing's-working day. He was having little success in determining whether Humphreys' murder was random or deliberate.

From the number of complaint letters in her personnel file, it was obvious she'd pissed off more than a few people. He put in a call to Jemimah in her capacity as the forensic psychologist for the County and invited her to lunch. Maybe she could offer a few insights into the case. Besides, he hadn't seen her for a few days and was missing her presence in his life. They had shared an intimate, romantic night on Valentine's Day and the relationship had become more serious since then.

Both Rick Romero and Tim McCabe had met Jemimah at the same time, through a series of serendipitous events that had begun with a shooting on the San Lazaro Indian Pueblo. A degreed psychologist, she relocated to New Mexico from Dallas and purchased a small ranch in the hills near the Ortiz Mountains near Cerrillos. From the moment they met, Romero was smitten, but it took over a year before they went on a first date. He was attracted to the cowgirl with honey blond hair and blue eyes. More your girl next door type than model material, but stunning nonetheless.

Shortly before noon, Romero watched as Jemimah drove her 4Runner onto the gravel driveway of the San Marcos Café a few miles from his office. The place was a quirky but popular spot for both locals and tourists, with a homey atmosphere and a menu to match. Local police stopped by often, as much for the food as to flirt with the perky waitress. Jemimah paused as a peacock in full bloom took his sweet time strutting along the sidewalk, followed by a young employee chasing the big footed emu that had escaped from its pen at the rear of the restaurant. She chatted with the owner and then strolled toward Romero. He stood and they shared a warm embrace. He kissed her lightly on the lips and she smiled.

"Excuse me, Detective, how's it going to look when Sheriff Medrano gets a phone call from some busybody that a couple of his employees were making out in a well-known restaurant?"

"That was just a small token of affection. If you'll meet me in the back seat of my cruiser, I'd be glad to demonstrate what the term 'making out' constitutes," he chuckled.

"I'll take a rain check on that offer," she laughed. "Right now, I'm hungry. Let's go inside and order. It smells yummy in here."

Between bites of a green chili smothered beef burrito and swallows of iced tea, Romero brought Jemimah up to speed on the two murders that were high on their list.

"Anything light a spark, there?" he said.

Jemimah put down her fork and said, "Let's assume that Gilda Humphreys was just taking the day off. Maybe she liked to hike the trails in those mountains. They're quite beautiful this time of year. You and I took a day off last year and spent it sitting on the rocks, just watching the river float by, remember? What's to say she couldn't do the same?"

Romero shook his head. "We've interviewed most of her co-workers. She *never* took days off to hike, in the mountains or anywhere else. In fact, she had hundreds of unused vacation hours and sick leave on her record. Of course she did do a lot of walking as part of her job checking out sites and giving people hell, but there wasn't one person who indicated she was an avid hiker. Avid bitch was more like it, according to all sources."

Jemimah shrugged. "Sounds like she wasn't on the top of anyone's favorite boss list. Let's explore another avenue. Tim McCabe told me that on a number of occasions Humphreys had been hanging around the fringes of San Lazaro, bound and determined to make him halt the excavations. She had it in for him and was spending a lot of time looking for an excuse to be out there."

"Did McCabe actually allow her access to the ruins?"

"No, at least not when he was there. He wasn't about to

give her permission to snoop around, particularly when she was being so nasty about it. He said she had no business being there and I believe him."

"But that doesn't mean she didn't go out there on her own," Romero said.

"It doesn't," Jemimah replied, "but there was nothing for her to see. All the excavations are monitored, mostly conducted by private archaeological firms and university students."

Romero waited for the waitress to take their plates away before continuing, "That opens up a whole 'nother direction. I can't see any connection between her, Tim McCabe, San Lazaro and Taos. McCabe said he's been so occupied lately with setting up his treasure hunt with Foster Burke that he hasn't spent any time out at the ruins."

Jemimah thoughtfully stirred sugar into her iced tea. "What about maybe *she* was looking into this treasure herself?"

"That's a bit of a stretch, Jem, but why not? I know I'd sure like to find a buried treasure. First off I'd buy you that house in the country you've always wanted."

Jemimah laughed. "I already have a house in the country. By the way, I didn't tell you about my afternoon with Sister Rita."

"The fortune teller? Were you hoping she was going to confirm that you were going to meet some tall, dark and handsome guy who was going to sweep you off your feet?"

"I've already met him, for your information."

He gave her a quick peck on the cheek. "That's good to know. So did she dust you off with a feather duster or clean your aura with crystals?"

"As a matter of fact, she probably did."

"You don't remember?"

Jemimah smoothed her hair. "Of course I do," she insisted. "It's just a little hazy."

"Just kidding, Jem. I've known about Sister Rita for some time. I personally have never consulted her, but she's been in business ever since I can remember."

"She did get me to relax a bit, and that was refreshing."

"So what was your reason for going there, if you didn't want to know what the future holds for us?" He grinned.

Jemimah tapped her index finger on his forehead. "Focus. Let's get back to the case, here. I found her number on a card in Gilda Humphreys' purse and went there to see what I could learn."

"Did she give you anything we could use?"

"Nothing other than that Gilda was bound and determined to find some hidden treasure."

"Are we talking about McCabe's treasure?"

"I'm pretty sure that would be it. I think she might have been actively considering a search in the mountains near Taos to see what she could find."

"So we can assume she did have a reason to be in that area," Romero said.

"Looks that way. What was the Humphreys' financial situation?"

"I had Martinez pull their bank records, and it looks like they had a few bucks saved. George Humphreys indicated they weren't struggling to make ends meet."

"Everybody's struggling to make ends meet, Rick. What else you got?"

"I was going to ask you the same question. Now that we've made the connection to McCabe's treasure hunt, I think it's worth following up, don't you?"

"Yes," Jemimah replied. "That theory seems the most likely, unless she was killed for getting too close to discovering something that nobody wanted her to know."

"Maybe she had stumbled onto illegal shenanigans in that area. That might be another avenue we can explore."

"Now," Jemimah said, sipping her tea, "what's going on

with the murdered woman from the casino, is that headed for a shelf in the cold case room?"

"Glad you asked, Jem. For a while there it looked like these two cases might be connected, what with both of them being strangled before being shot."

Jemimah cocked her head. "So what happened to change your mind?

"Before I left my office to come out here, the forensics lab called. We don't have the bullet yet in the Humphreys case but the method of strangulation doesn't match. Gilda Humphreys was choked with a guitar string; Amy Griego had a scarf wrapped around her neck."

"It can't just be a coincidence that two women are strangled and shot within a short period of time and in a hundred mile radius? There has to be a connection, don't you think?"

"Forensics didn't seem to concur. In Gilda's case the strangling appeared deliberate; in the other case it appeared to be an afterthought. We won't dismiss the possibility, but hopefully something will break on one of these cases sooner or later."

"I'm not convinced that one case doesn't have something to do with the other," Jemimah said. "Just because there's been more activity with Gilda's case is no reason to dismiss the similarities."

Romero shrugged. "It's up to us to make the connection; otherwise one case is going forward and the other is standing still." He looked at his watch. "Time to get back to the grind. Well, pretty lady, I have no doubt you'll put that amazing brain of yours in gear and find something we can work with."

"Thank you, Detective. I'll try to live up to your expectations."

As she got up to leave, he kissed her on the cheek. Jemimah grinned all the way to her car. Early on, she had resisted every move Romero made to get closer. Now, she was falling in love and eagerly anticipated the nights they could spend together.

CR

Romero headed back to his office. He checked for messages and spent the afternoon on his least favorite task: reviewing employee files to determine who needed to be called on the carpet and who deserved a recommendation for a raise.

At four-thirty he shoved his briefcase and case material into a file cabinet and drove home. After a dinner of Chinese takeout, he picked up the book McCabe had given him, propped himself on the recliner, and read it from cover to cover. Toward the end, he considered Jemimah's theory that there might be a connection between the treasure, Bart Wolfe, and Gilda Humphreys. Earlier in the day, Detective Martinez had reported what the bartender had told him—that Gilda was the woman who had come to the bar asking questions about Wolfe and that he had told her Bart mentioned he was going fishing near Taos. Bart's cell number came up several times on the list provided by the cellular company.

No matter, he was going to have to haul Bart in for questioning. That guy was all over the place. Knew everybody, knew everything. Maybe Romero could shake a few piñons off this tree.

CHAPTER FORTY-ONE

Later in the week, Romero and Jemimah met again, this time in the conference room, to exchange theories about the case. The briefcase found in Gilda Humphreys' vehicle contained a file with a number of aerial maps and photographs of canyons in Northern New Mexico. Romero perused a sheaf of magazine and newspaper articles about McCabe's treasure that had been tucked neatly in one of the side pockets. They had spread everything out on the large table.

Jemimah broke the silence. "It looks as though she was seriously considering joining the treasure hunt, don't you think?"

Romero nodded. "I spent a few hours reading McCabe's book. From my point of view, the whole treasure hunt thing might be out of an Indiana Jones movie. It's going to appeal to thousands of people, mostly men, who have an adventurous spirit and the kind of spare change that would allow them to drop everything, grab their shovels and camping gear and load up the SUV. The UPS guy told me he and his son go out every weekend to search. It's brought them closer together. They've got just as much chance of finding it as anyone."

Jemimah sat down and took a sip of water. "I agree. Listening to McCabe and Burke talk about the way they put it together was really exciting. I was mesmerized," she said. "I could have listened to them talk all night."

"So, getting back to Gilda. From what I've gleaned from the case file and recent interviews, she just doesn't seem to be the type who would go out searching for something that might never be found, at least in this lifetime."

"What are you saying, Rick? That the treasure's hidden so far away it's unlikely to be discovered?"

"More like it's hidden *so well*. McCabe and Burke are dead serious about making this a legitimate treasure hunt. They're adamant that whoever finds it is going to have to work for it. Otherwise they could have just set it out in the middle of the Plaza, in plain sight, and the first person who spotted it could have it."

"I see what you mean. They've given this a lot more thought than the average person."

"Nothing *average* about those two. They're like Siamese twins, joined at the chest."

Jemimah chuckled. "Yeah, Laura told me they've been inseparable ever since they met."

He took a seat and folded his arms across his chest. "You know, Jem, it doesn't appear to me that Gilda Humphreys knew anything more or had any more information than anyone else did. It was too early in the game. The book hasn't been out that long and the television interviews aired right after its release. She had to be operating on sheer conjecture, and for whatever reason, she set her sights on the Taos area. The odd thing I found as I read the book is that there didn't seem to be any indication that the treasure was even buried that close to Santa Fe. She just got some wild notion in her head."

Jemimah nodded thoughtfully. "Some people do that. Fixate on an object or an idea and that becomes their focus. Gilda also believed that seeing a psychic would give her something more to go on. Although there may be psychics who are able to sense specific events, I don't believe they can actually direct a person to hidden treasure. Otherwise they could find it themselves."

Romero smiled as Jemimah related her experience with the egg and the aura cleansing. As a child he had learned never to doubt psychic phenomena.

His grandmother had a whole collection of stories she related when the occasion warranted, and some were harder than others to dismiss. Many of the tales were handed down through generations and were designed to impart a moral lesson. She had recounted them in a grave undertone, speaking almost in a whisper. One had concerned two young sisters who wanted to go dancing on Good Friday during Lent. Their mother said no; it would be sacrilegious. No matter, as soon as she was asleep they snuck out of the house and made their way to the dance hall, where they peeked through the windows and observed everyone having a grand old time.

As the evening wore on, a drop-dead gorgeous man stepped into the room. The women swooned as he took each one of them out on the dance floor, much to the chagrin of their escorts. After being twirled around to the music, one woman happened to glance down at the man's feet and saw that they were hooves. Just then a long tail began to emerge from beneath his jacket. Everyone headed for the exit in a thunderous panic, only to find the doors locked. But one of the men grabbed a hatchet and broke the door down and everyone fled into the night. The girls left their window perch and ran home in terror. Romero believed every word of the story.

Jemimah continued, "There are other aspects of this case to consider. I question the extent of Bart Wolfe's involvement."

"You've interviewed him in the past, haven't you?"

"Yes, on the San Lazaro murders case. At the time he existed in a purple haze—lots of weed and alcohol. He was a bar-stool cowboy who tried to put the make on every pretty face that graced the bar. Also the not-too-pretty ones. Sometimes he lucked out. He was really full of himself. I remember he joked he never went to bed with an ugly woman, but he sure woke up with a few. It was apparent then that his worst sin was being a philanderer. I didn't see him as a murderer, and it turned out he wasn't."

"But this is two years later, Jem. Maybe things have changed. Maybe Bart has changed," Romero said.

"Anything's possible. Maybe you need to sit him down and make him come clean. His cell number showed up several times on the list of calls on Gilda's phone starting over a month before the murder. When I interviewed the bartender at the Line Camp tavern in Madrid, he said Wolfe and the victim were looking pretty gaga-eyed at each other a couple of times when they were in the bar."

Romero was incredulous. "Together? That might be a match made in hell."

"Yeah, he said that after a few turns on the dance floor and a copious amount of booze, they burned a path to the parking lot and probably ended up in his van."

"Anyone else see them?"

"Nope. I've talked to a few of the regulars so far, but the barmaid who waited on them quit her job a week later and Detective Martinez has been trying to find her. She'll show up eventually, probably working another bar job."

Romero thumbed through the file. "Any of the vic's credit card charges reach out and grab you?"

"Nothing. It appears she was a bit frugal, but she did make a purchase at Undies Galore on the Internet for forty-eight dollars."

"I thought she and her husband had separate bedrooms," Romero said.

"Yeah. Strange as it might sound, maybe she was planning to spend some quality time with Bart."

"If they were romping around in the van, there wouldn't be much call for fancy undies."

Jemimah grinned like a Chinese Buddha. "It's a woman thing, Rick. Guys just don't get it. I'll spare you the details on that intriguing subject, as it would take more time than I have right now. Anyway, you work on Bart. There's a whole box of notes and books taken from her bedroom and office that nobody's gone through and I'm going to take on that task this evening."

"So much for popcorn and a movie," Romero said.

CHAPTER FORTY-TWO

Jemimah arrived home in the early afternoon, arms laden with an evidence box from the Humphreys case. She greeted her enthusiastic dog, spent some time mulling through the refrigerator and decided on a salad and the remainder of the green chili burrito from lunch.

Emptying the evidence box on the kitchen island, she stacked each item according to category. The majority were books on various subjects relating to the anthropology and archaeology of New Mexico. She skimmed through each book to make sure there were no loose papers or notations inside that might be relevant before returning them to the box. All that remained were three manila envelopes containing various memos distributed to employees, a copy of a letter from the Director notifying her of the upcoming freeze on hiring, and three canvas field books.

Written in neat penmanship, the field books contained notes of Gilda's daily comings and goings. Jemimah thumbed through the first ten pages, which referred to various dates and excursions to locations throughout New Mexico, and decided there wasn't going to be much useful information in the first field book; the dates were from previous years. The next contained similar information. Jemimah stifled a yawn. She slid down from the kitchen stool and walked to the refrigerator, where she retrieved a pint of Ben and Jerry's Chunky Monkey ice cream and scooped out a bowl's worth.

Like snuggling up in a fuzzy blanket, the ice cream break

provided a feeling of contentment. Jemimah was tempted to set her task aside and watch the ten o'clock news, but decided to press on. She reached for the last field book, expecting to read more of the same. Halfway through the pages she was surprised to see the notations had turned into paragraphs. She read the first entry dated over two months earlier.

> I can't believe what happened tonight. I'm walking on a cloud. I felt like a teenager, making love in the back of a van, of all things. This experience has made me realize something about myself. I'm not such an ugly duckling if I can attract a strange man without trying. Interesting. Maybe there is life out there beyond George. He doesn't even bother to try any more, hasn't for years. Just because he's dead, I guess he assumes I am. Tonight proved him wrong!

There were several columns of numbers in the next two pages that appeared to be related to a parcel of land. Gilda had scribbled "San Lazaro Pueblo" on the side and "No errors found in transfer, damn!" Jemimah assumed she had been exploring ways to harass Tim McCabe. Other notes appeared to relate to her continuing investigation of McCabe and his property.

On the pages that followed, Gilda described her second liaison with Bart in terms Jemimah thought would make a sailor blush. She wrote about putting blonde streaks in her hair and trying to lose a little more weight so she could fit into a pair of jeans she had bought at the mall. Amazing what a box of Clairol could do for a girl.

As Jemimah read on, she could see that Gilda was warming to the idea of exploring her sexuality, a notion that had been simmering for some time. She had also decided to divorce George. In her own mind, she was three-quarters out of the marriage. Any fool would tell you, Jemimah thought, that when a woman makes up her mind to do something, watch out. It was the classic psychological profile of transformation. The butterfly had begun to emerge.

The journal entries ended abruptly, as though Gilda had been interrupted. The final entry appeared to be quickly scribbled.

> I'm going to see what little honey I can pick up tonight. As much as I hate work related events, I have to attend this one. I have my eye on someone, and I'm sure he's going to be there.

CHAPTER FORTY-THREE

Dressed in a checkered western shirt and Levis, Bart Wolfe smelled of cheap aftershave and cigarette smoke. To diffuse his alcohol breath, he chewed noisily on a wad of peppermint gum. The SFCSO had requested that he come in voluntarily for questioning on the Gilda Humphreys homicide case. The complex was only a few miles north of where he lived, but he drove there with an uneasy hand. His legs were unsteady as he walked up to the main office of the Sheriff's Department across from the old State Pen, which also housed the Detention Center/Adult Corrections Facility. He was no stranger to these parts, having spent more nights than he cared to remember in an eight by ten cell with nothing more than a mattress and a toilet to keep him company. New paint and plaster didn't change its reputation for making the orange jumpsuit clad prisoners toe the line.

The receptionist directed Wolfe down the hall and to the right, where he spotted Romero, standing at the door in Sheriff Medrano's side office. Romero shook his hand, which by this time was clammy.

"Bart, thank you for taking the time to come by," Romero said.

"Didn't think I had much choice, the way that detective was talking. It was either come willingly or he was going to handcuff me, shove me in a cruiser and haul me over here."

"I'm sure that's a misperception. We're just out to get some answers."

"Harsh way of going about it. A man has to have some dignity, you know. We're not all criminals."

"Let's settle down, Bart. I just need to ask you a few questions about Gilda Humphreys."

Bart stopped chewing his gum. "Who?" He shoved his hands in his pockets. "Can't say I know that name."

"Gilda Humphreys. Her body was found a while back in the Taos canyon area."

"Hmmm. I still can't recollect. Never heard of her. Taos, you say?"

"Cut the crap, Bart. Maybe this will refresh your memory." Romero pulled out a photograph from the file in front of him and put it under Bart's nose.

"Oh, yeah. I might have seen her somewhere or other, come to think of it."

"I understand you two were pretty tight."

"What? She ain't my type."

"I'll ask it another way, Bart. We have information to indicate that you two were hitting the sheets, if you know what I mean. Got a couple of eyewitnesses who saw you dancing up a storm at a bar in Madrid. Were you two lovers?"

Bart changed his tone. "All right, dammit. So we screwed around a couple of times, no big deal."

"You knew she was a married woman."

"Hey, it didn't bother her, why should it bother me? If someone spreads it out for free, I take it."

"When was the last time you saw her?"

"I dunno. Maybe three, four weeks ago, maybe longer. I don't keep a calendar."

"Where was that?"

"We had a couple of drinks at a bar."

"Were you celebrating something?"

"Huh? No. We were having a drink, that's all."

"The bartender said that wasn't the first time you two had cozied up."

"None of that asshole's business. I get a lot of action out of that bar. I'm pretty popular with the ladies, if you get my drift."

"All right, Bart. Let's get serious here. The woman is dead. You were seeing her on the side. What's the real story here? You two have an argument? Did things get out of control ... maybe end up in the heat of passion?"

"You trying to pin this on me, Detective? If you are, you can kiss my ass. I got nothing to hide."

Romero stood and leaned against the table. "You have to admit your story's a little squirrely. Nothing comes together, just a bunch of holes, like Swiss cheese. First you don't know her and then you do; then you're not screwing around with her then you are. And some people might even say you have a little bit of a temper, Bart. That true? According to your rap sheet, you've been involved in more than a few skirmishes."

"Listen, I've gone a few rounds, had a few brawls, and I ended up spending some time downstairs, eight by eight square room courtesy of the County, but I ain't never hurt no woman. Never have and don't plan to. I'm not that kind of guy."

Romero returned to his chair. "Well then, help me out here, Bart. You two must have meant something to each other. She didn't appear to be the kind of person who hung around bars and went around having one night stands. There's a lot of mystery surrounding this woman, and we'd like to clear it all up. How about a little respect for someone who ended up being murdered for no apparent reason?"

"Okay. But I need a cigarette. Is it okay to light up in here?"

"Yeah, go ahead." Romero offered him a light and shoved an ashtray in his direction. He could see the sweat starting to form on Wolfe's brow and the way his fingers were shaking as he lit up.

"I'll go get us something to drink, Bart. I'm a little thirsty myself." Romero went into the employee lounge with the intent of giving Bart a few minutes to compose himself.

Bart's head was spinning. He sure as hell didn't want to have anyone suspect he was capable of killing somebody. *No siree.* That would play hell with his reputation. He wasn't having any of it. *Might as well come clean and tell them what I know. There wasn't no cause for someone to kill that woman. She had started to grow on me, only I didn't want to have to deal with no husbands. I should have gone out there with her and walked her around the canyon. Shit.*

Romero brought in a couple of cans of Coke and set one in front of him, flipping the top off the other. "What do you say, Bart. Can we get on with it? Tell me all you know about Gilda Humphreys."

Bart crushed the cigarette in the ashtray and lit up another. "Detective Romero, I just want to say up front that I had nothing to do with that woman's murder. I might be a piece of shit in a lot of people's minds, but I would never kill anyone. I ain't got it in me."

"I believe you, Bart. So what's the story here?"

Bart told him how they met, what she wanted him to do regarding the treasure, and all the rest of it, including walking into Tim McCabe's house looking for any kind of drawing that might indicate where the box might be buried.

"So you're saying that you went out looking for this treasure yourself, based on some of the things she had discussed with you?"

"That was *her* plan. She had this idea that finding McCabe's treasure was going to be a slam dunk. She was bound and determined that it was where she said it was, like someone could just walk up to a spot marked with an X and start digging. It would take years to find something buried out in that canyon. I couldn't have changed her mind if I tried."

"So you just gathered up your gear and drove off half-blind, figuring it wouldn't be long before you were rolling in dough?"

"No. I had another plan."

"Oh, a Plan B. And what was that, Bart?"

Bart wrung his hands, as if debating what he was going to say. "Truth is, while I was at McCabe's I found another map and made a copy of it. I didn't show it to Gilda, and it looked more promising than that piece of paper she was interested in."

"Tell me about this other map, Bart," Romero said. "Take your time."

Bart puffed on his cigarette. "Well, there was a letter attached to it from an inmate at an Arizona prison somewhere near Chandler, and he wanted McCabe to finance him to locate a box he and a couple of other criminals buried around Taos Canyon."

Romero rolled his eyes. "What kind of box was that, another treasure? Was his name Captain Hook?"

"I'm serious," Bart said. "I looked it up on the Internet and the guy was telling the truth. In the seventies, these guys had robbed a Brinks truck as it left a Taos bank, and as the cops chased them down through the canyon, they pulled off the road and buried it. The other two were caught and this guy was free for about a week until they caught him, too, but he had time enough to draw a map of where they had hidden the box."

"So that's what you went after? Didn't you ever stop to consider that if McCabe thought there was any truth to it, he would have gone to look for it himself? The guy likes a little adventure in his life, you know?"

"McCabe had written a note on it and I guess he just filed it away."

"What did the note say?"

" 'This is bullshit,' or something like that."

"That should have told you something, don't you think,

Bart? Now let's get back to Gilda. Did you finally tell her you hadn't been out searching for the treasure she was looking to find?"

"No. I made up a story that I had been out there several times and that it was like looking for a needle in a haystack. I told her she might be better off going to look for it herself."

"Meanwhile, you were searching for this other treasure. Did you find it?"

"I thought I had, but when I went back to get it, I couldn't find it again."

"So why did you get involved with Gilda Humphreys in the first place?" Romero said.

"She was paying me. She made it sound easy, that all I had to do was follow this map of hers and I would find it. Only I must have had rocks in my head to believe something that farfetched. She was so damned sure that I was going to find something for her, and then I gave up on everything and told her so."

"So you think maybe she went off to look for the treasure herself?"

"Probably. She was determined to get her hands on it, one way or the other. That's the impression I got from our last conversation. She seemed to think she would round a corner and find it sitting there waiting to bite her in the ass. I tell you she was going to have to hike a hundred miles. I don't think those guys made it that easy, no sir. I gotta give them a lot of credit for their smarts."

Romero reached across the table to empty the ashtray. "Do you know what made her think the chest was buried somewhere near Taos?"

"Well, she thought she had a map of sorts that was going to lead her to the treasure."

"And that map came from where?"

"I already told you. I went into McCabe's ranch house and took it for her. She paid me."

"Ah, the ranch house, where you got the other map, too. And was Mr. McCabe aware of what you had done?"

Bart cringed. "No, man, and I'd appreciate you not telling him. I didn't touch nothing. She told me what to look for and I thought I'd found it. I didn't take nothing, either. I just took pictures with the digital camera she gave me, got the hell out of there, and gave it to her."

"You're asking me to overlook what amounts to breaking and entering. Can't do that, Bart. I'll run it by McCabe and see what he has to say. A lot of cooperation on your part will pave the way for that. Maybe I can talk him into not pressing charges."

"Anything you want. I ain't going to jail. I didn't kill that woman and I don't know who did or why. You're just going to have to believe me."

"I'd like you to look at something else, Bart." Romero shoved a photo of the casino victim in front of him. "Have you ever met this woman?"

Bart glanced at the photo. "Can't say that I have."

"Take a good look. You hang around the bars a lot, maybe you've seen her somewhere."

"No, sir. I only hang out at bars in Cerrillos and Madrid. I can say for sure I've never seen this person. Who is she?"

"This is another woman who was murdered a couple of months ago in similar fashion to Gilda's murder and her body was found in the foothills of the Ortiz Mountains. That's not too far from where you hang out, Bart."

Bart shifted in his chair. "Hey, wait a minute, Detective. You're not trying to connect me to this woman, too, are you? I swear, I don't know her. Never have seen her. I might be a lot of things, some of them not good, but I sure as hell ain't no murderer."

"Well, somebody killed her, and we're going to keep looking, so keep your nose clean, Bart," Romero said.

"It wasn't me. Can I go now? I'm about to wet my pants."

Romero scraped his chair back. "All right. That's all for now, Bart. Don't go taking any long trips until we've solved these cases."

"You don't think the killer might come after my ass, do you?"

"Not unless you're holding out here. Might be a good idea to start locking your doors." Romero couldn't keep from smiling. His last remark was designed to ruffle Bart's feathers, and from the look on the man's face, he had accomplished that.

He dialed Tim McCabe's number.

McCabe was glad to hear his voice. "Hey, Rick. Long time no hear."

"Back at you, Tim. You been hiding out in plain sight again, doing the celebrity circuit?"

"Just a bit. But I'm sure you didn't call to talk about how many autographs I've signed lately," he chuckled.

"Actually, you're right. I just finished interviewing Bart Wolfe on the Humphreys case. He said at Gilda's direction he'd been out at your ranch looking for a map to the treasure you and Burke were getting ready to launch."

"Bart Wolfe, that scoundrel? He's a shady character, that one. He was looking for what at my place?"

"It was about the time construction was almost completed out there. Said he went through an unlocked sunroom door."

"Yeah, I can see where he'd have no trouble getting in. Did he find anything? I never noticed anything out of place."

"Apparently he found a couple of things in your files. Didn't steal anything, but shot some photos, kept one and delivered the other to Gilda Humphreys."

"Why in hell would that unlikely pair be looking in my house for anything? What was it he took a photo of?"

"Bart said one was a drawing; he thought it might be a map of your treasure. The other was an old letter from some convict in Arizona who wanted you to pay his expenses to go looking for a box they buried after a robbery."

McCabe paused. "Jeez. I had forgotten about that. Thought I threw it away years ago. It was some kind of scam these cons were trying to pull. And as for a map of my treasure hunt, I don't know what he's talking about. No such thing exists," McCabe said.

"I'll fax a copy out to you. Take a look at it and get back to me. Bart is shaking in his boots that you might want to press charges against him. I'm going to keep him on the hook about it and maybe it will jar his memory a little more."

"Just let him keep thinking that. On another note, Rick, I'm going to be leaving on a trip this afternoon. Is it something you need an answer on immediately, or can it wait? I'll be back toward the end of the week. The house is already closed up, but if you need me to, I'll take a look at the fax."

"That's okay, it's probably not anything so earth shattering it can't wait. It's just part of the investigation into Gilda Humphreys' murder."

"Speaking of which, can I assume you've eliminated me as a suspect, or should I maybe postpone this trip?"

"Never really thought you were involved, McCabe. Just doing my job."

"That's sure a load off my mind."

CHAPTER FORTY-FOUR

Jemimah's office overlooked the Santa Fe Plaza on San Francisco Street. She took a moment to open the windows, just in time to see a stretch Hummer rounding the bend toward the La Fonda Hotel. *Probably Oprah or Cher and their entourage stopping off for a quick lunch. Shades of Hollywood.* Each Friday the local newspaper published a blurb about alleged star sightings around Santa Fe hot spots and called it *El Mitote*, the gossip. Jemimah smiled as she wondered who would be the one to catch a fleeting glimpse of the latest visitor to the popular hotel and call it in.

Hoping to make headway in the Humphreys case, she put in a call to the manager of the KOA Park just outside of Pilar where the victim's car was found.

"Kerry, this is Jemimah Hodge in Santa Fe, we spoke previously about the green Subaru that the Taos Police sent a tow truck to retrieve?"

"Yeah, so what do you need?" the man asked. "I already talked to the cops about it."

"I was wondering if you remembered anything else since our conversation about the week leading up to that car being parked there."

"You know, that's weird that you should ask. Me and my girlfriend were talking about it yesterday, and this probably doesn't mean anything, but one night we were sitting out on the porch, enjoying the sunset and having a few beers. We don't live too far from the river. You can hear it running from the porch. Our house faces the highway, and the river's across from that."

"Yes, I believe there's a note in the file to indicate where your house sits in relation to the river."

"Anyway, we were sitting around just shooting the bull, and I remember seeing a light winding its way down one of the trails next to the river. I figured someone had just stayed too long on the mountain and found themselves in the dark. There are worn paths along the way, so it's not as though someone would have to hike through the brush."

"Did you notice anything else?"

"I'm pretty sure there was a full moon out that night, but it was still dark enough where you needed some kind of light to find your way if you were on one of the trails. When the traffic noise gets louder, you can always tell you're on the right track."

"Did you see any vehicles parked anywhere near that open spot across the road from where you live?"

"Well, you know there's always traffic up and down the canyon, no matter what time of day or night, but come to think of it, it was kinda quiet for a while and I think I heard a car start up. The only reason I remember that is you know when you turn the key in the ignition more than once you get that screeching sound when the engine's already on and you don't know it?"

"Yes, I do. Did you actually see a car moving onto the highway?"

"No, Ma'am, I can't say that I did. I just remember hearing that screeching sound. I couldn't tell where it came from, and truthfully, I didn't give it no mind. Done it often enough myself to recognize the sound. I just heard it and then dismissed it."

"About what time was that?"

"It hadn't been dark for too long. We close at nine, so sometime before that."

Jemimah thanked him and thoughtfully placed the phone on the cradle. The other thing that was driving her nuts was that she couldn't figure out how a boat fit into the scenario. Was it just someone's idea of a cruel joke? Did they expect the body to float down the river and never be seen again? So far, ownership of the boat was vague. Nobody seemed to remember how long it had been moored at the rafting company, or even if it had been tied to a post there at all. She also wondered if the killer had known the boat was there.

CHAPTER FORTY-FIVE

It was early morning and the streets were deserted except for a young couple with two children emerging from the Starbucks across the street. Jemimah walked east on San Francisco Street, headed for her office. She thought she heard someone walking up behind her and noticed they slowed their pace when she did. She ducked into a storefront and waited for that someone to pass. *Dammit,* she was sure now she was being followed. She crossed the street against the light, pausing at another store window to see if she could catch a reflection.

"Detective Martinez! *Damn you.* You scared the hell out of me."

"I'm sorry, Dr. H. I was just trying to catch up with you. You walk at a pretty mean pace," he said. "It looked like you were in a marathon."

Clyde Martinez had a *pachuco* look about him. The appearance of slicked back dark hair and a few strategically placed tattoos stemmed from 1950s Santa Fe gang wannabes. He modeled his tough-guy appearance after his father's teen years, and it helped anytime he was interviewing young hoods and gang members. They weren't intimidated by him as they were by most cops.

"What can I do for you?" Jemimah said.

"Just wanted to go over these two murder cases with you. The boss wants us to log in a few more man-hours on the Humphreys case and then he'll decide whether he wants to continue on it or ship it all back to Taos PD. Do you have a few minutes? I don't think it will take very long."

They walked up a flight of steps and down a long hallway to her office. "Have a seat, Detective. I just need to check my messages." Jemimah scribbled a few notes and then sat across from him. "Nothing here that can't wait." She turned her chair to face him. "So how's this investigation going? Anything new I should know about?"

"Not much. We haven't been able to come up with a viable suspect in either case. At first we thought the two were related, but once it's down on paper, the similarity ends."

Jemimah interrupted. "I'm not sure I agree, but go ahead."

"As for the Humphreys case, obviously there's someone out there who hated her enough to kill her."

"So where do we go from here? Have you plotted a timeline of the victim's last days?"

"Bits and pieces. In a nutshell, it started off as a regular work week, she spent some vacation time around Taos, and a day or two later she was floating in a boat near Taos Canyon, dead."

"Have we determined the identity of the last person to see her alive?"

"Other than our killer, no. She might have been perceived as a total bitch, but that's hardly an excuse for murder. I know a few of those myself."

"What about her neighbors? Has anyone talked to them?" Jemimah said.

"I canvassed the victim's neighborhood. Most of them are upper middle class, retired, play a lot of golf. It's not a moms-dads-kids-and-dogs kind of neighborhood. The Humphreys didn't seem to cultivate friendships with any of them. They were unfriendly sorts, or maybe just anti-social. You would think that having a high paying job with the State she might come off as a little friendlier."

The coffee maker beeped as the light blinked to green. Jemimah walked to the kitchen and poured herself a cup and offered one to Martinez, who declined. "What kind of a read did you get on the husband? You think he's being cooperative?"

"Kind of a hard nut to crack. On the one hand he appears to be holding a lot of pain over his wife's death, and on the other hand, stiff as a board. He was all torqued because he thinks everyone considers him a suspect. Says the neighbors look in the other direction when they see him coming."

"I got the impression they didn't have much interaction with the neighbors."

"They didn't, but apparently he feels they're whispering behind his back because the police don't have enough intelligence to take a look at someone else, so they've zeroed in on him."

"Unfortunately right now there isn't anyone else. But in all honesty, I'm not leaning toward him being the killer. He's a little on the mousy side, don't you think?"

"My sentiments exactly. In my circle of friends it's referred to as pussy whipped," Martinez said, looking up.

Katie Gonzales, Jemimah's long-time assistant, walked into the office and unceremoniously dumped her designer purse on the desk. "Am I interrupting something? Is this pussy-whipped person anyone I know?"

Jemimah laughed. "Hey, Katie. No, we're just discussing a case."

An incurable flirt, Katie smiled broadly at Detective Martinez, who seemed to lose his composure and his conversational skills. She was short and perky, a little on the pudgy side, but her clothes accentuated all the right places.

"My, my, Detective Martinez. Don't you look handsome today?"

"How are you, Miss Gonzales?"

"Please. Not so formal. It's Katie," she tittered.

Jemimah could see the sparks starting to fly between the two, but she had a lot of work to do. Right now she was trying to figure out what the real connection was between Bart Wolfe and Gilda Humphreys. The task was one she would have preferred to put at the very bottom of her to-do list, but she knew the importance of developing a profile early in the game. Detective Romero's interview with Bart had unearthed some interesting dynamics between the two.

"All right, boys and girls. If you're hoping to collect overtime, it's not going to happen by making goo-goo eyes at each other," she said. "Clyde, let me know if you have any success with the remaining interviews."

"Will do, Doctor Hodge. Will do." He almost tripped over a chair as he made his way to the door.

Jemimah chuckled. "You do have an interesting effect on men, Katie. What are you doing here today?"

"Just wanted to get some of the recent interviews typed up."

Jemimah's eyebrows arched. "On a Saturday?"

"Well, I could have taken them home, but to tell you the truth, there's a low-rider event on the Plaza and there's no better vantage point than the windows of your office."

"I suspected there might be more to it," Jemimah smiled. "Let's sit out on the balcony. The view's much better from there. I need another cup of coffee to get me going, anyway."

Katie grabbed a mug and followed Jemimah out of the double doors leading to the balcony overlooking the Plaza. As they sat on the wrought-iron chairs, the noise level below began to escalate, from a hum to a din as car club members in low-slung cruisers revved their engines, ready to roll out onto the pavement for the main parade event.

A classic four-door Chevy Impala with a chop-top, reversible suicide doors and heart-shaped tail lights eased out in front of the line, its exhaust pipes rumbling. Cars lined up behind it and began to hop and dance as their hydraulics became engaged. Katie whistled and waved from the balcony. A handsome *vato* hollered out to her.

"Hey, *chicas locas*. Come down here and we can do it *suavecito*, low and slow."

She laughed and blew him a kiss.

Chrome bumpers gleamed in the sunlight as the last of the low-riders circled the Plaza. Jemimah and Katie returned to their desks, big smiles pasted on their faces. Between Detective Martinez and the guy in the car below, Katie was feeling the heat.

Nothing like a wave of testosterone to perk up a lady's day, even smack-dab in the middle of a murder investigation.

CHAPTER FORTY-SIX

Antoine Nelson resided in a small apartment complex in the South Capitol area of Santa Fe, next to Wood-Gormley Elementary School. Built in 1926, the school was attended by most of the area's bilingual population, who then migrated across the street to Harrington Junior High. The drone of playground sounds dissipated by mid-afternoon in this quiet neighborhood. The apartment was one-half of a duplex on Santa Fe Avenue, with Antoine's side being considerably smaller than the adjoining apartment. An old Volvo was parked in the driveway, the rear passenger side window covered with duct tape. A screened-in wood porch was painted bright turquoise with an apple-red screen door, someone's warped sense of Santa Fe style. The interior of the house was in perfect order, unlike Antoine's mind, which at the moment was reeling at the prospect of being questioned by police about his boss, Gilda Humphreys.

Antoine arrived at Detective Romero's office at the substation in Cerrillos with time to spare. Clarissa offered him water, coffee or juice. He politely waved his hand in refusal and rifled through the magazine rack.

Emerging from his office, Romero introduced himself and said, "Mr. Nelson, come this way, please," directing him to an empty office at the rear of the complex. The room wasn't an official interrogation room, but had the standard fluorescent lights and metal chairs surrounding the type of table used at craft shows and flea markets.

"Have a seat, Antoine," Romero said. "I'll be right with you. Can I get you something to drink?"

Antoine fidgeted with his watchband. "Uh, I guess so. Water will do."

Romero returned to the room, yellow tablet and bottled water in hand. He waited as Antoine screwed off the cap and took a long swallow. He set his coffee next to the yellow tablet on the table.

"I just have a few questions, Antoine. Just trying to tie up all the loose threads in our investigation of Mrs. Humphreys' death."

"Are you getting ready to arrest her killer?"

"Not quite. We're working on a few leads. Most cases aren't really that cut and dry. That's why we sometimes call witnesses in for a second and third round."

Antoine shifted in the chair. His hands were clasped in his lap. He repeatedly brushed miniscule pieces of lint from his pant legs. He hoped there wouldn't be a second round in his case. He felt like he was going to have a nervous breakdown with just this one.

"Tell me about your relationship with your immediate boss, Gilda Humphreys."

"Well, I've worked as her assistant for three years. I did everything. Set up meetings, typed up reports, kept her calendar up to date, and made phone calls."

"How did she treat you?"

"About like she treated everyone else, maybe worse."

"In what way was it worse for you?"

Antoine took a sip of water, carefully replacing the cap. "It seemed more personal. Like she really didn't like me. She was always making hateful slurs and off-color remarks."

"About what?"

"Personal things."

"Don't be embarrassed. This isn't going anywhere else."

"She was always implying that I might be gay. She never

came out and said it, but the nuances were there. Little smirks on her face when she thought I wasn't looking at her after she said something."

"What was the reason for that? Did you ever get the impression she was homophobic?"

"Just because I liked to keep things neat, and did things she might have considered effeminate, she was on my case all the time. People can't help how they appear to others. We are what we are. And I got tired of trying to convince her I wasn't a homosexual."

Romero scribbled on his tablet. "So I take it that made you angry?"

"Yes, of course it did, but I learned to live with it. I needed the job, and I figured she wouldn't be there forever."

"Why was that?"

"She was always having me check the state personnel website to see about better paying jobs. I kept thinking maybe something would show up and she'd go for it."

"What was the worst thing she ever said to you?"

"She could be a real bitch sometimes. She was always going on about envisioning my mother dressing me in little girl dresses and that kind of crap. It was pretty disgusting. She never let up. Sometimes it was all I could do to keep from strangling her. Oh, I'm sorry," he gasped, "I didn't mean it that way."

"Why didn't you ever file a sexual harassment proceeding against her?"

His eyes widened. "Are you nuts? You don't know what she was like. She would have crucified me. I figured it was my word against hers. She was the one getting paid the big bucks, not me."

"And did you resent that?"

"Yeah, but like I said, I learned to live with it. My coworkers kept telling me to report her, but I knew better. They would have never ruled in my favor. I would be hung out to dry and have hell finding another job."

Romero paused to stir his coffee. "When was the last time you were in the Taos area?"

"I don't know. Probably never."

"Can you tell me what you were doing on the day Gilda was killed?"

"Do you know what day she was killed? I thought the newspaper said the police didn't know for sure."

"Let me rephrase the question. During the three day period between the time she didn't show up at work and the body was identified."

"I was at work the whole time. I don't have any vacation time left, and I haven't missed a day for months. I clock in every morning at seven-thirty and clock out at five. You can check with the records department. Why are you asking me all these questions?"

"As I mentioned before, we're just tying up some loose ends. Do you have family?"

"I have a sister. Dina. Haven't seen her for years."

"Does she live around here?"

"Last I heard, somewhere in Washington. What's that got to do with anything?"

Romero closed the file folder and stood up. "I think that was it for my questions. I'll let you know if I need you to come in again."

"Am I a suspect?" Antoine's eyes were wide and his hands grasped the arm of the chair even tighter.

"Everyone's a suspect until we solve this crime, Antoine. It's all a process of elimination. You can go now. Just don't schedule any long trips."

In the parking lot, Antoine could feel his breakfast rushing up to his throat. He pulled over next to the scenic overlook and upchucked.

That detective had no right asking me such personal questions.

CHAPTER FORTY-SEVEN

As part of their caseload, Santa Fe County Sheriff's detectives were required to attend autopsies of victims. Nobody knew the reason, but it became part of the investigative process. Detective Romero was scheduled to attend the autopsy on Gilda Humphreys' body. Since the victim was initially classified as a Jane Doe, any forward movement in the case had been delayed until her vehicle was located and her purse found in the trunk. Taos PD decided Santa Fe might as well perform the autopsy since they had taken the case.

The last autopsy he attended was that of the victim from the casino. Romero wasn't looking forward to spending another two hours with Harry Donlon, the pain in the ass Medical Examiner for the County. Donlon was an *über* bigot with a nasty bedside manner who managed to alienate everyone in his midst. Romero couldn't fathom how this M.E. managed to keep his job. There had been more sexual harassment claims filed against him than any other County official, which kept the County Attorney busy fielding and investigating claims. Yet Donlon always walked away unscathed. The *mitote* from the employees' lounge was that it all had to do with his brother, the powerful head of the Santa Fe County Commission. Donlon was hired under the wire before legislation passed disallowing relatives from working in the same sector as elected officials.

An assistant handed Romero a face mask as he walked

through the stainless steel doors. Donlon was ready to begin the autopsy. He wore his usual green jumpsuit and face mask, impatiently tapping a scalpel against the edge of the steel table. Gilda Humphreys' remains had arrived at the M.E.'s office in a black vinyl body bag and were now on the table tucked securely under a sea-foam green sheet.

Donlon picked up the chart and began dictating to his assistant, a nerdy young man Donlon had called *Hey You* throughout his entire four year employment, even though the assistant's name was embroidered on his lab coat. Donlon was perfectly comfortable with degrading his employees. Failing to acknowledge them was just one of his many methods.

"Any suspects, Romero, or are you people dragging your feet as usual?" Donlon said.

"Too early in the game. Body was Jane Doe'd for a while. Once she was ID'd, it took the Taos M.E. another seventy-two hours to transport the victim to this location."

"Why are *we* doing the autopsy? Surely there haven't been *that* many murders in the Taos area. Course, the place is inhabited by a bunch of barefoot savages."

"Law enforcement there is shorthanded right now. We offered to help ease their caseload," Romero said, ignoring the tenor of Donlon's remark.

"Toxicology report hasn't come in yet, but I doubt if a woman this age would be out partying in the Taos Mountains. Then again, you never know. Not a bad figure for her age. Calves look pretty firm."

Romero whistled. "Come on, Donlon—a little respect here."

Donlon ignored him. "Cause of death was brain hemorrhage triggered by a single bullet to the head. Blew her ear right off, coupled with what appears to be a failed attempt at strangulation. From the position of her head, she never saw it coming or she was turning to look at her killer, or maybe he wanted her to suffer before he blew her brains out. No defense wounds, nothing but a few bruises on the body, probably postmortem. No residue under the fingernails either, so it doesn't look like she had an opportunity to fight for her life. You see these marks on her knees? She might have been kneeling for a while, looking for something on the ground. The pants she was wearing have mud stains there also, according to the crime tech's notes."

It made Romero wonder if the victim had been forced to her knees before she had been shot, or maybe Donlon was right and she was already kneeling on the ground. His comment about strangling her just to make her suffer sent a chill through him. They were dealing with a coldblooded killer here.

After an hour of yammering on while dissecting the body, Donlon unceremoniously plunked the bullet fragment into the metal tray. He glanced at his assistant. "That's it. Clean it up. I'll sign the release papers so the family can get on with arrangements."

Romero walked out to the parking lot as Detective Chacon was alighting his vehicle.

"Hey, Boss. You look a little green around the gills. Everything all right?

Romero lit a cigarette and offered one to Chacon. "Just sat through another damned autopsy. As usual, that was brutal," he said.

"Donlon makes it a lot harder than it should be. He's a heartless SOB. Guess that's what makes him good at the job," said Chacon.

"If that's what it takes for him to get through the day," Romero said, snuffing out his cigarette. "I'll catch up with you later, Artie."

He headed for his car, stopping to check his cellphone. There was a playful text message from Jemimah. He smiled. It was exactly what he needed to put the day's events behind him.

CHAPTER FORTY-EIGHT

Romero was uneasy about Antoine Nelson's bland attitude over Gilda Humphreys' suggestive tirades about his sexuality. *This guy might be harboring a shitload of pent-up anger, but enough to kill someone?* He wasn't qualified to guess. He ran a records check on Nelson and faxed copies of all the interviews to Jemimah's office with a note for her to call him after she had completed her review. Between Bart Wolfe, George Humphreys, Antoine and a few others, there were enough motives in that file for half a dozen murders. At the moment he wasn't about to elevate any one of them to prime suspect, and there wasn't anything to connect them to the casino murder, either. He was confident Jemimah would pull something out of the hat and get back to him.

CR

Jemimah was a highly qualified forensic psychologist. She was thoughtful and serious, and comfortable interviewing even the most demented psychopaths. Over the years she had developed an uncanny knack for sifting through the B.S. She read through the file Romero sent and made several notes, one to call Antoine's sister in Seattle. She checked the white pages on the Internet and found a number for Dina Nelson. After explaining the reason for calling, Jemimah requested permission to speak with her about Antoine.

"Sure, I have no problem with that. Antoine and I have

never been that close," Dina Nelson said. "I haven't spoken to him for quite a while."

"Is there any particular reason for that?"

"Not really. We just drifted apart. I'm a few years older, so by the time he was a teenager, I was attending college in another state. I guess I could have called him, but I never had occasion to. I don't know, really."

"Can you tell me something about his childhood?"

"Is he in some kind of trouble?"

"We're investigating a case here in Santa Fe. Nothing I can go into detail about, but I would appreciate your giving me a little information."

She hesitated for a second. "What is it you need to know?"

"For instance, was he ever in trouble as a child?"

"Antoine was always in trouble."

"In what way?"

"My father beat him senseless every time he looked at him sideways. In his eyes, Antoine could never do anything right."

"Was he ever in trouble with the law?"

"There was one incident a long time ago involving one of his high school teachers. I never knew all the details. My parents threw him out of the house. I believe he left town shortly after that."

"Did he communicate at all with you?"

"No, I don't think he had my address. Honestly, I didn't know he was in New Mexico. Nobody seemed to know where he went, and since I never heard from him … is he all right?"

"As I said, we're looking into a matter here locally. He's just part of our routine investigation. Can you tell me the name of the high school he was attending?"

Dina gave her the information. Jemimah thanked her and hung up. *More here than meets the eye.*

She filed the notes of her conversation, indicating her

doubts about Antoine's involvement in Humphreys' demise. He didn't have it in him. His personnel records confirmed he had been at work every day during the last month. As Jemimah rearranged the file, she was intrigued that Gilda had entered personal information in her work logs. Maybe she didn't have a close friend to confide in, certainly not at work. She wondered if it was because she knew nobody would be interested in looking at her field notes, particularly her husband.

There was only one entry regarding Gilda's coupling with Bart Wolfe, but according to Bart it had been more than once. Surely if she wrote about the first, she would have written about the second.

But where were those journals?

CHAPTER FORTY-NINE

Romero directed Detective Chacon, head of the County Forensic Unit, to take turns with Jemimah in interviewing Gilda Humphreys' co-workers. Almost every colleague confirmed her very low approval rating. Not one single individual, including Director Tom Rodriguez, had a kind word for her. *Condolences, yes. Kind words, no.* Her husband hadn't been wrong on that account.

Jemimah's job was to interview suspects, review case files, study crime scenes, and then develop a personality profile on the killer. With so little information available, she was scraping both sides of the barrel trying to come up with something viable. Romero decided to bring George Humphreys in for another round. There were a number of gaps in Jemimah's preliminary interview. It was apparent she hadn't asked the right questions. He chocked that off to her lack of experience, but would never say that to her face. It was all a learning process and he knew she still had a ways to go on that.

Besides, you can't knock the interrogation style of the person you're sleeping with. That's dangerous territory.

❧

A few days later, Detective Chacon sat across from George Humphreys in the interrogation room. A seasoned detective, he tweaked his handlebar moustache as Humphreys fidgeted with his iPhone. Chacon noticed he couldn't sit still and kept looking out the window. He also noticed Humphreys' righteous attitude.

"What's this all about? Do I need to lawyer up? I already spoke to that woman psychologist," Humphreys' said.

"We're just trying to put two and two together here, Mr. Humphreys. All part of the ongoing investigation. You are, of course, entitled to seek counsel if you wish, but at this juncture, I just need to ask you a few more questions."

"You're about the fourth person I've spoken to. Have you found my wife's killer?"

"No, we haven't. We're following every lead we get, and there haven't been too many."

"Well, instead of wasting your time with me, why aren't you out there looking for him?" Humphreys' voice cracked. "I'm still trying to make funeral arrangements and her body hasn't been released yet."

"I apologize for that, but in matters such as this where the circumstances aren't so cut and dried, things take a little longer. The coroner just completed the autopsy. I'll see if I can get you the release papers before you leave here."

Spreading out the case file in front of him in a meticulous manner, Detective Chacon pressed the button on the recorder and flipped a few pages of his tablet. Humphreys raised his eyebrows.

"Why do you need a recording?" he said.

"Just standard procedure, Mr. Humphreys. Want to make sure the questions or answers aren't misinterpreted. Some people have short memories and can always come back and deny they made a particular statement. That's why we record."

"Do I get a copy? That would be *my* standard procedure. Especially if someone says I said something I didn't."

"I've never been asked that question. I'll have to check with the brass. Now, George, you are aware that the Judge issued a search warrant in order for us to check your wife's activities relating to her computer and also her bank records. This allowed us to go to your home and retrieve everything listed on the warrant. Is that your understanding?"

"Yes, I didn't have a hell of a lot to say about that. The last batch of detectives came by the house and took everything they could find. I hope they choke on it. The least they could do is return the damn computer so I can keep up with my emails."

"In reviewing your joint bank account we found that a sizeable withdrawal was made about a week before your wife's body was discovered. Can you tell me anything about that?"

Humphreys squirmed in his seat. "Would you please quit referring to her as *a body?* She has a name, you know."

"I'm sorry, but would you answer my question?"

"My wife did all the banking and the bookkeeping. I only used the checking account to buy groceries. She paid all the bills and kept track of everything else."

"Are you saying you knew nothing about deposits and withdrawals?" Chacon said, noting that Humphreys didn't inquire about the amount of the transaction.

"That's what I'm saying. My wife was the bread earner in the family. Consequently I was allowed only to purchase items necessary to keep the household running smoothly. She took care of everything else."

"So a ten thousand dollar withdrawal is not something she would have discussed with you?"

Humphreys was silent for a moment. "I don't know what you're talking about."

"The bank records show that a withdrawal was made from your joint account about a week and a half before your wife, excuse me, Gilda, was discovered. We have contacted the bank and will be going over their surveillance tapes to see exactly when and at what branch that transaction was made."

"Well, it wasn't me. I can assure you I know nothing about it. Did she have any money on her?"

"Nothing other than pocket change."

"Well, I don't know what to tell you, Sir. Maybe she bought something for herself. She liked jewelry, you know. She pissed and moaned that we were struggling, but I never saw it that way. We had enough to get along."

"So you were pretty much a homebody. What did you do all day, watch the soaps?"

"Look, Detective, this might not work in most households, but it worked in ours. She was in charge of bringing home the bacon and I was in charge of cooking it. I pretty much kept my nose out of our financial affairs. I made a few bad investments, and she never let me forget it. From that time forward she handled everything relating to money. I couldn't even buy myself a pair of Jockey shorts without her permission."

"Do you recall the last time you spoke to your wife?"

"About five days before the police came to my door to say her body had been found, maybe six."

"What was your reaction to that news?"

Humphreys glared at him. "What the hell kind of question is that, Detective? Tell me how you'd feel if you'd been told your wife was dead, murdered by some maniac in the mountains, where she had no business being?"

"Just answer the question. I'm gathering information, that's all. I'm on your side, trying to get all the facts together so we can make a little progress here. Nothing personal, you understand?"

Humphreys slumped forward. "I was in shock, of course. Took me by surprise. I thought she was out on a job somewhere, unearthing human bones from some archaeological site or another. She considered herself the protector of ruins on Indian reservations."

"Weren't you worried that she hadn't come home?"

"No, not really. There were other times she had stayed out for a week at a time. I didn't think about it either way. She rarely discussed her schedule with me. I just went about my business figuring she would show up whenever she had finished whatever she was doing. When she was home, she was still working anyway, so her absence never made a difference."

Detective Chacon refilled his coffee cup. "How were the two of you getting along, Mr. Humphreys?"

"Like most married couples, I guess. Some good days, some bad days. Nothing out of the ordinary."

"What would you say the past few months had consisted of, good days or bad days?"

"A few of each, I suppose. I don't know. I wasn't keeping track."

"How would you describe a bad day?"

George Humphreys expelled an audible sigh. "My wife was not the easiest person to get along with, Detective. She had a way about her that came off as condescending, bitchy, and irritating in general. It took some getting used to. I just learned to blow her off. If I didn't join the fuss, things would get back to normal all by themselves."

"Was there anything specific?"

"Not that I can think of. Lately she bellyached about everything. Her job, her employees, her boss, nothing in particular that I can pinpoint. It was just more of the same. As usual, I let it roll off me."

"So, let's backtrack here a minute. What you're telling me is, the last time you saw your wife was four to six days before her body was found? I'm going to take a little convincing here. Why didn't you report her missing?"

Humphreys pressed his palms together. "I didn't think she *was* missing, Sir. I thought she was out working or looking for some so-called hidden treasure she got wind of. It was making her crazy. That's all she talked about. Some damned box buried up in the hills somewhere."

"Treasure? In this day and age?"

"Yeah, she managed to get hold of a book by a couple of rich guys about a treasure they buried somewhere in the mountains, and she got it in her head that she knew where it was stashed. I saw them being interviewed on television a few times and they never mentioned the treasure being buried anywhere around here."

"So it didn't bother you that she hadn't called or come home for several days?"

"I've said this before. With all due respect to her memory, my wife wasn't the easiest person to be around. I kind of enjoyed her absence, if you know what I mean. Could pretty much do whatever the hell I wanted and there was nobody to bitch me out. She would take trips out of town every couple of weeks and be gone for a few days, sometimes longer. I figured she had gone off like she often did on a work-related investigation at an Indian Pueblo. She spent ten days in Las Cruces last year. It didn't bother me then, either."

"One more thing, Mr. Humphreys, George. May I call you George?" Chacon didn't wait for an answer. "I'm going to need a list of your whereabouts over the past several weeks. Kind of give me an idea of your daily schedule, would you do that?"

"Sure, if it will help. You mean like what I do and where I go every day? You know I don't work. I stay at home and take care of things. Our roles were reversed and I became the house-husband."

"Pretty much along that line, but maybe more so. Especially where you were on the day your wife disappeared."

"I'm telling you, I wasn't aware that she had disappeared. If what you're asking me is did I kill her, the answer is no."

"Same difference."

Humphreys was adamant. "I was at home. You saw my house. It doesn't just clean itself. And my wife didn't usually raise a finger to pick up after herself. So you might say I've been doing a little spring cleaning. You can ask the plumber, the baker and the candlestick maker," he said in his most sarcastic tone. "I don't go out unless it's to buy groceries or service one of the vehicles."

Chacon smiled. Come to think of it, the house did smell like a combination of Lemon Pledge and Mister Clean. He had to admit, Humphreys made no bones about liking what he did.

"Rumor has it you two fought constantly."

"Depends on who you talk to. My wife was opinionated and impatient. That's how she blew off steam. She couldn't help herself. I don't think she knew how to have a conversation without raising her voice. She couldn't do it at work, so she took all her frustrations out on me."

"What did you argue about?"

"In a nutshell, everything."

"Can you be more specific?"

"All right. She bitched about her day, the fact that I didn't have a job, whether the car had gas or not, if I hadn't changed my shirt before dinner, if I happened to fart at the table. Stuff like that."

"I don't know just how to phrase this next question, George."

"Well, just spit it out. It can't be any worse than everything else you've asked me. There are some things that don't have to be aired in public. My wife and I got along like most married couples in America."

"Are you impotent?"

"That's it. You have no right asking me such a personal question." Humphreys stood up and pushed the chair behind him. Chacon motioned for him to sit.

"Let me rephrase that. Were you aware that there was a half-empty packet of condoms in your wife's purse?"

Humphreys was silent. Chacon could see the vein in his forehead pulsating.

"I'm sorry but ... my wife, having an affair? That's

ridiculous. She probably picked those up on one of her forages into some nearby Pueblo. She couldn't stand the way the public littered without conscience."

"Were you and your wife intimate? When was the last time the two of you shared a romp in the bedroom?"

"What the hell kind of question is that? We've been married for twenty years. Of course we were intimate."

"I mean recently, in the past year or so. Is there a reason you had separate bedrooms? All her stuff seems to be in one room and all your stuff seems to be in the other. Can't get more separate than that."

"My wife was a cold woman, Detective. She said she couldn't stand the thought of sleeping with me. It was her idea. So are you happy now?"

"Are you sure it wasn't the other way around? Some couples tend to drift apart, especially when one's working and the other's not."

"Whatever arrangement we had worked for us. And frankly, it's none of your damned business."

"All right, I think we're done here. Just a reminder that I need that list of your whereabouts for the week before this all started," Chacon said.

"I'll get right on it," Humphreys said with a smirk.

"I have no more questions, but Dr. Hodge would like to ask a few. Relax for a minute while I bring her in, please."

Detective Chacon returned to the room with Jemimah.

Jemimah nodded her head at Humphreys. She sat in the chair the detective had occupied. "Mr. Humphreys, I know you've been here a while, but I need to fill in a few gaps. Did your wife keep some kind of daily journal or diary?"

"I wouldn't call it a diary—more like field notes."

"So you were aware of these notebooks?"

"I never looked through them. Figured it was all job-related and God knows I heard enough about that," he said. "She would spend an hour propped up on her pillows most nights writing down everything she did that day, right down to the time. She was obsessive about it."

"Where did she generally keep these notebooks?"

"A few of them were in her bedroom. I figured your people picked them up with the rest of the stuff. There's nothing on that shelf now; I know, because I dusted yesterday. I assumed she kept the others at work."

"So there were others?"

He shrugged. "There was a stack of them. I don't know how many."

"Do you mind if we come back to your residence and take a look just in case there are others that we might have missed? I can assure it won't take very long."

"Do I have a choice?"

"I could request another warrant, but that would mean sending the whole crew out there to take your house apart again. Your cooperation would help us move things along."

"Fine. So, are we done here?"

"Yes, thank you. And if you don't mind, I'll follow you home so we can take care of this and get out of your hair."

George Humphreys left the sheriff's compound and headed out to the parking lot. Jemimah drove out behind him.

From the hallway, Lieutenant Romero motioned Detective Chacon to his office. "I was listening in on the video. There's something about his mannerisms that bothers me. I can't help but think he knows a lot more than he's letting on. Maybe we should keep track of him for a few days."

"Will do, Boss," Chacon said.

CHAPTER FIFTY

George Humphreys unlocked the front door and directed Jemimah to enter.

"Knock yourself out," he said, walking down the hallway to the bedroom.

"I promise you, I won't be long. I'm certain there are other work logs in existence, as the ones we retrieved are out of sequence."

Jemimah looked in closets and drawers for half an hour as Humphreys expressed his impatience by standing with his arms crossed at the doorway of every room she entered.

She looked up at him. "Can you think of anywhere else she might have stored her books?"

Humphreys scowled. "This house has a small garret of sorts at the end of the hallway. I put a painting over the entrance because it stuck out like a sore thumb."

"An attic on a flat-roof house?" said Jemimah.

"No, not an attic," he replied. "It's just an opening where the electrician could reach an air conditioning unit on the roof, but when the house was being built we decided against it and settled for something that would sit on the side of the house and be easier to access. The compartment stayed and I know Gilda used to store Christmas ornaments and the like there."

"Do you mind if we check it out?" Jemimah asked. "If it yields nothing, I'll give up."

Humphreys grunted and retrieved a ladder from the

garage. He removed the painting and unlatched the hasp over the opening.

"You'll have to climb in there. There's a light switch to the right. It's about four by six, only enough room for one person, and I don't like spiders."

"I'll take my chances, thank you."

Jemimah scaled the ladder, thankful she was wearing jeans. She found the light switch and a dozen or so boxes stacked neatly against the wall, with labels indicating the contents. After assuring herself each contained what was listed on the label, she restacked them to her left. There were two boxes remaining, one marked "miscellaneous" and the other marked with the year. The miscellaneous box yielded nothing but articles related to Gilda's job. Jemimah exhaled as she opened the last box. Too heavy for her to move, it was filled to the top with books and magazines. After emptying the entire box, she was about to replace the contents when she noticed a loose cardboard on the bottom. She lifted it to reveal four journals.

"You almost done up there? It's time for my news program," Humphreys hollered.

Jemimah stifled her enthusiasm. "I think I found what I need. I'll be right down."

"Well, see yourself out. I'll take care of the ladder," he said.

Jemimah restacked the boxes, placed the journals in her satchel, and left.

☙

On the way back to her office, she stopped long enough to have the journals marked as evidence and photocopied. When she arrived at her office, Detective Romero was waiting. She had a big smile on her face as she plopped the evidence envelope on her desk.

"What are you so happy about, Jem?" he said.

"I had a gut feeling Gilda Humphreys had more journals. I can't wait to read these. They might just hold the answer to some of the questions we haven't been able to answer."

"I'm glad your visit to the Humphreys' home was fruitful. If you let me fix you dinner, I'd be glad to help you review them," Romero said.

"As much as I'd like to take you up on that offer, I'd rather do this alone, if you don't mind. Can I take a rain check?"

"Absolutely," he smiled. "Let me know your progress."

The next time Jemimah looked up it was after six o'clock. She waved at the security guard as she left the building and headed to her vehicle. So many thoughts were running through her head, she almost ran a stoplight on Highway 14. She made a mental note to call Romero when she got home.

"Hey, I was just thinking about you, Jem. You must be psychic," he said.

"Don't I wish. Listen, do you have a few minutes, or maybe longer, so we can hash out what I found in Gilda Humphreys' notes?"

"I've got all night if you want to come over," he said.

"Not tonight, dear. I have a headache," she chuckled. "Seriously, Rick, there are a few things I need to run by you."

"All right, I'm all yours. What did you find out?"

"According to the entries she made in these journals, or 'work logs,' as she called them, she had fixated on the chase and the hunt, not only for McCabe's treasure but for the excitement she hadn't experienced in her marriage. It was Bart Wolfe who triggered that by making her realize she still had a lot to offer sexually. But she needed more. Intellectual stimulation was something Bart wasn't capable of providing. His scope of conversation was limited to subjects revolving around the Dallas Cowboys, San Antonio Spurs, prospecting and hanging around a bar. Undaunted, she made a move on some guy, following the end of a conference at the Sheraton Hotel in downtown Albuquerque.

"Listen to this, Rick. 'He looked across the table at me. Every time I checked he was staring. The blue dress I was wearing hugged all the right places. I smiled at him and winked when I caught him looking at me. Wow, that was brave of me! Who cares? He's never given me the time of day. After closing remarks, he caught up with me in the hallway and made some small talk about the program and the menu. He told me how beautiful I looked and how he'd never seen this side of me. I could feel my whole body getting warm as we headed toward the elevator. He said it was still early and invited me to have a drink. We went into the lounge and listened to the piano player sing songs from the forties and talked until almost midnight. I could feel his warm breath on my neck as he leaned closer. By the time we finished the next round, we were headed up to my room. We slid easily into each other's arms. I took a deep breath and closed my eyes as he kissed me. My head was spinning. I have never experienced such passion! We made love until morning. We'll see each other again, I just know it. He kissed me softly when he left the room. Driving back to Santa Fe, I felt like I'd just won the Kentucky Derby!' "

Romero whistled. "Wow, Jemimah. That gut feeling of yours was right on. You've hit on something."

"That entry alone proves that she was having an affair with someone who attended that function. Now I just have to figure out who," Jemimah said. "It sounds as though that relationship took off like a Texas wildfire and she started believing there could be a future without her husband. This guy was everything she desired. They fed off each other's need for power. Her sexuality appears to have been reaching its pinnacle and they were insatiable. Clandestine as their affair had to be, she looked forward to his daily call. The complete turnaround in her appearance and demeanor didn't go unnoticed. I believe that for the first time in her life, she had a reason to indulge in some vanity. You remember that some of the employees said she had done a complete U-turn in both in her demeanor and her wardrobe?"

"Yes, and I'm surprised that of all people, George Humphreys appeared never to have noticed," Romero said.

"Or did he? Infidelity is always a compelling motive for murder of a spouse."

"What about this treasure hunt?" Romero asked. "Are you thinking it might have something to do with her death?"

Jemimah paused. "It's certainly a consideration in developing the big picture, and it's also the only motive that makes any sense. Money makes people crazy, we all know that. It brings out the worst in them. What bothers me the most is, just what could Gilda have done to help bring about her death? According to her assistant, she had a spiteful streak, but I can't see how that could lead to her ending up next to the Rio Grande with a bullet in her head."

CHAPTER FIFTY-ONE

George Humphreys had a secret. What he hadn't told the detectives was that his wife was planning to divorce him. A week before her body was found, he followed her to Taos. That morning he watched from his bedroom window as she tossed the overnight bag in the trunk. It was filled with the fancy underwear she had ordered on the Internet. When he discovered it at the bottom of her drawer, he knew right off it wasn't for his pleasure.

She had a ten o'clock meeting that morning, which gave him time to rent a car and wait outside her office. At eleven she drove out of the employee lot. He followed a safe distance behind her. Arriving in Taos, George parked across the street from a bed and breakfast a block north of the Plaza on historic Bent Street, named for Governor Charles Bent, killed in an 1847 massacre in Taos. He watched as another vehicle with official New Mexico license plates pulled in next to Gilda's car. He continued to watch as they greeted each other with an embrace and entered the Victorian building together. They were arm in arm as they emerged from the lobby hours later. George was shaking. He wanted to scream, to confront them right in the middle of the square. Instead he got out of the car and followed about a block behind as they meandered down Main Street.

A celebration was taking place on the Plaza. Music blared from the bandstand as throngs of people mingled around. It was a carnival atmosphere, but to George, it was all a blur. He was focused on the couple up ahead, holding hands and falling all over each other like horny teenagers. They stopped to look in a shop window, pointing and laughing and then going in, emerging an hour later, both carrying bright pink bags with silver ribbons cascading from the handles. George glanced toward the window as he passed by. It was a trendy jewelry store featuring rock-sized diamonds and Rolex watches. *Bitch.*

They walked to a popular restaurant off the beaten path. Gilda smiled as her escort opened the door ahead of her. George sat on a bench in a corner of the grassy area of the park. The music had become a hodgepodge of muted sounds, chords banging together the way they did in wind chimes. An eternity later, he looked up to see them coming down the stairs from the restaurant in his direction. For a brief moment he was afraid she had spotted him, but she smiled up at her escort as they joined hands and walked on. Undecided as to what he should do, he let them walk up ahead. By the time he stood up they were almost out of sight, rounding the corner of Main Street, where they stopped to watch a colorful parade.

George walked to the parking lot with his shoulders stooped forward, dejected, a broken man. He sat in the car for a long time, in shock at the turn of events. His knuckles were white as he grasped the steering wheel. The vein in his forehead pulsated to the rhythm of the music coming from the stereo. He closed his eyes.

She's not going to get away with this.

CHAPTER FIFTY-TWO

The information Jemimah gleaned from the log books helped to fill in the gaps of the last six months of Gilda's life. Everything pointed to her falling in love with the person she wrote so floridly about. It was as though Jemimah was reading an excerpt from a Harlequin Romance.

> Bought some sexy underwear. He'll be as excited to see it on me as I am to wear it. We're going to meet in Taos later today, away from the prying eyes of Santa Fe. It's been so difficult to see him every day and not be able to touch him. I'm about to explode with desire.
>
> On the way back I might take another day off and spend some time in the canyon. I know that treasure's there somewhere, even though when I mentioned it he had a good laugh. He said anyone with more than a tenth grade education wouldn't be caught dead chasing after it. I showed him the map, pointed to where I believed the treasure was buried, and he laughed again. We'll see.

The personal entries were undated, so Jemimah had to assume they were the most recent; the log books ran in consecutive order. Gilda never identified her companion by name, and it was obvious they worked together in some capacity where they interacted on a regular basis. She had so many incendiary relationships, it was going to be a task to zero in on any one person. Jemimah wondered, *where, amid the animosity, had love blossomed?*

She stood up to stretch and refill her coffee cup. She stirred the cream and sugar thoughtfully as she gazed out her kitchen window to see the sun coming over the horizon. She had never gone to bed. She luxuriated in a warm shower, hoping it would reenergize her before she left for work. Thankfully it was going to be a slow morning.

At nine o'clock, she walked up the steps to her office, anxious to finish Gilda's journals and review her notes. She spread the journals and the notes across the desk and found the place where she had left off. Right away she noticed the tone was different. Something had happened between a romantic three days and the final night.

> This morning turned out to be a disaster. I was such a fool to think he cared about me. In the throes of passion, I told him I loved him. His reaction was so unexpected. He stopped in mid-thrust and asked what I had said. I told him I wanted him in my life, that I was tired of sneaking around. I wanted to be seen in public with him. He had such a stunned look on his face as he rolled over and covered himself, as if he didn't want to look at me. Later, when I got out of the shower, he was on the phone. He said he was just checking tee times for the weekend. I tried to snuggle up to him and he stiffened and said we had to talk.
>
> "Hey, don't look so sad, Honey. We've had a good run. You knew it couldn't be anything more."
>
> "What are you saying? You said we were meant for each other."
>
> "And I meant every word I said, but right now isn't the time to get serious. Surely you can see that

if news of our affair got out it could do a lot of damage."

"Affair? I thought we had a future."

"Come on, Gilda. You're married, I'm married. What future is there in that? It is what it is, and now we've got to go our separate ways."

Gilda had been run over by a steamroller. Jemimah saw what appeared to be tear stains on the pages. She tried to imagine the scene and read between the lines for a clue to his identity. Gilda had recorded their conversation verbatim. Jemimah recognized that ability as a sign of a severe attachment disorder, one where the person can recall every single word a person has said, no matter what the circumstances.

"You bastard! I was ready to give everything up for you."

"So what's your problem? Things were going just fine between us. Great sex, lots of laughs. We were having a good time."

"I'm sorry, I need more."

"I can't give you more. And from the direction this conversation is going, I'm starting to think this was a huge mistake. You knew early into this there was no future. You're not that stupid, or are you?"

"Go to hell. I don't give a crap about your political aspirations. You played me for a fool. And believe me, I'm going to tell everyone who will listen that the aspiring candidate for Governor has been having a sleazy affair with a co-worker."

"Nobody gives a shit about insignificant affairs. It's your word against mine."

"How about corruption, then? I know a lot more than you think about the kickbacks you received on the parking garage downtown. You used your position on the PRC to give that contract to one of your buddies."

"You don't know what you're talking about."

"The hell I don't. You should learn to keep your briefcase locked. A person can get bored sitting in a car alone while you get a manicure."

"I don't believe you."

"You can be sure the Democrats would love to hear about your shady dealings."

"If I were you I'd think twice about making idle threats."

"Just watch me."

Jemimah noted that Gilda shifted into first person again for the final entry.

He was livid. For a moment I was afraid. He went into the bathroom and jerked the door closed. I sat on the edge of the bed, dumbfounded and devastated. My hands are shaking as I write. What a fool I was. The romance I craved so desperately just went flying out the window. I should have never let it happen.

I looked at the gold bracelet he gave me. I thought it meant something. I tossed it on the bed and slammed the door on the way out. He can stick it up his ass for all I care. Oh well, lesson learned.

Jemimah thumbed through the remaining pages. They were blank. She glanced at the time and fought back a yawn. She wondered how long after that last entry Gilda had been killed. Did her murder have anything to do with that last conversation?

She closed the journal and thought about everything

Gilda had written. The woman thought she had found love, went into the affair heart first, only to be disappointed at the end. It was apparent to Jemimah she believed her lover was going to leave his wife and continue their relationship. She would leave George, and they would live happily ever after. Surely she knew he'd had previous affairs. After all, she had worked under him for some time and heard all the gossip. What was it that made her think this time would be different?

Jemimah felt sorry for this woman who in six short months had emerged from her cocoon, only to be shot down in mid-air on her first flight.

CHAPTER FIFTY-THREE

Romero met with his deputies for an update. Clarissa had laid out donuts and coffee in the conference room. The detectives were stretched to the max on the Humphreys case and had relegated the casino case to the back burner.

Romero brushed some crumbs from his shirt. "Have we had any more contact withthe Pojoaque Pueblo Police?"

Detective Martinez raised his hand. "For a while there we thought we had our guy. One of the casino managers found some old footage from about a year ago and recognized the woman playing footsies with the guy at the machine next to hers. They ran a search on the machine and pulled up the ID of the player."

"Any luck on that?" Romero asked?

"Pojoaque PD pulled the man in. Turns out he had a one-nighter with the woman the previous year. His story was that she came on to him at the casino and suggested they get a room. He wanted to score some cocaine first and so they drove over to Tesuque. He pulled into the boonies for a snort and after a while they started making out. When the coke was all gone, she got belligerent on him, so he drove back to the casino and left her there. According to the PD, the guy says he never saw her again after that night."

"Any chance we can connect him to the Humphreys case?" said Detective Chacon.

"Medrano thought of that," Romero said. "The guy's worked at the asphalt plant in Bernalillo for a couple of years.

He'd been doing double shifts during the time both murders were committed. Time cards prove it and he was sharing a motel room with two other guys. Just a coincidence we happened to have two victims killed in a similar way. Let's get back to this Humphreys case before it gets any colder. What about this assistant of hers? Antoine Nelson. What kind of vibe did you get from him?"

"He couldn't really account for his time away from work that week, but that's not unusual," Detective Chacon said. "I'll bet Dr. Hodge would diagnose him as having Attention Deficit Disorder. He spends a lot of his spare time playing video games. Kind of a neat freak. Says that on the days his boss didn't show up for work, he took the opportunity to tidy up the office. Time sheets show when he clocked in and out. Didn't miss a day and stayed in at lunch most of the time. He's got a mousy little girlfriend who sits next to him making gaga eyes while he battles monsters on his laptop."

"I'm thinking we might want to question him again. I'll drop by his house. Might jar him loose a bit. Something about him bugs me," Romero said.

Detective Martinez looked skeptical. "You thinking he might have had something to do with offing his boss? He's kind of a puny thing. I doubt if he could have picked up that dead weight."

"He's got as much motive as anyone. Anger, resentment. Just add him to the list of every other employee who probably hated her guts," Romero said. "We're not ruling anyone out, particularly since we don't have any clear-cut suspects as of this moment."

After the meeting, Romero cruised into the South Capitol neighborhood and parked in front of Nelson's apartment. He strolled up the walk and knocked at the door.

When he answered, Antoine looked surprised. "What do you want, Detective? Do I have to talk to you again?" His eyes were puffy and the cowlicks in his hair were sticking up.

Quite a difference from the neatly composed person who had showed up for the interrogation last week. Wearing a pair of red checked pajama pants, he was noticeably thin.

Romero stepped into the open screen door. "I just have a few questions."

Before Romero could speak, Antoine slumped on the living room couch and broke down. "I didn't kill her. I had nothing to do with it. Yes, I hated her guts, more than I was willing to say, but I couldn't ever kill anyone. Someone has to believe me. I'm not a violent person."

Romero sat on the side chair next to the couch. "It's interesting you should say that. I pulled a rap sheet on you, Antoine, and something interesting showed up. Apparently you've had difficulties in the past controlling your temper and the like."

"That happened a long time ago," Antoine said, sniffling. "I did a lot of anger management therapy just like the judge ordered, but I continued it long after. I was ready to confront all those issues. Everything's been under control since then. That's why I had such a hard time with Mrs. Humphreys. It was all coming back to haunt me. She was pushing buttons I thought were long gone."

"Would you mind if I spoke with your therapist to get her take on the progress you've made?"

"Not if it will help get me off your short list. Believe it or not, Detective, I've made a lot of progress. I take my therapy serious. I have a good job, a nice girlfriend, and I'm saving up to buy a house someday. I knew I would never be able to find a job that paid as well, so I stuck with this one. I wouldn't jeopardize all that by getting myself in trouble again."

Romero found himself having a change of heart. Not a good sign for a seasoned detective. His experience was that every family's closet is loaded with skeletons. Nobody was immune. Antoine Nelson was no exception. You could have a Halloween party with all the skeletons in that one.

CR

Romero took the long way back to his office, driving down I-25 north toward Albuquerque and then heading west at the Waldo turnoff just past the rest stop at the top of La Bajada Hill. The dirt road wound around through a stretch of ominous rock formations and ended up on the outskirts of Cerrillos. The dark and dreary landscape he had driven through matched the mood Romero was trying to shake. He stopped for a milkshake at the country store in the village and drove the remaining two miles to his office, where he intended to dig into the burgeoning stack of files on his desk. He picked up his cellphone on the third ring. It was Jemimah, who brought him up to date on the content of the remaining log books.

"Good job, Jemimah. What was your final conclusion?"

"We can talk about that later, Rick. The most important thing I discovered was that she was seeing someone with political aspirations who was a public regulations commissioner and a political candidate for governor."

"That sure narrows down the field. There are a few who have thrown their hats into the ring."

"This one would have to work for an agency affiliated with Gilda's department."

"Call around to see what you find out," Romero said.

The office was quiet as Romero sat at his desk to review the investigative reports in the Humphreys file. Originally it appeared to him that George Humphreys was in the clear. His car had been serviced a week before the body was discovered and had less than a hundred additional miles. They hadn't found a rental car receipt on the credit card records, but he could have paid cash. Something about George Humphreys continued to nag at him. He called and scheduled another interview.

CR

George Humphreys was visibly nervous as he walked into the substation in Cerrillos. Romero led him to the back office, where he motioned him toward the table.

"Sit down, George. Thank you for coming in on such short notice."

"I thought you people had asked enough questions. What the hell do you need now?"

"I just wanted to clear up a few things that aren't making sense," Romero said.

"None of this is making sense to me, Detective. I'm damned sick and tired of shuffling back and forth just to answer questions. I'm going to have to start asking for mileage. You people act like I'm your main suspect. Why aren't you out there looking for my wife's killer instead of harassing me?"

"It's all part of the ongoing investigation, Sir. Tying things together so we can reach a few conclusions and move on. I just have a few questions."

"Well, get on with it." Humphreys shifted in his seat.

Romero asked a series of questions about Humphreys' relationship with his wife and the reason the couple rarely socialized.

He continued, "Are you saying you were content not to have sexual relations with your wife and that you didn't suspect she might be having an affair? Something like that could really bring up a lot of angry feelings, wouldn't you think?"

Humphreys spun around, venom in his eyes. "What do you want me to say, that I killed her? No chance of that. Yeah, you're right. I did suspect she was having an affair, and I followed her to Taos, but I wasn't crazy enough to confront them in public. They spent a hell of a lot of time acting like tourists, going to all the galleries and museums. Besides, the guy was pretty good-sized. I was going to wait until she came home, and then I was going to give her a good damned piece of my mind. But she never did. I figured the two of them had gone off somewhere to continue screwing their heads off."

"You could have saved us, and yourself, a lot of trouble by coming forward earlier," Romero said.

"I might have if you people hadn't leaned on me so damn hard. I couldn't think straight. Every time I opened the door or answered the phone, there one of you was."

"Getting back to this guy in Taos … Did you recognize him?"

"For a minute there I thought it might be Tom Rodriguez, but I knew they hated each other's guts."

"Did you ever meet Tom Rodriguez?"

"Only once, for a brief moment. I remembered him as heavy-set and taller, so I didn't think that's who she was with."

"Didn't you attend any of the social functions your wife attended?"

"Never. She preferred to go alone. Didn't like the way I looked in a suit. I guess I didn't clean up good enough to be seen with her."

"So tell me this, George. When did you notice the change in your wife's behavior?"

"It got to the point where I never knew what to expect from her. Her moods changed without warning. I was beginning to wonder if she might be going through menopause or whatever it is women go through as they get older. I read somewhere that a woman could start this nonsense as early as their forties. What do I know? I Googled the subject to see what I could find out. You can check my computer. It's all right there."

"I think I've asked enough questions for now," Romero said, noticing how Humphreys' face had drained of color. Last thing he wanted was to give the guy a heart attack. "That should do it."

"I sure as hell hope so," Humphreys said. "I'll see myself out."

CR

Romero continued to weed through the file. Although it was difficult to pin down the exact hour of the crime, Bart Wolfe could account for almost all his time, drinking either in Cerrillos or Madrid bars. Plenty of witnesses to verify that, such as they were.

Fifteen state employees were interviewed and, although not a one had a kind word to say about Gilda Humphreys, it appeared none of them had a strong enough motive to kill her. He decided Antoine Nelson was incapable of harming another human being, no matter how much they harassed him. He dialed Detective Chacon's cell.

"Artie, is everything up to date on this Humphreys' investigation, or are there more interviews scheduled?"

"I finished up the last of them yesterday and attended a press conference today. Media's trying to throw Sheriff Medrano under the bus about this case. Had to assure everyone there wasn't a serial killer floating around out there. They asked about George Humphreys, too. The husband is almost always the killer in these cases."

"I hope you told them he was cooperating with the police," Romero said. "You know how quickly the media can turn the slightest innuendo into a full-blown focus on a suspect. We don't want him tarred and feathered out in his front yard."

"I hear you, boss. We're trying to keep the vigilantes at bay in this case."

"How about suspects? Anyone sitting in the middle of the target?" Romero said.

"Everyone seems to be in the clear. Threw Tom Rodriguez in for good measure, but he had nothing much to say about her except their regularly locking horns about department policy and the like. He was attending a seminar in Albuquerque around that time. Everything checks out. His wife was with him, and the front desk confirms they were there. Of course, because there's no time of death for the victim, some of these statements might not be worth a whole hell of a lot."

Romero shoved the file into a drawer. "I might just call him in for a sit-down. Everything sounds a little too convenient. By chance has he ever been involved in politics?"

"Sure has," said Chacon. "He was appointed to the PRC some time ago and, in fact, I heard recently that he was considering a run for governor."

CHAPTER FIFTY-FOUR

Gilda Humphreys' funeral service was held during the rainiest day of the monsoon season. Early in her adult life, she had abandoned any form of religious practice, so there was only a graveside service.

Considering her status on the state's rosters and the fact that the Governor herself had given state employees the day off to attend the funeral, the turnout was sparse. There were just a few wreaths of flowers, nothing ostentatious. Gilda's husband stood by the graveside, his demeanor guarded and eyes shaded by dark glasses. Her assistant, Antoine, and his girlfriend also attended. Jemimah and Romero stood together under an umbrella.

The eulogy was given by an employee of the funeral home who kept referring to the decedent as Glenda instead of Gilda. For the few people in attendance, it was a sad affair, primarily because they all knew Gilda Humphreys deserved better. Jemimah gave her condolences to George Humphreys.

"Thank you. Whether anyone believes it or not," he said, "I did love her." A tear formed in the corner of his eyes and slid down the side of his face. "I hope the bastard who killed her rots in hell."

When it was over, the group departed across the soggy grass of the cemetery which, ironically, was located behind the house of Sister Rita, the psychic Gilda had visited in her search for information.

Romero returned to his office. He put in a call to Tim

McCabe. It had been a while since they talked.

"I'm not sure I'm worthy to be in the company of such a well-known celebrity, Tim," he teased. "Bestselling author and flavor of the month for all the network talk shows. Sounds pretty exciting."

"Nothing's changed about me, Rick. Still the same old country boy."

"Still the same old nationally recognized country boy, you should say. I expect to see you on the cover of *Rolling Stone*. How's the treasure hunt going? I've been so darned busy I haven't had a minute to give you a call."

"Well, my sabbatical from work is about to come to end, so we'll have plenty of time to spend together and catch up. This whole treasure thing has been exciting, but I miss being in the thick of things. Once a lawman, always a lawman. Can't get it out of my system."

"We've got plenty of backlog, so I'm looking forward to your help. It can't be too soon for me, Tim."

"Burke and I are taking the wives on a well-deserved vacation to Acapulco. We'll be leaving in the morning. I'll be sure to bring you back a t-shirt."

Romero laughed. "Thanks. I've been meaning to ask you, Tim. You explained the letter from the convicts with the map attached, but what was the drawing I faxed you that Bart took from your ranch? Gilda Humphreys was convinced it was the map to your treasure. Was it?"

"That? Oh, hell, that was nothing of significance, at least not to anyone else but me. One afternoon, when Burke and I were out on his porch having a pow-wow, his eight-year-old grandson was playing nearby with his action figures. You know how kids are, all ears, especially since we were talking about buried treasure. Well, the kid listened for a while and then went upstairs. A while later, he came back downstairs and handed me a sheet of paper. He said, 'Here, Uncle Tim. I drew you a map of the treasure. It's buried in a good spot, right by where Grandpa took me fishing.' The kid had a good imagination. He had drawn a realistic map from the memory of a fishing trip his grandfather took him on last year in Taos Canyon. He remembered all the details, right down to the trees and bushes. I was so touched, I planned to get it framed and hang it up in my office. Still do. Just haven't had the time."

Romero whistled. "So that's why Gilda thought it was a map of your treasure? Man, that just goes to show you how people can be misled by their own interpretation of something."

"Yeah, I can see where someone could misconstrue the drawing and go off half-cocked, looking for a non-existent treasure. At least non-existent in the Taos area," he chuckled.

"All I can say is that she sure threw caution to the wind on that one. It cost her her life."

"Are you any closer to making an arrest?"

"Not hardly. We don't have enough evidence to bring anybody in. I'm pretty sure Tom Rodriguez had a hand in it, but so far we can't prove it. The only thing we know for sure is that someone wanted her dead."

"Well, keep at it. That doggedness of yours will pay off. I'll bet when I return from our trip you'll have it all wrapped up and tied with a neat bow."

"Thanks for the vote of confidence, Tim. I wish the media shared your opinion."

CHAPTER FIFTY-FIVE

Jemimah was frustrated about the lack of leads on the case. Other than the small group of suspects, there was little to follow up on. Her visit with Sister Rita, the psychic/palm reader/fortune teller had generated only one fact: Gilda was looking for information on the treasure hunt. Jemimah hadn't taken the time to explore the difference between a fortune teller and a medium because she was sure it didn't matter. She was only interested in learning why Gilda felt compelled to see one, especially since she had already made up her mind exactly where the treasure was. She must have believed that psychic confirmation would make a difference. Who knew?

Coupled with this sudden baffling reliance on psychic phenomena was her blossoming affair with Bart Wolfe, the bartender intimating they were getting it on in the back of his van. Uncharacteristic behavior for a woman of her stature—a well educated, married, highly paid public official. Gilda's husband was another big question mark. How could he not have suspected something was amiss in their relationship? Maybe he was impotent and Gilda finally realized she missed the sexual aspect of the relationship. Maybe that's why she was so cranky and out of sorts. In Jemimah's view, all things seemed to indicate Gilda was experiencing an awakening. The butterfly within was spreading her wings and this transformation was accompanied by an explosion of emotions, the most intense of which were sexual. Or maybe she had just snapped.

As a psychologist, Jemimah was well versed on the pitfalls of sexual deprivation in a marriage, especially a long one. Gilda's transformation from frumpy housewife to sex kitten was intriguing. She wouldn't be the first woman murdered because she had stepped over an invisible line in the course of an indiscretion. Jemimah wondered if that's what had happened after the affair with the no longer anonymous co-worker blew up in her face. Gilda had all but said it was Tom Rodriguez. He was the only member of the Public Regulations Commission considering a run for the governorship. Were Gilda's threats to expose their affair taken seriously? Even more so, her threats about exposing an alleged kickback on a contract.

Adding to the mix, Gilda's co-workers hated her and her boss barely tolerated her. Her husband saw her as a necessary evil—a meal ticket—and Bart Wolfe was another opportunist, going along with the buried treasure idea in exchange for money and sex.

Jemimah closed the windows of her office and looked out over the plaza. It was a good day to be inside. The sun was blazing hot and the pollen levels were at their highest for the season. She cranked up the air conditioner, reached for a tissue in mid-sneeze, and clicked the remote of the DVD player. She had watched all available video of Gilda Humphreys' lectures, which on the surface portrayed an intelligent woman with a good grasp of her subject matter. Her lectures were concise but informative, speaking in terms even a layman could follow. She was considered one of the best in her field, having conducted various studies on the excavation of indigenous ruins.

But beneath that veneer, Jemimah sensed a palpable loneliness, a need to fit in. You could see it in Gilda's body language. She believed the woman had been experiencing a mid-life crisis, suddenly aware of how others perceived her and how she perceived herself. All the signs were there. A renewed interest in sex, looking outside the marriage for fulfillment, becoming increasingly conscious of her looks and making changes to enhance them.

Jemimah dialed Detective Romero, from nine to five her working associate, the rest of the time her significant other. It was becoming more and more difficult to keep their personal lives separate from their work.

"Hi, sweet cheeks. I saw your name on the ID. Made my heart flutter. What's up?" he said.

"I hope you're not surrounded by detectives who are probably going to make your life miserable when you hang up. Sweet cheeks indeed," she laughed.

"Nope. All by my lonesome. Could use a little company. You free for lunch?"

" 'Fraid not. I'm drowning in paperwork."

"So what can I do for you, since I can't have the pleasure of your presence?"

"I'm glad you asked. I've been going over this whole Gilda profile. Can I run some stuff by you?"

"Sure. Hold on while I get a refill and settle in here." Romero hurried into the lounge, poured himself a fresh cup of coffee and returned to his desk. "Okay, I'm all yours. Shoot."

"So what's going on with George Humphreys? I understand you called him in again?"

"I just can't wrap my brain around the reason he didn't file a missing person's report on his wife," Romero said.

"He said he didn't think she was missing."

"He followed her to Taos and spied on her long enough to see her with another man. Then he went home."

"So? He probably figured she stayed with the guy."

"That's the problem," Romero continued. "It was the last time he saw her. Don't you think maybe he wanted her to come home so he could confront her?"

"He doesn't strike me as having enough balls to stand up

to her. That's why he didn't get in her face in Taos. The guy might have beat him to a pulp. More like he went home and had a good cry, swearing he would make things right. He claimed he never saw her after that."

"Scumbag."

Jemimah agreed. "While we're on the subject, what did the coroner have to say about Gilda?"

"Murder. No question about it. Failed ligature strangulation followed by gunshot wound to the head. The kicker is, it's impossible to set a time of death. He figures a week, maybe three days, who knows? Leave it to Donlon to declare something that far-fetched. The last time she was seen was four or five days before her body was found. Only an idiot would conjecture she'd been dead for a whole week. That by itself blows a couple of theories out of the water."

"I understand his ego is bigger than his behind."

"So they say. What's your overall take on this, Jem?"

"Based on initial reports, my clinical impression of Gilda was that she was an intelligent, domineering woman, who had long been a victim of sexual deprivation in her marriage."

"Yeah, I gathered that from the separate bedrooms thing, particularly since it wasn't because one of them had a snoring problem," Romero said. "Go on."

"It didn't surprise me that she had been molested as a child. I interviewed her best friend from high school, a woman who hadn't heard from her for years. She told me that Gilda's grandmother had practically given her to strangers when she was an infant. And there was no doubt in her friend's mind that Gilda had been sexually abused by her foster father until she left town less than a week after graduation. When they were teens, Gilda confided to her that, in fact, the man had been raping her for years, but she was so terrified of him she couldn't tell anybody."

"Isn't that always the case," Romero interjected, disgusted at the revelation of Gilda's childhood trauma.

"So, after leaving the town of Velarde, she enrolled at UNM and went on to receive her Masters and a PhD."

"*Velarde?* That's interesting," said Romero. "Velarde is a small community on the apple belt in Northern New Mexico, a few miles before you enter Taos Canyon. Maybe that's why she was so familiar with the area, having grown up near there."

"Could be. Now I also understand that she was raised in an Evangelical home, and probably would have never thought about having an affair. So she threw herself into her work like a madwoman. After years of repressing her sexuality, she went overboard, first by throwing herself at Bart Wolfe, and then going after the man she hated most, her boss. One of the employees who attended the conference in Albuquerque indicated she saw Gilda and her boss getting cozy at the bar. She didn't dare repeat what she saw to anyone for fear of losing her job."

"What exactly did she say?" Romero said.

"Here, I'll read a few lines. 'Miss Pacheco, in the statement you gave Detective Martinez you said you had observed Tom Rodriguez and Gilda Humphreys becoming cozy at an event in Albuquerque?'

'Yes, I said that.'

'Can you go into a little more detail?'

'Well, from where I was sitting in the lounge, they were making out pretty heavily. She was wearing this sexy low-cut dress that accentuated her figure. Even my husband said she was a knockout. They were still at it when we went up to our room.'

'What did you think about that?'

'I thought it was very odd since everyone at work knew they couldn't stand each other.' "

"So Gilda was dipping into a couple of cookie jars, I gather," Romero said.

"Yes, and she confirms it in her log books, even though

she doesn't identify her lover by name. Putting two and two together equals Rodriguez as the mystery man. Both he and Bart were womanizers in their own way, only Bart was less subtle and less particular about who he ended up in bed with. To top it off, her husband knew about Rodriguez, even though he denies seeing him up close in Taos. I doubt George knew about Bart. He seemed not to have caught any of the early signs."

Romero put his cold cup of coffee in the microwave and waited while the seconds counted down. "What else are you thinking, Jem?"

"It became obvious early on that there had been no loyalty lost between Gilda and Rodriguez. When a few of their co-workers were asked if they had any idea the two were romantically involved, most were incredulous. As one of them put it, 'No way, those two were like oil and water. Everything he said rubbed her the wrong way and vice versa.' A few other employees also said they noticed an extreme change in her demeanor and physical appearance in the past couple of months. She was carrying herself differently. She was no longer dressing like a frumpy housewife. Her hair was styled and had blond streaks running through it. It changed her appearance completely. This new version of her was a striking contrast to the woman they referred to as their bitch of a boss. 'Attractive' is the word they began to use more often."

Romero scratched his head. "What I don't understand is why she would get involved with her office nemesis," he said. "Doesn't make sense to me. Under those circumstances, most people would go out of their way to avoid unnecessary contact, particularly physical in nature."

"I guess just to prove to herself that she could. I imagine the combination of power and sex were very enticing to Gilda. Tom Rodriguez had always considered himself a ladies' man. His wife knew he fooled around, but she strikes me as someone who likes the big house and all the amenities that go with a high-paying job and was willing to overlook his indiscretions as long as he came home to her."

"Why would he choose someone like Gilda? She doesn't appear to be his type."

"Sounds like he's been serenading one too many *señoritas*. Gilda was the wrong one to court. Not only was she vulnerable, but she was ready. Turned out to be a fatal combination."

"I understand he's considered one of the most powerful members of the PRC."

"Yes, and in our last conversation, you confirmed that he was considering a run for the governorship in two years."

"I'd like to have that sanctimonious bastard spend the next two years politicking in a cell at the State Penitentiary to keep from becoming someone's boy toy," said Romero.

"Easy there," she laughed. "I understand you've scheduled him for an interview?"

"Yeah. We're running out of gas here. I'm curious what he has to say. His alibi's pretty tight. I might ask you to take the interview, though. I have a conflict that I'm trying to reschedule. In any event, he might respond more favorably to you." Romero glanced at his watch. "Gotta go, sweetie. I'll call you tonight."

"Why don't you come by instead? I owe you a home-cooked dinner."

"I'll take you up on that. Especially if it includes dessert."

CHAPTER FIFTY-SIX

Romero scanned the headlines of the morning paper as he motioned Clarissa to hurry up with the coffee. He was stunned how quickly it had become public knowledge that Sheriff Medrano was planning to call Tom Rodriguez in for questioning.

He read aloud, " 'Confidential sources revealed that a high-ranking state official has been summoned for questioning about the recent murder of State Archaeologist, Gilda Humphreys. Tom Rodriguez is a professional and a politician. He is highly regarded in the community and happily married to his childhood sweetheart. This reporter can see no connection to the case other than Rodriguez was her immediate superior at work. Surely the move is politically motivated as the Sheriff's Office continues to grasp at straws ...' Dammit, Clarissa. Where does that freakin' reporter get her information?" he fumed.

"You don't really want me to answer that, do you, boss?" Clarissa smiled. "She's been gathering information with those Barbie looks of hers for as long as I've been working for the department."

"Yeah, I've seen Detective Chacon ready to give up everything—including his Social Security number—anytime she blinks those baby blues at him. Sheriff Medrano threw the ball in my court since I'm responsible for agreeing to take the case off Taos County's hands."

"I take it he's not too happy with the way things are going?"

"You take it right. What started out to be a slam-dunk-across-the-board favor has turned into a nightmare. We're no closer to solving this case than when we started."

Later that afternoon, on his way out, Romero glanced behind the two-way mirror at the County Sheriff's complex on Highway 14 and took a long look at the gentleman sitting at the table contemplating his fingernails as though he thought it was time for a manicure. He hoped Jemimah would be able to peel a few bits of information out of him.

Tom Rodriguez was borderline handsome, well-dressed, and meticulously groomed. He had a squarish face with back-to-the-fifties sideburns and a thick head of dark hair graying at the temples. Among his peers, he also had a squeaky clean reputation, but in-house rumors tagged him as a womanizer.

Rodriguez looked up as Jemimah entered the room and introduced herself.

"Do I need to have my attorney present?" he said, ignoring her outstretched hand.

"Not unless you feel it necessary," she said. "We're interviewing pretty much everyone who knew Gilda Humphreys."

"Then let's get this over with. I have a tight schedule," Rodriguez said. "I don't have time to play footsie with law enforcement."

Jemimah sat down across from him. "All right, Mr. Rodriguez. We can do that. The Sheriff's Department has reviewed Mrs. Humphreys' cellphone records and there are a number of calls both to and from your cellphone. Were you two having an affair?"

Rodriguez smiled. "That's straight to the point, Doctor Hodge. I admire that. But to answer your question, no. Gilda Humphreys was an employee. I oversaw everything she did.

Everything in her department cleared through my office, including ordering supplies."

"Some of these calls lasted for as long as thirty minutes. That's a lot of time to discuss work-related matters, particularly since your offices were in the same building."

"Look, Gilda spent a lot of time out in the field. Sometimes she needed an approval on the spot."

"Six months ago the records show very few calls between the two of you."

"My conversations with Mrs. Humphreys were all work-related. I run a very busy division of the state government. In addition to serving on the PRC and everything else, I'm in charge of overseeing hundreds of archaeological sites throughout the entire state."

"Sounds like you're a busy man, Mr. Rodriguez, but that still doesn't explain the reason for the number of phone calls between you and the victim. I notice some of them were after hours."

"I didn't keep track of when she called."

"Was your wife aware of the number of times you two chatted?"

Rodriguez leaned forward. "Keep my wife out of this. There's no need to keep harping on the conversations I had with Mrs. Humphreys. They were business-related and that's it, and I don't think you can prove otherwise, unless you have a crystal ball."

Before she could ask another question, Jemimah was interrupted by a knock on the door.

"Excuse me, Dr. Hodge, but John Snead is here to see his client," the aide said, stepping aside as he pushed ahead of her.

Rodriguez stood up. "What are you doing here, John?"

"Your secretary said I might find you here." Snead gave Jemimah an oily once-over and shook her hand. "If you don't mind, Miss, I need a few minutes with my client." He pulled out a chair, dusted it with a silk handkerchief, shook it and put it back in his suit pocket.

John Snead was a well-known attorney in Northern New Mexico, having represented both the lower and upper echelon of criminals for over twenty years. It was rumored he came from a long line of attorneys who bilked unsuspecting *Hispanos* out of their lands on upper Cerro Gordo in Santa Fe, buying cheap and selling high. There was no question he was good at his profession, which provided not only the latest model in the BMW series, but accommodated a string of alimony-oriented ex-wives as well. His trademark pinstriped two-piece suit was accentuated with a blue silk shirt and matching tie. Tanned skin and a neat salt and pepper ponytail finished off the picture. Snead had everything going for him. Money, class, a killer smile and male-model good looks—even in his sixties. Jemimah suspected he and his client made a good pair.

Five minutes later, Snead stuck his head out the door to the conference room and motioned to Jemimah. "I think my client has answered enough questions. Unless the Sheriff has a reason to keep him here, this conversation is officially over."

"Whatever you say, Mr. Snead," Jemimah smiled sweetly as she gathered the contents of her file.

"Tell your boss the D.A. will be hearing from my office. My client's reputation has been damaged by these insinuations and false accusations of a sexual involvement with the victim."

"I'll be glad to relay the message, Mr. Snead."

Rodriguez left the room with his attorney, but not before giving Jemimah a stiff smile. As he smoothed his silver hair with his left hand, the thick wedding ring and gold rimmed Rolex watch caught the reflection of the bright office lights.

He reminded Jemimah of a pimp, all decked out in bling.

"Nice watch," Jemimah said.

"Yes, isn't it?" said Rodriguez. "Gift from a secret admirer."

"Could that secret admirer have been Gilda Humphreys?"

"It wouldn't be a secret then, would it, Doctor Hodge?"

After she watched the two leave, Jemimah noticed Romero standing nearby. When she informed him that Tom Rodriguez had lawyered up with the best criminal attorney in the Southwest, he nodded.

"Yes, I caught most of the interview," he said. " My other appointment was delayed at the last minute and I didn't want to interrupt. Anyway, Snead's appearance managed to cut it short."

They both knew the D.A. wasn't about to petition the court for a warrant on any aspect of the case related to Rodriguez. There was just not enough evidence to justify it. All the State had was a pound of hearsay and a foot of circumstantial evidence. Ongoing rain in the Taos Canyon had washed away any physical evidence that might have existed.

Romero was sure that the cocky SOB had killed Gilda Humphreys to keep her from going public with their affair. He also figured Tom Rodriguez was determined that *nobody* was going to scuttle his rise to the Governorship. Not Gilda, not his wife. He would be on that ticket in November. Already, he was a seasoned professional liar and a good actor. He knew all the right answers and hit all the right notes. Once again, the biggest holdup in making an arrest in this case was that it appeared investigators would never know the actual time of death of the victim. It was going to be impossible to poke holes in anyone's alibi, including that of Tom Rodriguez.

"I figure that's where the ten-thousand dollar withdrawal from Gilda's account had gone," Jemimah told Rick, "along with the gold bracelet she mentioned in her journal. It wasn't listed as missing because nobody except the two of them knew it existed. But again, we have no way to prove it. There's nothing that precludes one person from giving an expensive gift to another, particularly when they are exchanging sexual favors."

Both were sobered by the interrogation. Rick gave Jemimah a quick kiss on the lips before leaving for his own appointment.

CHAPTER FIFTY-SEVEN

Romero called his detectives in for a confab in the middle of the week. Maybe three heads were better than one. This case was a definite puzzler with no clear suspects other than Rodriguez, and it quickly became a challenge to link that one.

"Let's see what Rodriguez's wife has to say. She's probably pretty pissed to be caught in the middle of her husband's affair," Romero said.

"Good idea," said Detective Chacon. We need to have a visit with her before she forgives his sorry ass."

"Take Dr. Hodge with you, Artie. I'll see if Mrs. Rodriguez is available for us to pay her a visit," said Romero. He dialed the number and clicked on the speaker phone.

A woman with a lilting voice answered with the efficiency of a secretary. "Millie Rodriguez here, how may I help you?"

Romero introduced himself and inquired when it would be convenient for his detectives to stop by and interview her.

"If it will help get this distasteful matter over with, of course you can come by any time," she said.

"How about one o'clock this afternoon?"

"That's fine. I'll be here," she said. "The maintenance crew is working on the driveway, so you'll have to park on the south side of the house."

Romero gave Detective Chacon directions to the Rodriguez home and called Jemimah to say Artie would pick her up after lunch.

CR

The Rodriguez home was in an exclusive gated compound off Hyde Park Road en route to the ski basin. This was no ordinary subdivision. Every house for miles around had been designed by a leading architectural firm. Chacon drove up to the locked gate and punched the intercom button. A disembodied recording buzzed them in, while asking that they not disturb the peacocks in the garden. He pulled the vehicle around the circular drive and parked. The gardener pointed them toward the entrance.

Jemimah let out a low whistle. "Wow. We're not in Kansas anymore, Dorothy. Looks like we just came up the yellow brick road to the castle in the sky."

"No kidding. On my budget I probably couldn't afford the light bill."

Millie Rodriguez greeted them at the door. She was the perfect hostess, even to detectives who, although invited, showed up at her door following her private Pilates session, giving her little time to pull herself together. She was in her early fifties, with wavy auburn hair in a stylish pouf that barely touched her shoulders. Even dressed in black tights and a light sweatshirt, she was regal and attractive, with a honeyed voice that seemed to candy coat her words with a hint of a southern lilt. This was definitely not a local girl. Noticing Detective Chacon's blank stare, Jemimah felt the need to nudge him with her elbow.

"Mrs. Rodriguez, thank you for agreeing to see us on such short notice," he stammered.

"Yes, as I told Detective Romero, as long as it will help put this distasteful situation to rest so we can move on with our lives." She accompanied them to a sitting room in the west wing of the house.

The adobe house was tastefully decorated in a Southwestern theme, with paintings by major Native

American artists—Namingha, Scholder and Lomayesva. The floors were covered with Mexican tile; the foot-thick walls were hand-plastered and polished to a high sheen. A large bronze of a buffalo dancer by Alan Houser stood in the center of the atrium, surrounded by bright red and yellow hibiscus plants. There was no doubt this property fell under the category of desirable Santa Fe real estate. The panoramic 180 degree view was breathtaking, visible through the eight foot windows in each room.

"I'm sorry I can't offer you something to drink. The maid is out shopping for dinner."

"No problem, Mrs. Rodriguez, we just had lunch," Jemimah said.

"Call me Millie. Mrs. Rodriguez is so formal." She enunciated her last name as *Raw-dree-gus*, elevating it out of the realm of local Hispanic surnames into something more sophisticated. "Now, can we just get to the gist of your visit, detectives? I have a number of appointments scheduled this afternoon."

Chacon jumped right in. "Doctor Hodge here isn't a detective, Ma'am. She's the Forensic Psychologist for the County."

"A psychologist? What on earth would a psychologist have to do with anything regarding murder?"

Jemimah smiled at her reaction. "I assist the Sheriff's Department in profiling suspects."

"You're such an attractive woman. I would have imagined you working in a profession that isn't so unpleasant."

"Thank you, but I like my job," she said. "There's always something interesting going on."

The comfort level between the two women annoyed Chacon. It wasn't his idea of a witness interrogation. It was more like a coffee klatch. He chimed in, "How well did you know Gilda Humphreys?"

"Not very well, other than occasionally bumping into her at state functions and the like, work-related, of course. I never had any reason to see her socially."

"So she never attended gatherings at your home?" Jemimah said.

"Heavens, no. My husband barely tolerated her at the office. I would never invite someone like *her* to any of my parties."

"I take it you didn't care much for Mrs. Humphreys?" Chacon said.

"I didn't know her well enough to care either way. My husband abhorred her, and I was just being considerate of his feelings." She looked at Jemimah. "You understand, dear?"

"Of course. These are questions we need to ask as part of the investigation," Jemimah said.

"You are aware that there has been some talk that they spent time together at a bed and breakfast in Taos?" Chacon said, throwing Jemimah a subtle glare.

"That is just a coincidence. Look, my husband is the head of the department; she's somewhere down the line. They're going to run into each other on a regular basis. Whoever makes arrangements for these meetings books everyone in the same hotel, don't you think?"

"I wouldn't know. Let me ask you this, then. Do you believe your husband was having an affair with Gilda Humphreys?" Chacon said.

"Is that what everyone's saying?" she chuckled. "Well, they're wrong. My husband would never do anything like that. We have a strong relationship. Leave it to the state gossip mills to churn that one out." She smoothed the front of her shirt. Jemimah observed the subtle shift in her composure.

"Mrs. Rodriguez, Millie, are you aware that there were a number of phone calls from Gilda Humphreys to your husband's cellphone?" Chacon continued.

"Well, I'm sure there were. That woman was incompetent. She couldn't make a simple decision without calling my husband at all hours to get his approval."

"So you're saying that the calls were business-related?"

"Of course they were. He was more than patient with her constant harangues. It annoyed me to no end that my husband couldn't just fire her and be rid of the situation. I can't tell you how many times he had to leave the house after dinner to go fix one of her messes."

"I couldn't help but notice your lovely watch," Jemimah said. "Does it match the one your husband wears?"

"Heavens no. His is far more expensive. He bought it at some benefit auction at the prep school for a give-away price."

"Well, I think that's all, Mrs. Rodriguez," Chacon said, reaching out to shake her hand. "Thank you for taking the time to see us."

"You're welcome, Detective. I hope I was able to provide the information you needed to erase this matter from our midst." She led them to the door, closing it quietly behind them.

On the drive back to the substation in Cerrillos, Jemimah jumped on Artie. "What was that back there, rolling your eyes every time I asked a question?"

"It appeared to me that you two were acting like old schoolgirl chums, not participating in an interrogation."

"Not every witness has to be treated like they're headed for the gallows. Besides, didn't you know you can catch more flies with honey than vinegar? Anyway, I noticed she didn't bat an eyelash when you questioned her about her husband and Gilda at the bed and breakfast in Taos. Sheer coincidence, my foot."

"You think she's the long-suffering wife who's being kept in diamonds and expensive cars to maintain the veneer of a perfect marriage? Those were some nice rocks she had on her fingers, and that Mercedes convertible in the driveway still had the dealer sticker on it."

"It was apparent she considers Gilda a step down," Jemimah said. "I'm sure it infuriates her that her husband might have been having an affair with someone less beautiful and desirable than herself."

"I'll say. She's in pretty good shape for being in her fifties. You think we should consider her a person of interest?"

"In my opinion, those manicured hands wouldn't know how to hold a gun, let alone shoot one."

"But her kind of money can sure hire someone to get the job done, don't you think?"

"Hard to say, but she doesn't seem the type. She has to know her husband likes to play around. I'll bet Gilda's not the first one to get caught up in his silver tongued web," Jemimah said. "I imagine he's left more than a few broken hearts in his wake. I didn't see any sexual harassment claims in his file, so this may be the first time he ventured this close to home."

"Something about her bugs me, though," Chacon said. "She's probably in denial about his indiscretions."

"Most women are, Detective. They don't want their happy homes to fall apart and force them to start over. It's easier for men to move on. They carry less baggage. Within a few days, every twenty-five-year-old within a ten mile radius would be hanging on to his arm and the wife would be sitting at home watching Oprah and eating Frito Pies."

"I agree. But I will say she does appear to be the kind of woman who would like nothing better than to be New Mexico's first lady, no matter what the cost."

"I could picture that," Jemimah added. "She'd probably have no trouble walking those shapely legs around the Roundhouse and entertaining at the Governor's Mansion. On the surface, they enjoy all the trappings of success. But who knows what goes on behind bedroom doors. And she's not ever going to admit he stepped out on her."

"Even if the proof's practically staring her in the face?"

"Lesson number one, Artie. A true social climber can overlook a multitude of sins. You can count on it."

CHAPTER FIFTY-EIGHT

Detective Martinez strolled into Romero's office, sat on the couch and put his feet on the table.

"Make yourself at home, Clyde," Romero quipped.

"Thanks, Boss. Don't mind if I do." He reached into his pocket for a cigarette.

"Don't even think about it," Romero said. "Clarissa will have your hide."

"When did the satellite office become a non-smoking area? You're pretty far from the main office. The rules don't apply here."

"Clarissa makes the rules around here. She said she's tired of her office smelling like a casino."

"I can see who the boss is."

"Gotta keep the hired help happy. I couldn't run this place without her."

"All right." Martinez slipped the cigarette back in the pack. "Any breaks on the Taos case?"

"*Nada*. Zilch. Nothing. I've reviewed this file a dozen times and nothing pops out at me. It's the shits when a case goes cold long before its time."

"I just might have something we can go on."

"Well, spit it out, Clyde. Don't keep me in suspense."

"Detective Tenorio was reviewing the roster of calls on the tip line. Most of them are dead ends, but, there's a woman who works as a housekeeper for a bed and breakfast near the Taos Plaza."

"*And?*" Romero said.

"And when she was in Santa Fe last week visiting her sister, she saw the victim's picture in the local paper. I guess the Taos paper ran the story but not with photos. Anyway, she was pretty sure this woman stayed at the B and B where she works."

"When was this?"

"She was fairly certain that it was about a month ago. The manager had just changed her shift and it was the first time she had to work until late afternoon. I figured one of us might want to interview her."

"That coincides with what George Humphreys said about her being at a bed and breakfast. I'll send Dr. Hodge. She's pretty good about peeling information from witnesses."

"Does the good doctor speak Spanish?"

"Does the cleaning lady speak English?"

"*Sí, Comandante,*" Clyde smiled.

∞

Jemimah parked in front of the bed and breakfast on a side street in Taos. The exterior was Victorian, but the interior was all modern Southwestern, decorated as it was in vibrant colors.

She walked up to the front desk and introduced herself.

The clerk smiled broadly. "And how may I help you?"

"Mrs. Diaz is expecting me. She said to meet her in the lobby."

"Oh, yes, have a seat. Let me dial housekeeping."

Christina Gomez Diaz walked toward Jemimah. She was a small woman with large hips and an ample chest, made more noticeable by the buttonholes on her uniform stretched beyond capacity. She smiled at Jemimah, exposing an even row of small white teeth.

"Mrs. Diaz?"

"Everyone calls me Christina."

Jemimah introduced herself. "All right, Christina. I believe one of our detectives spoke with you over the phone."

"Yes, Detective Martinez."

"I'd like to ask you a few questions about your conversation with him. You said you recognized a photo of a woman who was killed in the mountains down the canyon?"

"Yes, there was an article in the Taos News, but they didn't show a picture of her." Christina put her chubby hands on her cheeks. "*Pobrecita*. The poor thing was all alone out there with nobody to help her."

"Where did you see her photo?"

"When I was in Santa Fe. I was visiting my sister and the newspaper was on the kitchen table, and when I spotted the article I knew I had seen that face somewhere."

"You recognized her?"

"She was a guest here over a month ago. I remember because they spent a lot of time in the room, and for two days I had to send the maids in after they went to dinner."

Jemimah's ears perked. "They?"

"Yes. She was with a man. I thought they might be newlyweds."

"Sounds like they were late sleepers?"

"Oh, I think they were doing more than sleeping," she giggled.

Jemimah reached into her briefcase. "Is this the woman?"

"Oh, *sí*. That's the one. She laughed a lot and smiled, like she was very happy and having a good time."

"Can you describe the gentleman she was with?"

"He was tall, nice looking. Very, how you say, distinguished. Maybe a little gray at the sides. He spoke very good Spanish, and was very generous with tips."

"Do you happen to know what his name was?"

"No, the room was registered in the lady's name."

Jemimah showed her a photo of Tom Rodriguez. "Was this the person she was with?"

She looked closely at the photo. "It looks like him. I can't say for sure. But maybe. I don't know. He was mostly in the background, you know what I mean? She was the one who requested things they needed. Most of the time I just saw his back."

"Were you on duty when they checked out?"

"Yes, I had to watch the front desk because my assistant Loyda called in sick."

"Did either of them say anything?"

"No, he went straight out the door with his luggage. He was wearing dark glasses and I really couldn't see his face. But I could tell she wasn't so happy no more. She looked very upset and her eyes were red, like she'd been crying. I wanted to hug her."

"Did she pay with a credit card?"

"No, I remember she handed me a bunch of hundred dollar bills. She wadded up the receipt and tossed it in the trash on the way out."

"I just have one more question, Christina. Did they embrace or kiss before they got into their cars?"

"No, they were pretty quiet as they checked out. Not at all like when they checked in. They got in different cars and that was the last I saw them."

Jemimah thanked her and as she walked out into the bright Taos sunlight, she wondered if they would ever be able to shed enough light on this dark tableau.

CHAPTER FIFTY-NINE

Romero was determined to schedule another interview with Tom Rodriguez. He contacted Rodriguez's attorney, John Snead, knowing he would probably oppose the request. He was right.

"What? You're kidding, of course," he said. "I assumed your department wouldn't even consider dragging my client through the mud again. The D.A. assured me the case was closed as far as Rodriguez is concerned."

"You of all people should know that a case is never closed until it's solved. Dr. Hodge interviewed the cleaning woman at a bed and breakfast in Taos. She's pretty sure the woman can identify your client as the man with Gilda Humphreys."

"So what? He already admitted they were screwing around."

"So that makes your client the last person to see the victim," Romero said.

"It's her word against his. Is Dr. Hodge one of your detectives, Romero?"

"No, she's our criminal profiler."

"Why is she still focusing on my client? You've already admitted there's insufficient evidence to connect him to anything other than an indiscretion."

"Maybe it intrigues her. Unsolved cases have a way of sticking to law enforcement's craw."

"Well I suggest you rein her in, Romero. My client's

ready to get his campaign on the road. We don't need a nosy female stirring up the pot again. In case you've forgotten, let me refresh your memory. My client has a rock-solid alibi. He was where he said he was and there are witnesses to prove it. There has been no date or time of death established, and the probability for that changing is zero to nil."

"You keep thinking that, Snead."

Millie Rodriguez was busy giving directions to the gardener when her husband drove up. She waved as he rounded the corner and parked in the three-car garage.

"You're early," she said as they walked toward the patio.

"Did you forget? We have to be at the Country Club at seven. The Elks Club is having their annual candidates' roast."

"I'm sorry, Hon. Those detectives threw my entire schedule off."

Rodriguez spun around. "What detectives, Millie? What are you talking about?"

She told him about the call from Detective Romero and that she agreed he could send someone by. "I just wanted to get this distasteful situation over with."

"And just what did you tell them?"

"The truth, of course. That this Gilda person was nothing to you."

Rodriguez reached for the decanter on the sideboard and poured himself a drink. "What else did you talk about?"

She put her hand on his arm. "You sound upset."

"I am upset. First of all you should know better than to talk to law enforcement without me being present. I'm getting ready to launch my campaign and I don't need any adverse publicity. You know how people manipulate things and spin out another story."

"Oh, I doubt that would happen. The detective and the woman were both very nice. It seemed as though she was certain you were having an affair. I set her straight on how I felt about those terrible rumors."

"The woman? Was she a detective?"

"No, some kind of psychologist, I think she said. But she was very sweet."

"I'm sure she was. Millie, next time someone calls you for an interview on this case, let me know, please. Now just get yourself ready. We're going to be late."

Rodriguez's mind was racing. He knew his wife could be a bit chatty, but he wasn't about to arouse her suspicion by harping on the subject. He was paranoid enough to think that Jemimah might have just connected the dots and decided he was involved in Gilda's murder.

At the dinner, he and John Snead discussed the latest developments and his conversation with Detective Romero. Rodriguez clenched his fist as he listened. He walked out to the patio, scanned his iPhone and dialed a number.

"We need to talk. Let me know when you get into town."

∞

Early Saturday morning, Rodriguez drove to the country club on Airport Road. The caddy met him at his car and helped him unload his clubs.

"What took you so long, Rodriguez? I've been here since seven."

"Ran into a reporter. They're all over the place."

"Yeah, Mr. Almost Governor. I imagine you're pretty newsworthy these days. What do you need now?"

They loaded the gear into the golf cart. A roaming photographer snapped a photo of them. Rodriguez flashed a big smile and waved.

"I thought my job was done," he said.

"Might have another one for you. You still owe me," Rodriguez said.

"This is starting to look like that debt of mine's never going to be paid off."

"Hey," Rodriguez said. "You would be spending ten years in lockup right now if I hadn't covered for you."

"Covered for me? If you hadn't been so quick to let that PRC contract out to one of your buddies, I would have had time to cover my tracks."

"Ancient history. Here's what I need you to do."

"Well, this is the last one."

CHAPTER SIXTY

Jemimah, Romero, and Chacon had been in Albuquerque the entire day for a State Police seminar. Jemimah was anxious to get home, jump in the shower and curl up with her dog Molly and a good book. A tinge of sadness hit her as she realized how much she'd been neglecting her dog lately, what with her schedule crammed with long hours. She'd hardly had time to take her for a decent run. It was a good thing her ranch had a couple of fenced-in acres for the dog to entertain herself chasing after rabbits and small rodents and of course, the cat, Gato. Every so often Jemimah arrived home to find them snuggled up together on the porch swing.

She pulled into the gas station at San Felipe Pueblo casino about twenty miles out of Albuquerque, where gas was considerably cheaper than in town. She poured herself a soda from the fountain, returned to her car and swung out onto the highway, accelerating to catch up with the speeding traffic. She tuned the radio to the NPR station and listened to a discussion on the problems of addiction and alcoholism on Indian reservations. Interested in the subject, she made a mental note to pick up the book the narrator cited.

Traffic was starting to pick up in both directions. Jemimah looked up and saw the sign for the Waldo exit. A coal mining community during the turn of the century, Waldo had become a ghost town in the 1950s. Although the road to Waldo was mostly dirt, it ended at the outskirts of Cerrillos, just a few miles from her home. She knew Detective

Romero used the road often. Taking the exit rather than continuing on the interstate would cut her trip short by more than forty minutes. She noticed several cars behind her taking the same exit, but made nothing of it. The first car, full of teenagers, passed her in a blaze of dust after a few minutes of tailgating her on the two-lane road. She took her time maneuvering the steep hills and sharp curves. The road had become as bumpy as a washboard due to recent rains.

The sun, as orange as a bowl of Cheetos, was preparing to make its slow descent into the horizon. Jemimah figured she would be home in less than twenty minutes, with more than enough sun left to enjoy her dinner out on the porch. Lost in thought, she was surprised when she looked in the rearview mirror to see a vehicle speeding toward her. She jerked the wheel to the right to give the car room to pass. The driver zipped by her at high speed, loosening dust and gravel and sending it flying into her car. She pulled over to get her bearings as the car rolled up the hill and pulled out of sight. "Bastard!" she muttered. "I hope he gets where he's going in one piece."

The next ten miles were uneventful, as she took in the surrounding scenery. She was approaching the turnoff to Devil's Throne, an eerie group of obsidian mountains with a dark overhang in the center that stretched over a shallow cave. The place gave Jemimah the willies every time she passed it and this time wasn't any different. She was startled to hear her cellphone ring. It was Romero.

"Hey, sweetie. Are you almost home?"

"Actually I'm on the Waldo Road, right before the turnoff to Devil's Throne. What's going on? Have you left Albuquerque?"

"We're about twenty minutes out from the Waldo exit, but since I don't have to stop by the office in Cerrillos, we're going to stay on the interstate and head home."

"Hold on a second, Rick."

Jemimah spotted a barricade ahead on the road. She took the left turn as directed by the arrows and returned to the phone.

"Rick, I just passed a detour with an arrow directing traffic onto the park road. Will that road circle around and get me back to Cerrillos? I'm not familiar enough with this area and it's going to be dark soon."

"You mean right there next to Devil's Throne?"

"Yeah. It's marked Cerrillos State Park."

"No, Jemimah. Turn around. That road ends about five miles in. There's nothing beyond that but a few hiking trails."

Jemimah heard the screeching of tires as a car pulled in behind her. She stepped on the accelerator, jolting the car forward. The driver pushed forward and banged into her bumper. She screamed.

"Jemimah, what the hell's going on?"

"Rick, someone's trying to run me off the road!"

The next shove almost made her lose control of the wheel as her phone went flying onto the floorboard.

CHAPTER SIXTY-ONE

Jemimah watched in shock as the driver swerved sharply in front of her, sped ahead and then slammed on his brakes, forcing her to come to a stop behind him. He got out of the car and began to walk toward her. She felt around the floorboard for her phone. As he sauntered over, she cut the wheel to the right and sped ahead, leaving him standing in the middle of the road. The dust storm she kicked up precluded her from seeing if he was back in his car, but she could only assume he was.

She drove without lights, flashing them occasionally to keep from ending up in an arroyo. Up ahead she could see a fence where the main road ended. She took a right. A mile up the road the sign read:

DEVIL'S THRONE—NO VEHICLES BEYOND THIS POINT.

Jemimah ignored the warning and plodded ahead. Rocks banged against the underside of her car. Hoping to circle back to the main road, she popped the gear into four-wheel drive as the vehicle moved forward like an army tank. Her elation was short-lived. Up ahead, a barrier of natural stone blocked her from going any farther. Devil's Throne stood before her like a menacing giant. She jumped out onto the rocky ground in time to hear the grinding of gears coming toward her like a bulldozer as she ran toward the safety of the darkness, where she lay quietly. Night sounds came to a quick halt, as though all its creatures waited to see how the dark drama was about to unfold.

Flat on her stomach, Jemimah slid quietly toward the edge of the monolithic outcropping, moving like a snake slithering across the desert. It crossed her mind that there were rattlers in the area, hopefully bedded down for the night. But which was worse—being bitten by a rattler or discovered by a predator? She would take her chances with the denizens of the night. In the quiet she could hear the crunch of footsteps moving in her direction, pausing by her car. She saw a man's shadowy form returning to his vehicle, open the door and reach in. The headlights went out and the footsteps resumed, this time accompanied by a flashlight. Jemimah groaned at the prospect of being not only without light, but also a sitting target.

The darkness was inky, the moon having retreated behind the clouds. Jemimah heard a sound, spun around expecting to see the man behind her. A coyote raised his head and howled as if to warn his companions of her presence. She was certain the stalker could hear her shallow breathing and the pounding of her heart as she staggered to her knees and stood. She broke into a sprint, running along whatever part of the trail was illuminated by the moon, banging her shins on rocky obstacles as she ran. By the moonlight she could make out a bike trail leading back to the road. Her leg brushed against a cholla cactus, the spiny needles latching onto her skin. She stifled a scream, the pain throbbing as she ran.

The trail led back to the barricade where the road ended. With renewed energy, she plowed her way across the road and ran blindly in the direction of the lights of a nearby house. Barbed wire fences glinted from security lights at the ranch coming up fast on her right as she ran. The gate was locked. If she screamed, it would draw the predator closer.

She slowed to a walk, sticking close to the fence several feet away from the road where she would be an easy target.

She leaned against a gigantic boulder to catch her breath. She saw the reflection of headlights coming toward her, a flashlight pointed out the driver's window, scouring the landscape. Tires crunched noisily against the gravel. The driver spotted her footprints in the sand to the right and braked to a stop. Within seconds he was out of the car. Jemimah peered over the rock. Illuminated by the headlights, he appeared to be a tall man, muscular with broad shoulders and a goatee. He had long hair tied at the neck. She gasped as he bent forward in front of the headlights to retrieve his flashlight. She recognized him from the cover of the morning paper as the man pictured with Tom Rodriguez at the Country Club. The realization made her shudder.

CHAPTER SIXTY-TWO

Artie Chacon was riding shotgun in the silver and black cruiser. Romero redialed Jemimah's number without success.

"What's wrong, Boss—romance going south?"

"No, man. Some creep just tried to run Jemimah off the road." He flicked the siren switch and jammed the gas pedal to the floor. "How far are we from the Waldo turnoff?"

"Three, maybe four miles."

Romero slowed down from ninety as he reached the turnoff. The vehicle fishtailed as he drove onto the dirt road. "Keep your eyes peeled, Artie. Jemimah said the road was blocked at the turnoff to Cerrillos Park."

Driving at fifty-five, the SUV jolted and bounced. "Damned County never gets out here to grade this road," Romero fumed.

"Up ahead, Rick. There's some orange barrels pushed to the side of the road. Looks like someone might have set up a temporary barrier to fence her in."

"Who the hell would want to do this to her?"

"Someone might have just picked her out. This isn't a well-known shortcut, you know. Road's too damned rough. Mostly locals use it. Practically impassible in the winter."

Romero veered around the turn and pulled off to the side. He turned his lights off. "We need a plan here, Artie, and we don't have much time."

"We know the road only goes up a short distance—can't

be more than four, five miles. There's a bunch of dirt trails leading off, some wide, some narrow."

"Bottom line, anyone can see us approach."

"It's getting too dark to see much without light. There's a house about two miles up on the left. Gate's probably locked at this hour."

Romero speed-dialed Detective Martinez.

"Clyde. Need some help here. No time for chitchat."

"Sure, Boss. Shoot."

"Get on the horn and find out who owns the first house on the state park road outside Cerrillos. Sign out here says McCarthy Enterprises."

"Yeah, I've heard of them. They're some kind of green company. Give me a minute."

Romero drummed his fingers on the steering wheel. "Come on, Clyde. Time's running out here."

Martinez came back on the line. "Here it is, Rick. Carl and Mindy McCarthy. Number's unlisted, but the phone company is patching you in. Hold on."

An operator came on the line. "Detective Romero, I have Carl McCarthy on the line."

"Thank you," he said. Romero identified himself and explained the situation, requesting that they allow the Sheriff's Department to use their home as a temporary base. McCarthy agreed and walked outside to wave them into the driveway.

"You can park here. Come on, I'll show you where you can set up."

Romero notified Martinez of the situation, gave him directions and ordered out a SWAT team. The homeowner provided maps of the area, indicating there were a number of places a car could travel once it was off the road. The most likely, though, was the area on the east side of the park, where old trails outnumbered the new ones.

CHAPTER SIXTY-THREE

The killer scoured the surroundings with his flashlight, annoyed that Rodriguez had called him out of seclusion for another job. This was going to be his last 'favor.' He was finding it to be more challenging, more difficult. The last one up near Taos had been a snap. *Bang, Bang. You're dead.* The one before that had been a freebie—just to keep in practice. *Too bad that chick at the casino freaked out after the coke.* He surmised the Doctor Shrink here had a brain on her shoulders. Not so willing to drop to her knees and beg for mercy. She had to be close by.

Once he finished this one off, he was going to spend some time playing golf in England. He was ready to put his weapons down for a well-deserved rest. Rodriguez could find another idiot to take care of his vendettas.

Jemimah held her breath. Waiting and hiding were her only hope. The scent of skunk was carried on the cool night breeze rushing past her as she edged closer to the ground, hoping to become invisible. It crossed her mind that the bright yellow t-shirt she was wearing stuck out like a neon sign in the darkness. The moonlight had dimmed, reduced to a faint glow. She was certain he was closing in on her, as the night sounds escalated to a loud din, drowning out the muted silence of moments before. *Where is that bastard?* She considered running but instinct cautioned her to remain still. The chances of him finding her before she reached the ranch house were too high. She heard footsteps plunking down on the gravel behind her. Before she could turn, she felt an arm around her shoulders and a hand over her mouth. She struggled to break free, but he easily overpowered her.

"Hold still, bitch." He dragged her to the road and pulled her toward the passenger door. "Don't make a move or I'll shoot you right here." He tied her hands with plastic ties and threw her into the front seat. The radio was tuned to an eighties station. Englebert Humperdink was belting out his popular song, "The Last Waltz." The irony didn't escape Jemimah.

CHAPTER SIXTY-FOUR

Intending to drive to Petroglyph Pass and drop the woman's body into Waldo Canyon, the killer started the car and pulled back onto the road. Less than half a mile later the sound of sirens broke into the night. He saw the headlights of an oncoming car off in the distance, followed by whirling red and blue lights. He drove forward, only to find the road blocked by a police barrier. *Where the hell did they come from?* The ranch house glowed in the dark as vehicles aimed their bright lights toward the road. He slammed the brakes hard, almost sending Jemimah crashing through the windshield.

There was no time to think. He reached for the pistol in the console, pushed the driver's side door open and lunged into the illuminated road, dragging Jemimah along.

"Freeze, don't move!" Romero blared through a megaphone, his voice echoing through the canyon.

The man put his arm around Jemimah's throat, the gun aimed at her head. "Back off or I'll shoot her right here," he hollered.

Romero motioned for his men to stand down. He continued speaking through the megaphone. "Look, I don't know what's going on here, but let her go. We can work this out."

Police sirens came screaming up the road. Caught off guard, the killer suddenly shoved Jemimah forward and leaped into the darkness. He stumbled as he crossed the arroyo and kept running.

Romero rushed to Jemimah. "Are you all right?"

She nodded as he clipped the ties on her wrists and wrapped his jacket around her shoulders. He noticed her disheveled hair and her ripped clothing.

"Jeezus, Jemimah. What the hell happened? Where's your car?"

"Back there in the hills somewhere. My purse and everything's in it."

"Don't worry. I'll send a couple of the deputies to retrieve it."

He led her to the cruiser and helped her in. She was still shaking. "Stay here. I'll be back."

Romero dialed Sheriff Medrano's number to request a helicopter and bring him up to speed.

"So, did you arrest the guy?"

"No, he escaped."

"What do you mean, he escaped?"

"He had a gun pointed at Jemimah. We couldn't get a bead on him and take a chance on hitting her. My men are out beating the bushes looking for this guy, but it's pitch black out there."

"I'll notify State Police to put a BOLO out on him. Do we even know who he is?"

"I haven't had a chance to talk to Jemimah."

"Well, get on it, Romero."

The detectives and the SWAT team had the area lit up like the Fourth of July with spotlights pointed toward the arroyo. Two helicopters flew into view, illuminating the night sky. Romero returned to his cruiser and slid in next to Jemimah. Her head dropped onto his shoulder. He put his arm around her and gave her a firm squeeze.

"How you doing?"

"Better now. For a while there I didn't think I was going to make it."

"We've put out a BOLO on the guy, based on what he was wearing. That's not going to get us anywhere. We ran the plates and the car was stolen from the mall earlier today. Looks like a dead end."

"No, Rick. I know who he was."

"Well, who? Why didn't you say something?"

"I mean I've seen him. I don't know his name. Take me home; I'm sure there's a newspaper still sitting on my porch."

Romero thought she was delirious. "What are you talking about, Jem? You feeling all right?"

"Yes, yes. The man who chased me down was pictured in this morning's newspaper. You'll never guess who he was with."

"Tell me."

"Tom Rodriguez."

CHAPTER SIXTY-FIVE

Early the next morning at the main office, Romero's suspicions began to crystallize. There was no doubt in his mind Jemimah's abductor was a hired gun. That's all there was to it. Unfortunately the guy was a pro. There were no usable prints in the car, not even a soda can with DNA. The photographer gladly provided him with the photo from the previous day's paper. Detectives interviewed the staff of the Country Club only to find that nobody seemed to recognize him. A security guard conjectured the guy might be Rodriguez's caddy or golfing buddy. Guests could play a few rounds with members without having to register.

Detective Romero had long believed it was far too convenient for Gilda Humphreys to end up dead a day or two after she screwed around with Rodriguez. Her journal entries and Jemimah's interview with the hotel cleaning lady confirmed the affair had cooled considerably by the time the two checked out. Video from the jewelry store showed a vivid picture of Gilda and a grainy image of her companion purchasing an expensive watch and a gold bracelet and paying cash, but that also proved nothing.

Somehow the killer knew exactly where Gilda was going. Romero presumed that instead of returning to Santa Fe, she stayed overnight somewhere along the way. The next day, dressed in her hiking gear, she stopped to scope out some of the places where she thought the treasure was hidden. She had clearly been followed. It was an unlikely background for a crime, but altogether convenient. There was no indication that Rodriguez had ever been anywhere near where the body was found. He claimed he drove straight home from Taos and there was nothing to disprove that. He had produced a gasoline receipt with a time stamp on it from a gas station twenty miles north of Santa Fe. That coincided with the time he left the bed and breakfast. Following that, he and his wife attended a symposium in Albuquerque for several days.

Romero was still determined to question Rodriguez again before the news hit the afternoon papers. His attorney showed up instead and blocked the request.

"Without a warrant I'm advising my client to stay put and keep his mouth shut. And even if you convince some back-door judge to issue a subpoena, he has nothing to say. You've got nothing, and you know it."

Romero shoved the photo of Jemimah's assailant under Snead's nose. "Take a look at this guy, Snead. Look familiar?"

"Sure, that's a photo of our next Governor getting ready to play golf."

"Not him. The guy next to him."

"Never seen him. What's he got to do with anything? It's common knowledge my client is a golf nut."

"It so happens the man in the photo with Rodriguez tried to abduct Dr. Hodge yesterday. Fortunately we were able to rescue her before he finished the job he was hired to do, by your client."

"So where is he now? There's no way he can implicate my client. Tom's not responsible for every joker who comes up for a handshake and a photo with a well-known figure."

"Looks to me like these guys are golf buddies," Romero said.

"So, is he in custody?"

"Unfortunately he escaped before we could pin him down, but there's a state-wide search going on and he won't get too far."

Snead snorted. "I'm going to tell you something, Romero. There's still nothing here to tie my client to anything, let alone murder and now an alleged abduction. I've said all along that the most Rodriguez is guilty of is lack of discretion. We all use poor judgment from time to time. So what if he and the victim hit the sheets together; that doesn't make him a murderer. You have nothing to tie him to anything other than mattress hopping. In my books, that's hardly a crime."

Snead left the room in a huff. First thing he was going to do was call that mangy bastard and drop him as a client.

∞

An article in the front page of the newspaper that afternoon related the story of the attempted abduction of the County's forensic psychologist, Dr. Jemimah Hodge, by an unidentified man shown in a recent photo with Tom Rodriguez, gubernatorial candidate. The reporter asserted that the FBI was investigating the connection between this high-ranking state official and the suspect, who had been captured by authorities early that morning as he attempted to board an international flight out of Albuquerque.

Romero decided to bide his time, letting Rodriguez get comfortable while the D.A. negotiated a deal with Henry Hawes, the man Jemimah identified as the suspect who chased her through the hills of Cerrillos with the intent of killing her. Hawes admitted that Rodriguez had paid him $50,000 to get rid of Gilda Humphreys and an equal amount to kill Dr. Hodge. Payback was coming around the bend.

At the end of the month, Tom Rodriguez launched his gubernatorial campaign full force, with interviews on state-wide news media, where he dismissed the accusations against him with a wave of his gold-ringed fingers. Down the path somewhere, Detective Romero looked forward to walking into the Governor's office at the Roundhouse on Paseo de

Peralta and arresting the cold-blooded son of a bitch.

He reached into his pocket for the Chinese fortune cookie that accompanied his lunch. He clipped the plastic wrapper with scissors and crushed the cookie with his thumb and forefinger. A smile crossed his face as he read the words on the strip of paper and then stapled it to the inside of the file.

> He will win who, prepared himself, waits to take the enemy unprepared. —Sun Tzu, *The Art of War*

EPILOGUE

On a clear day in early fall, Rick and Jemimah sat on an iron bench on the grounds surrounding the Federal Building next to the downtown post office, flipping through the local paper. Federal agents had taken Tom Rodriguez, gubernatorial hopeful and head of the State Cultural Division, into custody, based on the testimony elicited from the golfing buddy he hired as a hit man. As they had hoped, Rodriguez had cooked his own goose. Romero smiled. He and his detectives, with Jemimah's help, had constructed a beautiful case, and it wouldn't be long before it went to the Grand Jury.

Henry Hawes not only implicated Rodriguez in Gilda Humphreys' murder, but also in a scheme to bilk the state of over a million dollars, spawning an investigation into his activities related to the PRC. The detectives were working toward connecting Hawes to the unsolved murder of the casino woman, Amy Griego, but even if that didn't happen, Hawes was sure to spend the rest of his life in prison.

With that behind them, Romero and Jemimah turned their focus to a more enjoyable task. They spent their free time sifting through the clues in Tim McCabe's memoir, planning a long vacation to engage in some treasure hunting of their own. They broke in their boots on weekend hikes at the Nun's Corner Trail in the mountains above Santa Fe and were ready to embark on some well-deserved time away from their hectic jobs.

It had been a challenge to unravel McCabe's cryptic

clues. The couple decided a drive through Colorado toward Wyoming might be fruitful. Between them, they had compiled a long list of possibilities that wouldn't make sense until the right place was reached. Once there, they planned to search for a hot springs from which a descent could be made into a steep canyon where the water ran fast and high. Then they were going to look for a blaze on a tree and dig right below it. Rick and Jemimah knew their plan was a long shot, but they had the adventuresome spirit McCabe said was necessary to locate the treasure.

As he loaded up the rented SUV in front of Jemimah's ranch house, Romero had a grin on his face.

"What are you smiling about, Rick?" Jemimah said.

"Hey, even if we aren't fortunate enough to locate the treasure, there's a few great spots on our journey that would be perfect for a honeymoon."

"Is that a proposal, Detective of my heart?"

"Is that a yes?" Romero smiled, pulling her close.

Jemimah wasn't sure if she was ready to say yes or not, but she wasn't about to kill a romantic moment.

Marie Romero Cash was born in Santa Fe, New Mexico, to a family that would eventually number seven children, and has lived there most of her life. After graduating from Santa Fe High School, she took a job as a legal secretary, a field that would provide a lifetime of employment. But then, in her mid-thirties, she discovered the traditional arts of Northern New Mexico. After twenty years of creating award-winning art, she began to write about it, but decided she needed a higher education to do so. At fifty she enrolled in college and, five years later, graduated with a degree in Southwest Studies. In 1998, she received the prestigious Javits Fellowship to pursue her education. Since then Marie has written several books about the art and culture of the southwest, including a memoir about growing up in Santa Fe.

Treasure among the Shadows is the third book in the Jemimah Hodge Mystery Series. The first two books were *Shadows among the Ruins* and *Deadly Deception.*

You can find Marie on the Web at
MarieRomeroCash.camelpress.com.